Printed in the United States of America

Chuck,
You are such a sweetheart. I was so glad to see you. I hope you get lost in my characters

TIME RELEASE

by

Jeannie Brown

Love in Light,
Jeannie

triacia31@comcast.net

ACKNOWLEDGEMENT

First and foremost, I would like to thank God for giving me the gift of writing. This is my first conspiracy. It was a wonderful experience to use my gift for something so exciting. I appreciated every moment of it and I hope you do too.

Secondly, I would like to thank a fellow writer and a wonderful friend, Arjay, who has spent endless hours reading, editing and teaching me the ways to being a better writer. He is a warm, giving, intelligent and caring person, without whom, this book would never have been finished. I have the imagination, the wonder and the words, as he does, but he adds or subtracts the commas and helps me to keep my thoughts in the right order. Also when I decided to set up a website, he stepped up again and helped me to build it. No matter what sort of help I needed, he was there. Thank you for everything, Arjay.

I would also like to thank my sister, Nancy Bobbit and to all who read the many different drafts of my book and to those who gave their comments. My Mom, Kitty Brown, my brother-in-law Terry Bryant, my sister's friend, Terri Herman, my life-long friend, Connie Heider, my good friend, Rochelle Kramer, my brother, Tom, my brother, Jim and his wife, Terri, and my brother, Bill and his wife, Lucy. A special thanks to my sister, Terry Waldrup and a good friend, Lynn Wolfe, who took an extra amount of time to look for inconsistencies, misspelled words, etc. I apologize now for the missing commas and run-on sentences that you endured, but your attention to detail before and during the editing process, made it possible to take care of them at the same time.

Also, I would like to thank the rest of my family. Even though some were not a part of this particular book, they have each added something special to my life.

PROLOGUE

On Sunday, September 20, 2009, The Chicago Lake News released this headline:

Massive heart attacks plague the Nation... Who's Next? In Chicago alone, dozens of healthy people have already died of massive heart attacks. Several others hospitalized. The culprit is still living with us...what is the government not telling us?

"Send the copy to print," said Clyde, the Editor-in-Chief. He initialed it. As he turned to walk away, he clutched his chest and fell to the ground.

CHAPTER 1

Turning sideways, Sara eyed her image in the mirror. A short wrap-around burgundy dress that showed off curves in all the right places, long slender legs in modest pumps, and silky brown hair that framed a delicate face and flowed past her shoulders.

I don't think my looks should stop me from getting the job…I hope, she thought, raising her left eyebrow and the corner of her mouth.

But who really knew anymore. It's not about the looks, the talent or anything else, one might think mattered. It's all about who you know.

Taking a deep breath, she sighed. "Unfortunately, I don't know anybody."

Sara turned and glanced at her backside.

"Hmmm. I've gotta get this job or one like it before my next birthday. Thirty. Once you hit thirty, if you haven't had a national commercial yet, you're finished."

Sara faced the mirror. *Pretend you're here, in this room*, she thought. *It's comfortable, romantic and safe.* She glanced around her bedroom - vertical light blue cloth-covered blinds from floor to ceiling that were always opened enough at night to cast shadows on the far wall. Romantic and warm. She had an oak four poster bed with a blue and white lace comforter and two royal blue throw pillows. An oak nightstand with brass handles that matched the dresser, took up most of the interior wall.

This is so me, she thought.

She backed up, sat on an oak bench that leaned against the end of her bed, and sighed.

"This commercial can be me too."

After several moments, she looked back at the cheval mirror between the bedroom door and the walk-in closet and she stood. Then she smiled.

Okay, Sara Ann Parkins, this is it. All you need to do is be yourself. You love romance, so what could be better than a national wine commercial. You don't need to know anybody else, because you know yourself.

Both sides of Sara's mouth moved up and her blue eyes sparkled off the mirror before she shut out the light and headed for the front door.

Locking the door behind her, she strode down the red and gray carpeted hallway to the mirrored elevator. *The hallway always has a clean antiseptic smell, but it's nice because I know it's clean.*

Down the hall, a door opened and out peeked an elderly woman.

"Hello, Sara."

"Hello, Anna."

Anna waved an aged hand over her head, hiding the yellow foam curlers and picks that were wrapped tightly in her short auburn hair. She bent and retrieved her newspaper.

"I'll stop by tonight with that curling iron." Sara said, giggling.

She remembered the first day she met Mrs. McClusky and was immediately told to call her Anna. Seventy two years old and she wanted to be one of the girls.

Anna closed her door swiftly, as five doors down, a man stepped into the hall.

"Break a leg, Sara," she squeaked from behind the wooden door.

Sara smiled to herself as she stepped around a roman pillar to reach the elevator. She stepped inside and placed the palm of her hand on the rubber strip.

"Going down," she called out.

"Thanks! Sara is it? said the man, quickening his steps toward her.

Sara cocked her head to the right.

"Sorry, I overheard," he said as he grabbed the rubber strip.

"Yes, yes it is…and you are?" she asked, taking in his perfectly pressed gray suit, brown hair and green eyes as he stepped inside.

"I'm Jason, Jason Forest. Just moved in Saturday. Neighbors pretty nice?"

"Yes, they are," said Sara glancing at the newspaper under his arm.

“Wow! You’re getting your paper delivered already? It took them a month before I received Saturday’s and Sunday’s.”

Jason pushed the paper further into his armpit. “Just got lucky and talked to the right person. I guess. So are you a model or an actress?”

Sara raised her eyebrows.

“Again, sorry, but I overheard the well wishes. Break a leg?”

With a small giggle, she replied, “Yes well, I’m neither. I’m a hopeful actress.”

“Well those are the best kind in my opinion. Full of dreams and possibility.”

Sara shifted from one foot to the other. “So, what do you do, Jason?”

“I work in a lab with enzymes and medications. It’s a pretty boring job. But when we find a cure for somethin’, it’s worth it.”

“Wow! Now I feel silly. You’re out there trying to save people and, um, I’m going on a commercial audition? Okay! So are you a doctor?”

“First of all, you should never feel silly about being beautiful. Everyone has different gifts and if one of yours is beauty, I’d take it. A lot of people would love to have that problem, including me.” Jason’s smile broadened and his eyes sparkled.

Sara felt her cheeks get warm. She shrugged her shoulders and shook her head.

"Thank you. That's sweet." Grabbing a tube of pearl lipstick, she quickly applied it. *Stop getting so nervous. I thought I got over that,* she told herself.

"Lips get dry sometimes," she said,

"And, as for me," continued Jason, "I have a Ph.D. after my name, but I don't work in a hospital or anything like that. Not much for taking medications myself, just research the effects they have on other people. I like to figure out why things happen," said Jason.

"Well, I'm like that with the medication thing too. I didn't even get a flu shot. I guess I have the mentality, 'if it's not broke, don't fix it'."

Sara realized neither one of them had pushed the button. She leaned forward at the same time Jason did. Brushing hands as they hit L for lobby, Jason's newspaper slipped to the floor.

A strong scent of Paco Rabanne sifted past Sara's nose. She pursed her lips and smiled, then saw the exposed headline on the front page of the paper, '*Two women struck down by progressive heart attacks*'.

Jason bent and swiftly replaced the newspaper beneath his arm.

Sara glanced at him. "Too bad you couldn't help those women."

"Excuse me?"

"Two women that died of heart attacks …the headline on the paper!" Sara re-iterated.

"Oh! yeah! I haven't read it yet. I wish we could help everybody."

Jason smiled and his eyes stole all the light in the enclosed space. "You really are very beautiful you know."

Sara felt the heat rising. She tilted her chin down and to the right and quickly opened her bag and began rifling through it.

"Oh, no! I must have forgot it," she said. Sara extended her index finger as they passed the 8th floor and pushed 7. Shuffling the papers in her bag, she mumbled. "Have to get off here and go back up for it. Sorry!"

"No apology necessary," said Jason, placing his left hand on the rubber strip as the silver doors separated. "I forget things all the time. Don't be late for your audition."

Once again Sara nodded. "Thanks."

Jason leaned forward toward the closing doors. "Oh! and break a leg."

The mirrored doors closed and Sara's heart raced. *What's wrong with me, getting off the elevator for no reason?* she thought. *He seemed like a nice guy, and really good looking too. Why didn't I give him a chance?* The right corner of Sara's lip ticked upward and her eyelids fell to half mast. "He was cute, wasn't he?" she muttered to herself. *When it comes to guys, my nerves always get the best of me.*

Sara waited five minutes, and then took the next elevator to the lobby. She glanced from left to right as she walked swiftly through the lobby to the revolving doors.

Walking to the curb, she raised her hand to flag down a cab.

A cab pulled in, stopped one foot from the curb, and Sara lifted the handle and jumped in. *That's the nice thing about Chicago,* she thought. *There's always a cab when you need one.*

"Six fourteen North Wabash please," she said as she settled onto the ripped vinyl seat in the back, opposite the driver. She angled her legs to the right, so as not to catch her nylons on the tear or the spring she saw hidden within the seat. She discreetly raised her hand to her mouth to stifle the stench of cigarette smoke.

"This must be a very old cab," she mumbled, without thinking.

The cabbie's eyes lit up in the rearview mirror.

"Yes it is, Miss. I made the final payment last month."

He pulled away from the curb and another cab driver took his place.

"That's wonderful," Sara replied, choking down her displeasure.

Shifting his eyes toward traffic, the cabbie rested an arm on the window. "The address you gave me, that is a talent agency, is it not?" he asked.

"Yes," said Sara, separating her index finger and thumb to speak.

"I thought that it was," said the cabbie. "I take many girls there throughout the week." Another cabbie attempted to merge in front of Sara's cab, but her cabbie cut him off and continued. "These girls, they are carrying leather cases the same as yours and they are usually very well dressed." He hesitated. "But, Miss, do not be fooled, a lot of these girls go home in tears. It is a very hard business to be in."

"Yeah! I know. But like my Mom always said, if it's your dream, you've got to give it a shot."

"That is very good advice, indeed."

The back of the cabbie's buzz cut faced Sara, but his rounded eyes and the wide bridge of his nose turned toward the rear-view mirror again. His eyes smiled at Sara, then he resumed his straight ahead stare into traffic. A business man attempted to cross in the middle of the street, but was forced back by an oncoming city service truck.

Sara shifted in her seat, opened her valise and breathed in the new leather smell. She carefully sifted through each headshot to be sure she hadn't forgotten one.

"Ninety degrees today with 80% humidity," said the voice on the radio. "It's gonna be a scorcher. Before the Cubs take on Cincinnati at Wrigley this afternoon, they'll be saying a prayer for all the lives lost on this day eight years ago. And let's not forget the Bears are getting ready for the season opener on Sunday against the Packers."

At the corner of Wabash and Ohio, the car finally pulled alongside a four-story gray Victorian building with green and white awnings.

"Here we are, Miss. Good luck to you."

Sara handed the cabbie $6.00, swiveled toward the door and stepped out. "Keep the change," she smiled.

The cabbie leaned over the passenger seat toward the open window and a medallion of St. Michael, the Archangel, swung forward from his shirt. "Miss?"

Sara stopped and turned toward him.

Tilting his head to the left, both corners of his mouth pulled up and his brown eyes glistening, he spoke. "When you make it big Miss, may I have an autograph?"

Sara grinned from ear to ear and shot her index finger and thumb toward him.

"You got it."

She turned and looked at the building. *The green and white awning gives it a quaint touch*, she thought. *It's been years since I've been to this agency.*

A large sign over the doorway read, "Riggati's PIZZA." Another Riggati's sign hung over the side of the building facing Wabash. Sara did her best to ignore them. Climbing the seven crumbling cement stairs, she reached the front door, where The Jada Agency was engraved on the window. She slowly opened the door and a wonderful smell sifted under her nose. *Hot bread, sausage, heavenly sauce and melted cheese. Mmmmmmm. Why in the world would a Talent agency rent a space above the best pizza place in town?* Sara shook her head and noticed a poster in the window halfway up the stairs. Get your flu shots downstairs from Thursday, August 13th thru Thursday, September 17th.

"Hmmph!" said Sara. *Only a few more days. Can't believe they started almost a month ago already.*

Sara took the steps two at a time, then walked the long hallway to the Jada agency. She opened an old rickety door and stepped inside. *There has to be over sixty girls in here*, she thought, as she glanced around the room. She could hear the mumbling of the other girls reciting their lines, but what she really noticed was how young they all looked.

Okay! So they're younger than me. I have a maturity about me and a level of confidence that they may be missing, she told herself. With that, she stepped up to the receptionist's desk and signed in. She handed her snapshot and resume to the girl behind the desk.

"Sara," said the girl handing her a document. "Here's the script you need to read."

She took the script and looked around for a place to sit. All the chairs were taken. To get one, she'd have to wait until someone got called in. Heading for the corner of the room, she commandeered a stool that had books stacked on it. She placed the books on the top of a cabinet and sat down. Other girls stood and leaned against the wall, so Sara was proud of herself for finding the stool.

The office was very old and beat up. *There's a sooty smell in here, probably from mold,* thought Sara. The ceiling was stucco, but it was crumbling in spots and the floor boards squeaked, and apparently the painter changed his mind several times before finishing the walls. One wall was a bleak orange, another, bland yellow and dark brown, and the one by the receptionist, a cheery lavender.

Sara placed her purse strap over her leg and held up the script. The lead-in read,

This shoot is for an International Wine Vineyard in France. It's all about emotion, romance, class and charisma. You are on a yacht with the man of your dreams and he is offering you more wine. He will place you in an embrace and you need to make the feeling work. Your line is: "More please."

"More please?" said Sara to herself. "There's only one line?" More pressure. One line meant you couldn't fix a mistake in the second or third line, it meant it was definitely about the delivery and looks.

Sara glanced around the room and noticed there were rows of black chairs, a group of gray chairs, and five or six newer white chairs, all filled, scattered about the room.

There was a creaking sound and the door behind the receptionist opened and a long leg with a black strappy stiletto stepped out. A hand wrapped around the door frame and half of a face followed.

"Laura Finder," said the voice that belonged to the face. The stiletto retreated and a curly haired blonde, wearing a canary yellow mini skirt and four inch orange wedged heels, jumped up from her chair. She grabbed a piece of gum from her mouth and stuck it on a piece of paper pulled from her purse.

I don't know, but I don't think she really fits the style they're looking for, thought Sara.

Sara moved quickly and secured the girl's chair and another girl grabbed Sara's stool. Some of the chairs were metal with a cushioned seat and some had no cloth seat at all.

"Ooooh! Cushie…lucked out," said Sara as she sat on one of the newer chairs.

They must have gotten these chairs from goodwill or something, they're so beat up, she thought. Her eyes scanned the room again. Two seats away, a redhead, maybe twenty-one, bit her nails, while the girl next to her, probably twenty- four, brushed her hair and applied lipstick over and over again.

I don't know if I'm calm because I don't care as much as they do or because I've learned that worrying doesn't help the situation, thought Sara. She retrieved two magazines she brought with and leafed through them.

Minutes later, the door creaked again and the girl in the yellow mini skirt walked out of the audition, sobbing. She wobbled in her shoes and finally stopped and removed them. She picked them up and carried them out, while wiping her eyes with a napkin.

Sara didn't want to stare, so she looked away. *I hate to say it, but it had to be the outfit.* Sara missed the next name called, but she did see a flash of someone going in behind the long legged woman. And she knew it wasn't her turn yet.

About fifteen minutes later, a lanky blonde haired girl exited the audition room and rushed to her friend's side.

"I was asked to do the line with a stand-in, were you?" she asked.

"No!" snapped her friend as they headed for the door.

Sara listened as each girl left the audition and only three girls had been asked to do their lines with a stand-in. *I hope they ask me too,* she thought.

Three hours and thirty girls later, the long leg and strappy stiletto that appeared periodically from the door behind the receptionist was followed by a matching leg and entire face. It was a beautiful, thirty-something face with a long, slender body beneath it. The slender body wore a black wrap-around skirt and a purple satin boatneck blouse.

Wow! What an amazing figure and a take-charge demeanor, thought Sara. *I wonder if she never got a national commercial and ended up helping others find their dream.*

"Lunch Break!" announced the leggy woman. "One hour. Be back exactly at 1:30pm."

Sara didn't have to worry about getting a chair when she got back, after all, there were less than thirty girls left. She walked downstairs to Riggati's to get a salad. *I definitely don't want to get full now,* she thought. A small side salad and another bottle of water and Sara headed back upstairs. She found another white cushioned chair and got comfortable. Twenty-eight girls later, the leg appeared, Sara leaned forward and…

"Sara Parkins?"

Sara stood and walked confidently in, matching the woman stride for stride.

The woman pointed to her right and motioned to Sara. "Stand on the X, please."

Sara stood on the X facing the video camera.

Okay! she thought, this is all about body language, so relax your leg, use your hip and give that famous head tilt...I know, I'm gonna pretend I'm standing here with Jason, she thought.

"Okay, state it," said the director.

"My name is Sara Parkins and I'm with the Jada Agency," she replied.

"Okay! Sara, your boyfriend has his arm wrapped around you and he kisses you gently. He has a glass of wine in one hand and the bottle of wine in his other, which is wrapped around your waist. He's looking in your eyes, asking if you would like more wine. This is where your line comes in," said the director.

Sara pictured Jason in her mind. She tossed her head, brushed her hair over her right shoulder, dipped her chin, lifted the left corner of her mouth and delivered her line.

"More please," said Sara.

And the director smiled.

"Very good," said the Director. "Let's try it a couple more times.

Sara repeated the line with the same feeling and body language.

"Very good, Sara. Now, I'd like to see you run your line with a guy standing next to you. So, I'm gonna have Mike stand in for this next one."

"Okay!" said Sara. *This is good. Now I'm one of four*, she told herself.

Mike, a 5'10," sixty-ish balding man with a large belly, stepped beside Sara and wrapped his arm around her.

"Okay! You've already kissed…"

Thank God, thought Sara.

"And you're looking into his eyes. And your line is…"

Once again, Sara threw her head back, tossed her hair, dipped her chin and delivered the line.

"More please."

The director smiled again.

"Very, very good," repeated the Director. "That'll be all. If you're chosen, we'll get in touch with you this week, otherwise the agency will call you. You definitely have something."

"Thank you very much," said Sara.

She looked at her phone for the time. *Wow! 5pm and I'm just leaving*. She rushed down the broken cement stairs, stopped mid-stride and stared into space. *There's a good possibility I could get this job,* she said to herself. *Oh my God! If that guy's breath had smelled any worse, I think I'd of passed out. I wonder if they did it on purpose*."

Sara smiled and before she raised her arm, a cabbie pulled in tight to the curb. She opened the door and slid in.

"How did it go, Miss? You were there a long time," said the cabbie.

Sara's smile lit the backseat. "You must be my good luck charm! What are the odds I'd have the same cab here and back? My name's Sara by the way. What's yours?"

"My name is Frank. It is nice to meet you, Miss Sara," he said extending his right hand over the seat.

Sara shook his hand hard. "It's very nice to meet you, Frank. Very nice."

"So how did it go Miss, Sara? They mustn't have given you the heave ho, if you're leaving now," he said.

He turned his hand over and squeezed a drop of hand sanitizer into it. Without missing a beat, he did the same for Sara.

Sara's eyes opened wide as she rubbed her hands together. *Wow! that was nice,* she thought.

Frank turned on the meter, pulled away from the curb and nearly got sideswiped by another cab. He hit his horn once and Sara braced her arm on the opposite door. Frank smiled in the mirror at Sara.

"Thanks, Frank! But, actually I was there a long time because sixty some girls showed up for the audition." Sara began. "What's nice is that as far as I can tell, only about five of us were asked to do our readings with a stand-in. At the end of my audition, the director said I had a certain something…whatever that means." Sara rolled her eyes playfully. "Hopefully, it means they'll want me for the job. It could be a couple of days before I know anything."

"I would not be surprised if you were chosen, Miss Sara," said Frank with a smile. "But, if they do not call you, it is their misfortune."

Sara smiled.

"I knew I liked you."

Sara released her grip on the door and relaxed as their conversation continued.

"Hey, Frank, someone left today's Trib in here."

"It is yours now. I believe it was the gentleman I dropped off at Midway right after I dropped you off this morning. He must have finished it."

Sara watched as Frank ran his hands over the steering wheel with precision. He talked casually and smiled as he swerved around a big yellow bus. The traffic light flashed red, Frank screeched to a halt alongside the bus. The light turned green, he laid on the horn, stepped down hard on the gas and cut over in front of the bus, as though that were the only thing to do. Sara gripped the door handle and closed her eyes.

"I dropped off two other young women at Jada's," he continued. "And two young men to a company down the street. One of the young ladies had blond curly hair and a very short skirt. She left crying within an hour of dropping her off. From what I could understand through her sobbing, they said she was pretty, but she did not have the talent necessary. I am afraid she was not very happy with them."

"I saw that girl with the curly hair. You're right, she left about five minutes after I got there. I felt bad because I don't think she realized what the product was. Unfortunately, I don't think the yellow mini skirt helped."

"Well, I hope that you hear from them, Miss Sara."

"Thanks. Me too!" she said sliding back into the vinyl seat. "How long have you been driving a cab, Frank? You sure have a knack for it." She unfolded the paper and peeked at the headline.

"Probably since before you were born, Miss Sara," laughed Frank. "It will be twenty-three years this Thursday."

"Thanks for the compliment. Wow! I can't imagine doing anything for twenty-three years. You must really like it."

"Yes! I do, Miss Sara. When my family moved here from Africa, I looked for a job that would help me to learn the culture. What better way than to talk to people of every ethnicity each and every day. It is always very different and very interesting."

Sara tilted her head. "If you don't mind my asking, why did your family move here?"

Frank glanced in the rearview mirror. "My grandmother was ill and we could not get her the help she needed at home. So my mother and father said we would move to America where my Grandmother would be better. She lived many more years because of the medicine she received here."

The sounds of an ambulance and fire truck blared through the slightly cracked window and Frank pulled to the side. They passed and carefully travelled through the intersection with Frank right behind them. Frank continued. "There are so many sick people in Africa, Miss Sara, that can't afford medical help. I knew that in America, when I had a family of my own, I would be able to take them to a doctor if they needed to go. Last month, I took my whole family for their flu shots. In Africa, you would have to be somebody, but not here...you can be anybody. And

America is truly a country where anyone can live their dream."

"Absolutely. I guess I'm proof of that too," said Sara. "At least I'm attempting to be." She turned the paper from front to back, her eyes scrunched and she read it under her breath. "September 11th Ceremonies: Victims of Sept. 11th attacks."

Frank pulled in tight to the curb in front of Sara's building, eyeing Sara in the rearview mirror. "Is there something wrong Miss Sara? You look puzzled."

"No, no, it's just…is this today's morning paper? There was a headline this morning about two women and heart attacks and now it's…" she waved her hand. "Well it doesn't matter. I'm rambling."

She looked up and realized the cab had pulled into the curb.

Frank extended his card. "If you ever need a cab, perhaps when they call to say you have the job," he said, smiling. "Give me a call and I will be sure to get you there on time."

Sara handed Frank another $6.00, pushed open the door and stepped out.

"Thanks, Frank. Have a great evening."

Frank smiled and waved as he pulled away.

Tucking the paper under her arm, Sara pushed through the revolving doors and entered the salad shop, *Garden Pure*, on the first level. The smell of hot sauce and cheese drifted under her nose from the pizzeria, *Italian Heaven*, down the hall. She hesitated while picking up the plastic container to build her own salad and scrunched her lips to the side.

"No pizza, Sara. If you get this job, you need to be in good shape. Salad is good for you."

"Something you recite to yourself often?" said a voice from behind her.

Sara jumped and turned toward the voice.

"Mr. Adashi, you scared me" she smiled.

"I seem to have that affect on a lot of women," he replied.

"Ha ha ha. You know I love your shop and I love salad and it is good for me, but every now and then I smell that wonderful sauce and melted cheese, and I start to cave. So, I recite my little mantra and I'm fine."

"Well good for you, Sara." He winked his right eye and looked around. "But you know, even I've snuck over there a couple times and had pizza...and it's pretty good. Sometimes it's a nice change. And with your figure, I wouldn't worry so much."

"Thank you. That's sweet. I'm sure I'll have it one day. But for now, I think I'll make myself a salad."

Leafy green lettuce, ripe tomatoes, sliced cucumber, deviled eggs, cubed turkey, real bacon bits, croutons, a few strawberry halves and seven grapes. *That's a lot of stuff,* thought Sara. *But at least I'm using grapes instead of dressing. That saves on calories and leaves room for a croissant.*

Sara smiled, put the cover on her salad, picked up a small croissant and took it to the counter, where she stood third in line. *Hmmph!* thought Sara. *I wonder where that guy, Jason, is right now. I've been so busy all day, I forgot about him. He was cute.* She glanced around the shop to see if he might be there, but he wasn't. She paid and headed for the elevator. Eight people occupied the elevator with her. They exited one by one, until Sara stood alone and the car stopped on 14. *I know it's really the 13th floor,* thought Sara. *Kind of like a hidden bit of luck.*

Exiting the elevator, Sara heard Anna's door creak open. Out walked Jason. Sara hid behind the pillar and eyed his physique. He wore a pair of gray, washed out jeans and a lavender button down shirt. Nervous, she plucked the tube of lipstick from her purse and applied it, and eavesdropped.

"Enjoy! Mrs. McClusky. I've been baking since I was fourteen. It's really a passion of mine," said Jason.

"Oh my! What a nice young man you are. Call me Anna. All my friends do. I'll have to have you for dinner some time."

The left corner of Jason's mouth ticked upward. "That would be wonderful, Anna. I look forward to it."

This is so ridiculous. Why am I hiding from him? He's hot, he's sweet, so what's my problem? Sara gritted her teeth and exhaled as though blowing through a straw. *Next time,* she thought. "Wow! I'm pathetic," she whispered, rolling her eyes.

Sara watched Jason disappear into his apartment, then scurried to Anna's door. Knocking lightly, Sara swiveled her head to the right several times, to be sure Jason didn't reappear.

Anna's door opened.

"Wow! You looked radiant," said Sara.

Anna's auburn hair was in perfect curls and her makeup spotless as she twisted her hand in her multi-colored muumuu. Her eyes sparkled and the corners of her mouth pulled up further than Sara had ever seen before.

"Hi Sara. How did it go? Did you get the job? Come in," said Anna.

"My goodness, we're in a good mood today," remarked Sara. "Could it have anything to do with your gentleman caller?"

Anna blushed and waved an aged hand in front of her.

"Don't be silly dear. He's new in the building and he wanted to introduce himself is all."

She swung around like a prom date and then settled herself in the overstuffed yellow chair. Eyes glazed over, she scrunched her lips, and she let out a sigh.

"It was awfully nice to have a gentleman come to call. It's been a very long time. Even if he is thirty or forty years too young."

Her eyes focused and she looked up at Sara.

"Actually I think he'd be good for you, Sara."

Sara shifted her weight, squinted her eyes and tilted her head to the left.

"Now look whose blushing," said Anna.

"Ha ha ha! Okay! You got me. I'll admit he's a good looking guy, but I don't know anything about him. Good looks aren't everything." The left side of her mouth stretched up and nearly reached her cheekbone.

"He's hot," said Anna. She burst into laughter and Sara joined in.

"Yeah! I know he's hot. But I need more."

"Make yourself available, so you can find out more about him." Anna raised her eyes. "He bakes too, ya know."

"I'll think about it," said Sara. "And, since your hair looks gorgeous, how about we play with the curling iron this weekend. Would that work for you?"

"Absolutely. Besides I've already got a chicken breast in the broiler. Thanks for looking after me, Sara. I think I'd like to adopt you."

"Well, I'd be proud to be your daughter."

Anna turned her head and winked. "Hey! Maybe I could get a son-in-law out of the deal too."

"You're terrible."

Sara pulled Anna up from the chair and wrapped her arms around her. "I think you're gonna have to be happy with a daughter for the time being. Tee hee hee. Gotta go. Love ya."

"Love you too, honey!"

Sara started down the hall to her apartment. Once inside, she kicked off her shoes at the front door and walked into her living room. She placed her salad on the living room coffee table and poured herself a glass of water.

I'm gonna get comfortable first, she thought. She walked to the bedroom, untied her wrap-around dress, let it drop to the floor and stepped to the bathroom.

Sara leaned on two feet of gray and white marble countertop to the right of a white-washed sink and nickel-plated faucet. She opened the triple doored medicine cabinet, snatched a bottle of Vaseline and snapped off the cover. Dipping her index finger into the jar, Sara closed her right eye, then her left eye and massaged the gel over her lashes. She wiped it clean with a tissue and pumped Dove soap onto a washcloth and washed off the rest. Rinsing with cool water, she reached for a teal colored towel hanging on a towel ring behind her.

I'll take a shower in the morning, Sara thought, as she glanced at the rain-tinted shower stall at the end of the room. She applied L'Oreal face cream, then walked back to her bedroom and threw on a pair of sweats and a tank top. *Now I can relax.*

With that, she returned to the living room, stepped between the table and the couch and slid to the floor Indian-style.

Clicking on the TV, she picked up her fork to eat her salad. After two hours of mind numbing TV, she clicked it off, undressed for bed, brushed her teeth and slipped between her silk sheets. As soon as she lay her head on the pillow, her eyes closed and her mind relaxed.

***

"There's always tomorrow, for dreams to come true" played and vibrated on the nightstand. "The time is 10:13 pm," announced Sara's cell phone. Sara woke and reached for the phone, instinctively putting it to her ear before opening her eyes.

"Hello!"

"Hello Sara, it's Anna…I'm not feeling well. Help!

"I'm on my way Anna. I've got your extra key."

"Thank you."

Eyes wide open, Sara jumped from her bed, stripped off her t-shirt and threw on a pair of jeans and a tank top. With phone in hand, she grabbed her keys and purse and opened the front door. Locking the door behind her, she ran down the hall.

"Anna, I'm coming in," said Sara. She opened the door to find Anna on the floor with one arm clutching her chest.

Sara sat down on the floor next to her and dialed 911.

"I need an ambulance at Chicago Hi-Towers, 371 North Lake Shore Drive, suite 13 or that is 14-09…It's my neighbor, Anna McClusky. There's something wrong. She's in a lot of pain."

"My chest, Sara. It feels tight and my arm hurts."

Sara nodded her head. "Yes, she's breathing, but she's clutching her chest. She said it feels tight. Oh! And she has a pain in her arm. She looks very pale and weak. An aspirin? I don't know, let me see," said Sara.

"Anna, do you have any aspirin in the house?"

Anna pointed to the bottle of Fahrer Aspirin on the table at the end of the couch.

"She has aspirin. Should I give her one? Okay! I will. Yes, I'll stay with her until they get here. Oh! Okay, hold on."

Sara turned toward Anna. "It's gonna be okay."

Snatching the bottle of aspirin off the table, she flipped off the cover and placed a capsule in Anna's mouth.

"Here Anna…take this. I'll get you some water."

Sara ran to the kitchen, filled up a glass of water and returned to Anna.

"Here you go."

She held the glass to Anna's lips until she swallowed the capsule.

"I'm gonna stay right here with you." Sara put the phone to her ear again.

"Can I help her up to the couch?"

Sara nodded to the voice on the other end of the phone.

"Anna, can I help you up on the couch?"

"Okay!" said Anna.

Sara placed the phone on the table and dipped her right shoulder down. "Wrap your arm around my neck and I'll stand you up slowly," said Sara.

"Oooooh! My chest, it's really bad, Sara."

"Here we go. A couple more steps." Sara helped Anna sit down on the burnt orange couch and laid her head down on an orange throw pillow with a red embroidered rose on it.

Sara picked up the phone. "She's on the couch."

Sara listened. "Okay, Anna, the paramedics are in the building and should be here any minute. Anna, 911 is asking if you did anything different last night. Anything strenuous?" said Sara stroking Anna's arm.

"No…I ate my dinner…then I watched Jay Leno. I didn't do anything else. Ooooohhh! My vision's getting fuzzy."

Sara turned toward a sound at the door.

"Paramedics ma'am." Sara jumped up and opened the front door.

"Right this way."

Both paramedics made their way to Anna.

Sara put her phone back to her ear. “The paramedics are here. Thank you so much for your help,” said Sara.

Sara clicked off the call and leaned back against the living room wall and watched.

The first paramedic took Anna’s hand.

“Hello! Ma’am. I’m Jim and this is Bill. We’re gonna ask you a few questions and take your vitals, is that alright?”

“Yes of course,” said Anna, pulling herself to a sitting position, her face wincing in pain.

“Are you feeling dizzy?” asked Jim

“A little. I’m feeling weak and my vision is a little weird. I did get nauseated about half an hour ago. But I don’t know if that means anything.”

Bill placed a stethoscope on Anna’s chest and listened. “Have you ever had any heart problems, a murmur or anything like that?”

“No, I’ve been very lucky…I may be old, but I’m pretty darn healthy. “

Jim held her wrist, feeling her pulse. “Are you on any kind of medication?”

“No, not really.”

“Do you take over the counter drugs?” asked Bill.

Anna held her chest and breathed out. “Only Rilosac for reflux.”

Bill noticed the bottle of aspirin on the floor next to the couch and held it up. “What about these? How often do you take aspirin?”

"Oh, yeah! I forgot! Only once in a while for aches and pains."

"How many did you take tonight?" Bill asked while taking her pulse.

"I didn't take any tonight, until Sara got here. She gave me one. The 911 operator told her to. I took it right away."

"That may have helped you, but we're gonna have to get you to the hospital for some tests, just to be on the safe side," said Jim. "Is that okay?"

Anna's eyes opened wide and she ran her right hand through her hair.

"I must look a mess."

"You look fine. Are you feeling better?" asked Jim.

"Yes, I am kind of," said Anna.

Bill rolled the gurney in from the hall, stopping at the coffee table in front of the couch.

"Well, Mrs. McClusky, we're still going to bring you in," said Jim.

"That's fine," she said as she reached for Jim's hand. "But call me Anna, if you would. All my friends do."

Jim grabbed Anna's hand. He smiled as he helped her up onto the gurney. "Alright Anna, is there anything that you need to bring with you? Your insurance card or Medicare card?" Jim turned toward Sara, standing against the opposite wall in the living room. "Will you be coming with us?"

"Yes, definitely." Sara moved to Anna's side again. "Tell me where your things are and I'll get them for you."

"Oh Sara, you're such a dear. My cards are rubber banded together in the top drawer of my nightstand."

Sara released Anna's arm and walked swiftly into the bedroom.

"I've got them. I'll be right there," Sara called out, as she hooked an overnight bag on her pinky and lifted it from the floor. She quickly searched through several drawers.

"Packing a few personal items for you in case you need to stay at the hospital," she yelled.

Jim placed an oxygen mask over Anna's nose and mouth and Bill wheeled her down the hall toward the elevator. Sara rounded the corner into the hall behind them with Anna's red bag and information.

"She's going to be okay, isn't she?" Sara whispered to Jim.

"She'll be just fine. It looks like she may have had a mini-stroke or a minor heart attack, so we'll need to do a few tests. Did you say that you gave her an aspirin?"

"Yes, is that alright? The woman on the phone said I should," said Sara.

"You did just fine. That actually limits the chance of her having another heart attack by twenty to thirty percent."

Sara stared at Jim's broad shoulders and slim waist. *Nice physique*, she thought as he pushed the gurney out the front door. As he lifted Anna into the ambulance, she caught herself staring and raised her focus to his short brown hair and blue eyes. *Not as cute as Jason, but still pretty nice,* she thought.

Sara stepped up, placed the bag on the floor and took Anna's hand in hers. The back door shut and the sirens began.

Anna lifted her mask. "I feel like a queen…I'm getting so much attention," she laughed.

"Well it's about time," laughed Sara, as she put the mask back in place.

The sirens blared and the red lights bounced off buildings, reflecting back through the windows in the ambulance. Bill drove and Jim sat on the other side of Anna, keeping track of her vitals.

When Anna's eyes closed, Sara's face grew pale and her eyes found Jim.

"She's got good rhythm now and we didn't have to use the defibrillator, so those are all good signs."

"Be there in thirty," said Bill.

The sirens stopped as they pulled into the hospital emergency bay. The back doors flew open and interns grabbed the stretcher and brought it down in seconds. They wheeled her in past the front desk for immediate testing.

"Miss, are you here with the patient," asked the nurse at the front desk.

"Yes, I am," said Sara.

"My name is Nurse Fleur. Would you mind filling out some forms and giving us some information on your mother…is it?"

"Oh! She's not my mother, but I like to think of her like that. She's my neighbor and yes, I have all of her information. Her insurance card, driver's license, the medications she's taken recently, all of that," said Sara.

When Sara finished filling out all of the paperwork, Nurse Fleur took her into Anna's room.

"How is she? Is she gonna be okay?" asked Sara.

"She's sleeping now and her vitals are good. But, it was good that you called 911, because you never know. Much better to err' on the side of safety. But for now, you should probably go home, get a good night's sleep. We'll call you in the morning with the results."

Sara fidgeted. "Maybe I should stay in the room with her…in case she needs me."

"I know you wanna help, but it's after midnight. Trust me, if you get a good night's sleep, you'll both be better off. We'll keep an eye on her."

"Okay! But, please call me if she needs anything, anything at all," said Sara.

"I promise. You're down as the primary contact." Nurse Fleur turned to walk away. "Good night dear!"

"Thank you." Sara took one last look in Anna's room. "Good night Anna!"

CHAPTER 2

"There's always tomorrow for dreams to come true…The time is now 8:19am," announced Sara's cell phone. Sara lifted her hand and dragged her right arm across her body to reach for the phone. "Hello!"

"Is this Sara Parkins?" said a voice on the other end.

"Yes, it is. Can I help you?" said Sara.

"This is Dr. Gordon at St. Cecelia Hospital. I believe you accompanied Mrs. McClusky when she checked in late last night. She has you as a contact."

Sara's eyes popped open and she jumped to a sitting position on the bed.

"Yes, I am. Is everything okay? Did you get the results for the tests already?"

"Ms. Parkins, are you related to Mrs. McClusky?" asked Dr. Gordon.

"Not by blood, but I'm pretty sure I'm her closest friend," she said. Sara stood and began pacing back and forth from her closet to her bed. She snagged a light blue racerback tank top and a pair of faded blue jeans from the top shelf and tossed them on the bench.

"I mean, she's like a mom to me, she continued. "I'm her neighbor from down the hall. I've known her for a couple of years now and if she needs something, I can get it for her."

Sara walked into the bathroom and put on her shower cap.

"Well Ms. Parkins. I'm very sorry to tell you, but Mrs. McClusky had another heart attack early this morning. Unfortunately, this one turned into an episode of progressive heart attacks. We did everything we could. She passed away at about 2am."

Sara stopped. Didn't walk…didn't talk, leaned against the bathroom wall and slid to the floor.

"Ms. Parkins, did you hear me? I would have called sooner, but there was nothing you could do. Are you alright?"

A very quiet "yes" slipped from between her frozen lips.

"If you'd like to pick up her things, we can hold them for you? I'm really very sorry!"

"Of course," said Sara.

Sara clicked the off button and the phone slipped from her hand to her lap. She sat frozen in time. *What happened?* she thought. *Why couldn't they help her? They said it was a minor heart attack, but they got her in time. I can't believe she's gone. She was fine yesterday and now she's…* Sara's head dipped and a tear ran down her left cheek. "I said I'd be there for her," she said aloud. Another tear and another and Sara buried her head in her hands.

After several minutes, Sara grabbed the towel bar on the shower door and slowly pulled herself up until she stood. She reached in, turned on the water, stripped off her pajamas and stepped in.

Pulling the lever for the shower, she closed her eyes and allowed the water to stream down her face. The rush of water pellets bounced off her forehead and cheekbones, flowing over her shoulders and down her back.

A ten minute shower turned into a twenty minute shower as her tears mixed with the soap and water. Sara stared at the bubbles, watching them disappear one after the other. Turning off the water, Sara's eyes followed one large bubble, down the gray tiled wall, past the nickel-plated faucet to the waiting drain. She bent and tried to capture it, but the suction pulled it in.

Here and then gone, she thought. *So quick...I didn't have time.*

"I want more time," she shouted, pounding her fist on the wall. She leaned her head on her clenched hand and closed her eyes. Several deep breaths and she pushed up and away from the wall.

"You can do this…you can. You have to - for Anna," she told herself.

Sara stepped from the shower and methodically began getting ready. Body lotion applied evenly, she pulled her hair into a ponytail so she could apply her eye makeup. She then stepped into the clothes she had tossed on the bench. Her mind raced.

I have to get her bag from the hospital and what about her apartment...what about all her things? I don't think she has any family left. Her one brother passed away the year before we met. He'd been climbing a mountain in Peru and there was an avalanche. I remember Anna saying he died doing what he loved doing. But what about her? Why did she die?

Sara stopped and closed her eyes. "Okay, pull yourself together. You've got a lot to do."

She remembered Frank, the cabbie who was so nice. Reaching for her cell phone and purse, Sara pulled his card from a side pocket. *It would be nice to have a friendly face drive me to the hospital,* she thought.

"Hello! Is Frank there?" said Sara.

"I'm sorry, this is his wife Della. Can I help?"

"Frank gave me his card and said to call if I needed a cab anywhere."

"Oh! I'm very sorry dear, but Frank's mother took ill last evening and I'm afraid she passed away this morning. He won't be able to pick you up this time."

"Oh! Oh my God. I'm sorry. No, that's fine. I'll flag another cab down at the curb. I only called because he was such a nice man."

"To give you his card, he must of thought you were a very nice person too, dear. He doesn't give it to very many people."

"Thank you. I'm so sorry for your loss. Della, please tell Frank you're in my prayers.

"Thank you. I will," said Della.

Oh my God! Two people on the same night, thought Sara. She shook her head. *They always say it happens in threes.*

She checked to be sure she had her purse and keys, then pulled her front door shut, locked the deadbolt, and headed for the elevator.

"Good morning, Sara."

Sara turned slowly and saw Jason coming down the hall.

"Good morning," she said and continued toward the elevator. Reaching it, she pressed the button and waited. The elevator door slid open as Jason reached Sara. He stepped in and tilted his head toward her.

"You okay?" he asked.

Sara tried to answer, but her eyes welled up and she stopped.

"What's wrong, Sara?"

Sara held her eyes closed and swallowed hard. "Anna, I mean Mrs. McClusky, she…" Sara's tears flowed.

Jason moved in carefully, extended his arm and pushed the stop button in the elevator.

Eyes jerking wide open, Sara stared at him.

"I'm sorry! I just thought you might need to talk about it before you get wherever you're going. What's wrong with Mrs. McClusky?" Jason's face softened, his movement careful.

Sara's stare relaxed and she looked down at the floor.

"She got sick last night and she called me. When I got there, she was holding her chest, so I called an ambulance and…."

Jason reached for Sara's shoulders and held her firmly. "Sara, did she die?"

Sara's shoulders shook and her mouth dropped. "Yes, how did you know?"

He loosened his grip. "I-I didn't, but you seem so distraught and she is in her seventies…so I thought she might have."

Sara pulled from his grasp and hit the button for the elevator to proceed. "I have to get her things at St. Cecelia," said Sara.

"Sara, I'm so sorry. What'd they say happened?"

"I don't know. It's not making any sense right now. I mean, at first, they thought she had a minor heart attack, but it stopped by the time they got her to the hospital. So, I don't know. They ran a bunch of tests, and they said she'd be fine." Sara's tears started again. A steady stream made their way down to her chin before she used the back of her hand to wipe them away.

"If there's anything I can do, please call me," said Jason. He put his left hand gently on her shoulder, bent, took a Kleenex with thumb and forefinger from a packet in his pocket, and gently blotted beneath Sara's eyes.

"I know you did everything you could for her. Sometimes these things happen. Don't blame yourself."

Sara smiled a weak smile and took the Kleenex from him.

"Thank you," she said.

The elevator panel lit up button L, for lobby, and she exited.

Jason remained in the elevator and Sara sensed him watching her from behind.

The ride to the hospital was a blur. Sara made her way past the front desk and glanced at the clock on the wall. It was 10:30am. On to the bank of elevators around the corner from the ones she took last night. She pressed the button and the doors opened.

Like they were waiting for me, she thought. *Were they waiting for Anna? Was it simply her time?* She stepped inside and the doors closed. *A room of metal, no mirrors on the wall or carpeting. Funny, how I didn't notice these things last night. Of course last night, Anna was here and now she's...well I guess she's still here, but she's not.* Sara ran her fingers through her hair and leaned against the metal wall as it came to a stop on the 4th floor.

She stepped out, glanced one way and then the other. "Which way?"

The walls seemed different than they did last night, thought Sara. The white looked stark and cold and the corridors seemed to go on forever. The still life pictures seemed lifeless now and unimportant. Last night, when Nurse Fleur took her to see Anna, she had watched as interns wheeled a patient to their room. They almost ran the gurney into a wall, where Sara noticed a beautiful picture of a daffodil in full bloom. Now, only hours later, nothing looked beautiful. The daffodils looked sterile and frozen.

Heavy, quick-paced steps came from behind Sara and she moved to the side.

"Are you lost?"asked a short, stocky nurse with dark skin, silky hair and green eyes.

Sara glanced to the side and down. "My name is Sara Parkins and my friend, Mrs. Anna McClusky..." she stopped and took a deep breath. "She passed away this morning. I called 911 late last night because she was having chest pains. They said they wouldn't have the test results until this afternoon. I wouldn't have left if I thought it was serious, but they said there was nothing I could do and that she'd be fine. I don't understand what happened. I mean I..." Sara stopped and noted the look of surprise on the nurse's face. "Sorry! I didn't mean to go on. I'm just here to pick up her things."

"That's okay, dear. Follow me." She passed Sara, quickly reaching the nurses' station and turned left.

Sara hurried to the nurses' station, but saw no one.

A head of thick dark brown silky hair popped up from beneath the desk. "Ah! Here it is," she said. The same dark skinned, green-eyed nurse stood. She held Anna's red overnight bag in her left hand and a release form in her right.

"Oh! there you are. I thought I lost you," said Sara.

"I'll need you to sign this, dear, and I'll need some sort of identification. I'm sorry for your loss."

Sara took the clipboard and pen and signed her name on the release to claim Anna's things. She proffered her driver's license, got an approval nod, and returned it to her purse.

"Oh! And there's this as well," said the nurse. She handed Sara a potted plant of yellow daffodils, Anna's favorites.

"I forgot I'd gotten these for her before I left last night," said Sara. "Thank you."

As the nurse turned to walk away, Sara eyed her name badge…Amanda.

"Amanda," Sara's voice echoed against the cabinets and the long hall of stark white walls.

Amanda stopped in her tracks. "Yes?"

"I know you're really busy, but I need to talk to someone about the cause of death." Sara blurted out. She glanced around quickly and brought her gaze back to Amanda. "Is there a specific person that I need to see?"

Amanda doubled back to the nurses' station, grabbed a chart and moved her head methodically from left to right, all the way down the page.

"Yes, here it is. Dr. Gordon can give you all the information you need. Unfortunately, he left for the day, just a few minutes ago. He'll be back for the night shift. You can give him a call then." She smiled, turned to leave and turned back. "Or you could call Mrs. McClusky's brother…he called about 30 minutes ago and the doctor gave him all the details."

She glanced at the chart. I'm sorry, we didn't get a telephone number, but he was a very nice man.

Sara threw the overnight bag over her shoulder. "Thank you. I'll call Dr. Gordon tonight," said Sara.

Sara made her way slowly down the hall with the information spinning in her mind. *Mrs. McClusky's brother died over four years ago,* thought Sara. *That's so strange. She never mentioned having any other brothers. So how could it have been her brother that called?*

Ten minutes went by as Sara stared off into space in front of the hospital.

Oh my God! I wonder how many cabs already passed me by…wasn't even paying attention, she thought.

After she flagged down a cab and got in, she leaned back to think. Time flew and the cabbie pulled up to her building. Sara handed him a five dollar bill. The cabbie took it and turned forward.

"Keep the change," she said. *Not like he wasn't going to anyway,* she thought.

She gathered up the overnight bag, the potted daffodil, her purse, and slowly got out of the cab. She pushed the door closed with her foot and the cabbie took off.

Stepping quickly, Anna's red overnight bag hung over Sara's right shoulder as she pushed into the revolving doors. As she stepped in, the door pulled back and stopped. Face flush and unable to budge the door, Sara waved at the man at the desk inside. As she did, a gentleman outside pulled the door back and dislodged the bag.

"Thank you," said Sara. She raised her hand half way and waved a meager attempt of gratitude. Into the atrium she turned toward 'Garden Pure' for her usual.

Sara put her plant down on the counter nearest the cashier. At the salad buffet, she grabbed the tongs for the green leafy lettuce and leaned forward, but the red bag fell off her shoulder. She pushed it back up and it slid back down. She replaced the tongs, dropped the bag between her feet and scooted it sideways down the salad buffet. Deviled eggs, croutons, cubed turkey, grapes and grated parmesan cheese drizzled with ranch dressing filled three quarters of her square plastic container. Sara rounded the corner to the bakery section, bag in tow and ripped off a piece of wax paper and wrapped it around a medium size croissant. She then picked up the bag in her right hand, threw it over her shoulder, picked up her lunch and strode to the checkout counter. Placing her salad and roll on the conveyor belt, she selected a Hershey bar while she waited in line.

Sara felt a hand on her right shoulder and turned quickly.

"Sara, is everything okay?" asked Mr. Adashi. "You're not usually here so early and I don't believe I've ever seen you buy chocolate before. Are you going on a trip," he asked, pointing to the red bag.

Eyes listless, voice drained, she replied. "Mrs. McClusky passed away this morning."

Mr. Adashi squeezed her shoulder lightly.

"I'm so sorry, Sara. You've always been good to her. I didn't even know she was sick. Was it sudden?"

"Yes…I mean no…she wasn't sick and yes, it was sudden. She had chest pains, so I went with her to the hospital about 11:00 last night. I still don't really understand what happened. They said she might have had a mini-stroke or a heart attack, but then they said she seemed fine. They told me to go home and they'd call me when the test results came in." Sara shook her head. "I don't know. She was sleeping when I left last night. I still can't believe she's gone." A tear fell from her right eye and she wiped it away with the knuckle of her index finger.

"I went to pick up her things at the hospital." Sara glanced at the red bag and the plant. "But I didn't get to talk to the doctor…he'd already left for the day. I have to call him tonight. I'm sorry…I know I'm rambling."

She moved up to the register and Mr. Adashi put his hand on her shoulder and put a palm up to the cashier.

"I've got it Sara. You go and relax. I'm sure things'll look better soon."

The cashier bagged the salad, roll and candy bar and handed it to Sara. Lunch under her left arm, overnight bag over her left shoulder, purse over her right shoulder, she bent and picked up the potted plant on her way out.

"Thank you," said Sara. Walking carefully, she reached the elevator and pressed the button. The doors opened, she stepped forward and a man in a long black coat rushed out of the elevator. His left arm knocked her off balance and the potted plant fell to the ground and cracked. Regaining her composure by leaning back on the door, Sara turned toward the man.

"Sorry! said Sara. Didn't mean to…" but, he was long gone. She did her best to scoop up the dirt and put it back in the pot and pressed the button again.

The door opened, Sara stepped in and pressed fourteen with her right elbow. *Thirteen doesn't seem so lucky anymore,* she thought. Floor after floor, Sara's eyes focused inward. *Anna ate a regular dinner; she took a pill for reflux that she's been taking for over 3 months and then all of the sudden...she's sick and then she's gone.* "It doesn't make sense," she said aloud. The elevator stopped on 14, the doors slid open and Sara stepped out.

She walked in a slow stride. Her eyes shifted from the carpeted floor to Anna's door to her own door across the hall, three units down. As she drew nearer to Anna's apartment, her pace quickened and the palms of her hands perspired. *One long stride would pass up the door entirely,* she thought.

Sara stopped abruptly. "What's this?" *Mrs. McClusky's door is slightly open. I know I pulled it tight and locked it when we left for the hospital,* she told herself. *Didn't I?* Sara reached for the doorknob when the door pulled open from the inside.

Sara's mouth dropped and she stepped back. "What…"

CHAPTER 3

Jason stared blankly at Sara, until he found his voice.

"Mrs. McClusky's door was open and I thought it was odd, so I went in to make sure nothing was taken." Jason backed up, palms up, and glanced over his shoulder.

"But I – I realized I wouldn't know, so I was coming to see if you were home. If something was taken, you'd know a lot better than I would. Maybe you should take a look. I didn't want to just leave it unlocked."

Jason regained his composure and took the red overnight bag from Sara's shoulder and the potted plant from her left hand. "Here, I'll help you with these and we can come back and check out her place together."

Sara tilted her head to the right, but said nothing.

"I mean, I don't want you going into an unlocked apartment by yourself," Jason explained.

Sara followed Jason down the hall to her unit, unlocked the door and Jason followed her to the kitchen to put down the bag containing her lunch. He placed the plant on the table in the hall and the bag on the floor next to it.

"Sara, I know this is really hard for you. I didn't mean to scare you." Jason tilted his head to the right, to look her in the eye. Sara's eyes fixed somewhere between Jason's knees and the floor. He took his thumb and forefinger and gently propped up her chin. "It's gonna be okay. Really."

Lifting her eyes, Sara found Jason's eyes and held fast. "Thank you."

"It is," said Jason.

Sara turned toward the front door and Jason glanced over his shoulder into the living room - a contemporary layout with a couch and loveseat in blue and cream and a hint of gray, the carpet, gray, plush shag and statues of angels throughout the room. A 37 inch TV sat in the corner and an oblong oak coffee table sat in front of the couch.

Sara cleared her throat. "I like it here…it's big, but it's cozy too."

Realizing his focus had shifted, he turned toward Sara again. "Did you find anything out from the doctor? Anything about what might have happened?"

Sara stopped and looked back at him. "The nurse said that Anna's brother called. The doctor gave him all the information." Sara shifted her feet. "It's kinda' weird because the only brother that I knew about died four years ago climbing mountains in Peru. He was two years older than Anna. Obviously, pretty healthy too. I guess I'm trying to figure out who really called? Does she have a family member I don't know about?"

"Ohhhhh! I don't know" said Jason. "Maybe the nurse was confused. It could have been an old friend that's like a brother."

"I guess." Sara glanced at the red bag. "That's hers," she said.

Jason reached down, grabbed the straps and swung the overnight bag back over his shoulder again.

Sara held the front door open for Jason to step through. She locked her door and turned to walk down the hallway to Anna's apartment.

"Oh my gosh!" said Sara. "It looks like the potted plant had a leak. There's dirt all over the floor." She stopped. "I should get my vacuum."

Jason reached for Sara's arm. "Sara, they have people that clean every night. Don't worry about it. It'll be fine."

Sara nodded and they continued down the hall. Jason pushed open the front door to Mrs. McClusky's apartment. He dropped the bag inside and flipped on the lights as Sara walked to the middle of the living room.

"I'm going to check things out…be sure we're alone. Stay right there," said Jason.

Sara stood frozen in the middle of the room.

I never noticed the musty smell before. I wonder if it was always here, thought Sara.

Jason disappeared down the hall to the bedroom.

Meanwhile, Sara regained her strength and walked tentatively toward the bathroom. She stretched her arm forward and gave the door a push. It flew open and bounced off a rubber stopper on the wall. Leaning forward, she looked inside. Nothing! When she flipped on the light, she saw the shower curtain only three quarters closed. *That's odd*, she thought. *Anna had a thing about keeping the shower curtain completely closed.* Heart pounding, she leaned forward, and with thumb and forefinger, yanked the curtain open.

"Whew! Nothing! I don't know what I expected to find," she said aloud. Pulling the shower curtain back, she stopped. Her eyes had scanned the walls and fallen to the tub. *That's weird.* She tilted her head to get a better look. *Looks like footprints, definitely larger than Anna's feet. Is that possible? Why would there be footprints in the tub?*

Sara leaned forward to get a little closer look…when a hand rested on her shoulder. Sara screamed. She jumped and turned at the same time, almost falling into the tub.

"Jason!"

He grabbed Sara with one hand and reached across her and pulled the shower curtain closed with the other.

"I told you to stay put and I'd check everything first. Why did you come in here?"

"I don't know. I – I just thought I'd help," said Sara, still breathing heavily.

"Well next time, please wait. Everything is fine. You didn't notice anything did you?"

"Well I'm not quite sure, but…" started Sara.

"Alright then. Everything's fine," Jason reiterated.

Jason still had a hold of her arm and Sara dragged behind him.

"Who did you think would be here?" asked Sara.

Jason turned toward her...his eyes looked to the left, to the right and his chin pulled up toward his mouth.

"I –I don't know. A robber of some sort…a drug addict looking for cash. Now-a-days you never know." Jason took a deep breath, moved forward and placed his hand on Sara's shoulder. "I just didn't want you to get hurt."

"I'm fine, but…" Sara began.

"Good," said Jason. He turned toward the door and reached for the light switch. "Well, we should probably lock up then."

Sara stood frozen staring at him.

"What's wrong?"

"I thought you wanted me to look around and make sure nothing was stolen?"

"Oh yeah! Right. I'll wait right here. Take your time." Jason sat down in the living room chair and folded his arms. The left side of his lip pulled slightly upward, but the tension in his eyes remained.

Sara tilted her head, eyebrows furrowed, she stepped toward him. "Are you all right? You seem very nervous."

Hesitating, Jason pushed up out of the chair. "I'm sorry." He bit down on his lower lip. "I know I'm supposed to be all macho, but when I saw the door open it made me really nervous. My grandmother's apartment was broken into once and they hurt her pretty bad."

Sara's eyes softened, her top row of teeth bit down into her lower lip as she moved closer.

"I'm so sorry, Jason. I had no idea. And for what it's worth, you did great. Being stupid isn't being macho. You were being cautious and I appreciate that." Sara pushed up on her tiptoes and gently kissed his cheek. "I've been in a fog since this whole thing happened. I guess I'm still in shock."

"It's understandable," said Jason. "She was important to you. I get that. Maybe you could use a listening ear right now? I'd be happy to take you to lunch or an early dinner. But, only if you're comfortable with that."

Sara's bottom lip pushed her top lip slightly upward as she smelled that wonderful smell she noticed on the elevator the day before…Paco Rabanne.

"That would be nice! I could use a friend right now. Just let me grab my purse. Can you lock up?" said Sara.

"Absolutely. I'll wait for you at the elevator."

Sara hurried to her apartment, grabbed her purse and glanced in the mirror. "Okay! Don't block him out Sara. He's here for a reason," she told herself.

Sara closed the door, locked it and in her rushed state, dropped her keys. Bending to pick them up, she noticed two sets of footprints in the dirt, hers and Jason's.

"I've got the elevator Sara," said Jason.

Sara grabbed the keys, dropped them in her pocket and hurried to the elevator.

"Are you up for some Italian food?" asked Jason as he pressed the Lobby button.

Sara smiled. *That's really fattening*, she thought. "Normally, I eat very light, but today, I think it's just what I need."

"Great! We can grab a cab and see what we find."

The elevator doors opened and Jason and Sara walked side by side toward the revolving doors. There was a hustle and bustle of people in the lobby, coming and going from Garden Pure and Italian Heaven. The smell of hot pizza and mostaccioli with melted cheese drifted under Sara's nose. Plastic bowls containing healthy salads carried mostly by women, drifted past her. *I never really noticed how many people live here*, she thought.

Jason stepped in and pushed the revolving door for Sara and she exited.

Raising his arm, Jason hailed a cab, while Sara noticed an elderly woman walking her dog. Jason took Sara's hand as a yellow cabbie pulled in tight to the curb.

He opened the door, Sara slid in all the way to the other side of the cab and Jason took the seat by the right door. Both of them glanced at each other and squinched up their noses.

"Where to?" said the cabbie.

"We're looking for a reasonably priced, but good little Italian restaurant. Know of any?" said Sara.

"How far from here?" said the cabbie, an Asian man, gray, balding and unshaven. He had slits for eyes and his mouth appeared to be frozen with the corners turned downward.

"Within a couple of miles would be good," interjected Jason.

The cabbie didn't respond, but pulled rapidly from the curb, zigzagged in traffic, but kept his speed at 35mph. Jason and Sara held the back of their hands in front of their noses and glanced out the windows.

Not soon enough, the cabbie stopped in front of 'Trattoria's at Dearborn and Harrison. Without even looking at where they stopped, Jason noted the amount and handed the money to the cabbie with a $2 tip. He opened the door and extended a hand to help Sara. She took his hand and pulled herself up and out. The door shut and the cab squealed away from the curb.

"Ya think he was a little ticked off?" laughed Jason.

"Yeah! Just a little. He must've been hoping for an airport ride. And now that I see where we are, there was a much more direct way to get here too."

"That's my fault…I look like a visitor," said Jason. He offered Sara his arm and they walked beneath the green awning to the hostess stand inside 'Trattoria's'.

"Well at least he brought us to a nice place," said Jason, laughing. "The smells in here are fabulous."

Sara lifted her nose slightly. "Uh, huh! It smells very rich. And now that we're here, I don't know if I'm hungry for something so heavy."

"Don't worry about it," said Jason. Only eat what you're in the mood for." Jason picked up the menu at the hostess stand and glanced at the main dishes. "Looks like they make healthy salads here, too – a Chicken Caesar, an Antipasto, and an Italian Chicken salad."

"Right this way," said the waiter. He seated them at a small booth in a corner directly across from the bathrooms. "Here are your menus, water and silverware. I'll be right back for your order."

"Actually I know what I'd like. Can I get a Chicken Caesar Salad?" asked Sara, handing the menu back to him. Sara turned toward Jason.

"I'll have the Chicken Alfredo and a glass of Sprite with a lemon in it, if you wouldn't mind?" said Jason.

"Fine," said the waiter and he disappeared.

"He must have heard me say I wasn't that hungry," said Sara.

"It's a little crowded that's all." Jason threw his hands in the air and pointed at the bathroom signs written in Italian. "It just makes it easier to find the bathroom," he said.

Sara smiled and the muscles in her face relaxed.

Resting his arms on the table, Jason leaned in. "Maybe you could tell me a little about Mrs. McClusky. I'm sure you have some wonderful stories. The one time that I talked with her, she seemed like a delightful woman. I wish I'd gotten to know her better."

"You would have loved her," began Sara. "And I know she would have loved you. Actually, I think she had a crush on you."

"Really! Well, I feel honored, but what makes you think that?"

"Well, the day you stopped by, I saw her afterward and she said if you were about twenty-five to thirty years older, she'd ask you out herself." Sara smiled.

Jason laughed and threw his head back.

"She was great," continued Sara. "Always positive about everything, never looking at the negative. Such a joy to be around. On the weekends we played Yahtzee or we'd go to a movie. She loved to bring her micro-wave popcorn and her bite-size candy bars. I always insisted on taking them out of the wrappers before we left and putting them in a baggie. I told her it'd be easier for her because it's so dark in there. I didn't want to hurt her feelings, but the truth is, the noise was a bit much for the people around us," laughed Sara. "She had so much energy…I don't know where she got it. She was always offering me something to eat or something to drink. Even if we'd just finished dinner. It was always, 'is there anything else I can get you?' or 'I don't think you've had enough'."

Jason gazed into Sara's eyes. Her smile grew bigger and bigger, as she reminisced about Anna.

"The first time she invited me for dinner, she asked if I liked ham and mashed potatoes. I said I did and when I got to the table, she had a third of a five pound ham on my plate. I'm serious. So, I promptly picked up the other two thirds and said, 'this'll be fine.' I don't think she knew what to say, until she saw the huge smile on my face. We both laughed so hard. She learned really quickly that I wasn't a big eater. The two of us were always laughing about something or other."

Jason laughed, "She sounds like a hoot."

"She is…" Sara stopped. "I mean, she was."

Jason reached his right hand across the table and laid it on top of Sara's. "I know it's hard, but this is a way to celebrate her life."

"I know. It's just so strange. I was with her this morning and she was fine when I left. I just don't get it," said Sara.

"Did she have a heart problem? Maybe it was hereditary?"

"No, she always used to say how blessed she was that her family was so healthy. I mean my God, her brother was climbing mountains when he was seventy. And he didn't die of old age. There was an avalanche of snow or whatever that's called and he was pushed right off the mountain."

Sara pulled her hand from under Jason's and grasped his hand tight.

"Jason, you know the human body. If a family doesn't have a history of heart disease, what are the odds of somebody in that family having a heart attack with no exertion at all?"

"That's a good question," said Jason. "I can look into it if you like."

The corners of Sara's mouth spread up and out. "That would be great. I would really appreciate it."

The waiter rounded the corner with a large tray. "Water, Sprite with a twist of lemon, Chicken Caesar Salad for the lady and Chicken Alfredo for you," said the waiter. "It's a little hectic today. One of our waiters called in sick. My name's Antonio, so if you need anything, please let me know."

Antonio placed a basket of hot bread on the table. "The olive oil is there," he pointed his index finger toward it…"in the corner of your table."

"Antonio, do you think I could I get some butter, when you have a chance? I'm not an olive oil fan," said Sara.

"No problem, be right back."

Antonio returned before Sara got the fork to her mouth.

"Thank you so much. I really appreciate it," said Sara.

Jason and Sara ate quietly.

"Is everything okay?" asked Jason.

"Yeah! I guess I just drifted off. I was thinking about Anna and I remembered coming here once. I thought this place looked familiar. She knew where we were going, so I just enjoyed the ride. We were so engrossed in conversation, that I didn't even remember the name of the place after I got home. But, we did enjoy the food. I'm really gonna miss her."

Sara looked up into Jason's eyes. "I really would appreciate you looking into this. I feel like I wasn't there for her…" Sara raised the palm of her hand toward Jason. "I know, I know, they told me go home. But, it's just how I feel. Even if it wasn't my fault, I need to do this. To make sure nothing happened that shouldn't have."

"Sara, I promise I'll do everything I can to find out exactly what happened. But, I'm going to be honest with you, it may have been age that brought on the heart attack. But I will check for anything unusual, okay?"

"Okay," said Sara.

She patted his hand gently and glanced at her phone.

"Oh my God!" said Sara. "Do you realize the time? Thank you so much for taking my mind off things and for getting me to laugh. It's been a really hard day for me."

"Well I assure you, the pleasure was all mine," said Jason. He turned his hand over and caressed Sara's. "I haven't enjoyed a dinner so much…in I don't know how long. But before we go, give me ten more minutes and tell me a little about Sara."

Sara blushed. "What did ya want to know?"

"I don't know. What are your hobbies? What were you like as a little girl? Were you the girlie-girl who played the piano or were you the tomboy on the block?" said Jason.

Sara giggled. "Probably a little of both. I started out as the girlie-girl, when I forced my parents to let me take piano. Luckily, they were smart enough to rent a piano, cuz after one week of practicing, I got tired of it and quit. But, in all fairness, I was seven. Then when I turned eight, I wanted to be a ballerina. My Mom…she's got movies of me dancing around the house in a little tutu for hours on end. That lasted about a year. Then at age nine, I started looking through magazines and decided I wanted to be a model. I practiced walking down our long hallway between the living room and dining room. I used my Mom's scarves to look sheik," laughed Sara.

"So you've been modeling ever since?" asked Jason.

"Actually, I went on a couple of auditions, but I didn't get a call back, so I quit. Not really a stick-to-it kinda kid. That's when I became a tomboy. I wanted to prove I could do anything a boy could do. So, my Dad, being very supportive, decided to take me fishing. I learned to cast a line and skirt the water and I even caught a few fish, but it was too quiet for me. So, next he taught me how to play darts. Now, that I liked. And it went pretty well, until I started beating him on a regular basis, throwing side arm."

Jason laughed.

"Yeah! So of course, he said I wasn't throwing them correctly, even though I won. So, he decided to take me skeet shooting instead. Thing is, I got pretty good at that too. He was okay with that and got me into a bunch of competitions. He did the Dad thing and bragged every time I won a medal. But six months and six competitions later, I wanted to be a lady again. My Mom was thrilled and my Dad acted all disappointed, but I think he missed Daddy's little girl. I never told him, it was mostly because of Joey Parusa. Tee hee hee."

"Boy next door?" asked Jason.

"Yeah! Blond hair, blue eyes," Sara tilted her head. "He had this remarkable smile that melted my heart."

"What about your hormones," asked Jason.

"Well, a little of that too," laughed Sara.

"So what ever happened to this Joey?"

"Well, there was a Doug Carmichael who moved in down the block about two months later."

"Oh! so, you found a new guy?" said Jason.

"Not exactly…but Joe and Doug hit it off right away. I believe it was my first introduction to gay men," smiled Sara.

"Oh my! That must have been confusing," said Jason.

"Yeah, it definitely was. And it seemed like after that, every good lookin' guy I met, turned out to be gay. They say all the good looking ones are." Her eyes darted toward Jason. "You're not gay are you?"

"Absolutely not," said Jason.

"Just making sure," said Sara.

"They were both great guys…and I'm grateful they turned me back to my feminine side."

"I'd have to say, I appreciate the feminine side of you too." said Jason. "When did you come back to modeling?"

"Thirteen, fourteen, right around there. I started modeling in catalogues and I got pretty regular work. I did a few commercials, but it started getting leaner as I hit my mid-twenties. I'm hoping to get a 'National' before my career's over. The residuals would keep me going for a while," said Sara.

"That's pretty impressive," said Jason.

"Okay! Enough about me. What about you? What were you interested in as a boy?"

Jason scrunched his mouth to the side and bit down on his lip.

"Well, I was never very good with instruments or singing…" he began.

"Did you ever try any?"

"Yes. I try to forget about it, but…"

"Come on, you couldn't of been that bad."

"Oh! I think I could. Matter of fact, they called my parents from Band and asked if they could try and get me interested in something else because I was ruining the sound."

"No!!! No way," said Sara.

"Oh! Yeah! Of course, my parents said I was too good to be in band because I was making them look bad. They didn't explain until I was in my mid-twenties that it was because I was really making them look bad." Jason chuckled.

"Oh my God! That's too funny," said Sara. "So what did you do that you felt you were good at? What made you decide to be a doctor or biologist?"

"My dad was a medical doctor," said Jason quietly.

"Was?"

"Yeah! He passed away when I was seventeen. I think that's when I decided to go into Medical Research. The hospital gave him a drug that interacted badly with what he was taking."

"Oh my gosh! I'm so sorry."

"He was a great dad. You'd think being a doctor, he'd of been too busy for me, but he never was. I miss him. So many times, I wish I could pick up the phone and call him."

Sara squeezed his hand. "Thanks for sharing that with me. It makes me feel special."

"You are." Jason looked at his watch. "Whoa! I lied. I took up another thirty minutes of your time, instead of ten."

"I did most of the talking," said Sara. "As much as I hate to say it though, I should probably get back. I've got to call the doctor and find out what he says."

"Let me know what happens. I don't want you dealing with this on your own."

The left corner of Sara's lip rose again and her eyes twinkled. "Thanks Jason, I will."

Jason pushed his chair back, when Sara squeezed his hand. "Do you mind waiting just a couple minutes," asked Sara. I'd like to use the ladies room before we leave."

"No problem. Take your time." Jason scooted back in and crossed his legs at the ankle beneath his chair.

In the bathroom, at the mirror, Sara beamed. *I can't believe I actually met a nice guy for a change, she thought.* "Anna, you were right about him," she whispered. She re-applied her lip gloss and ran her fingers through her hair and turned to exit.

Walking back to their table, Sara saw Jason from across the room. *Wow! He's really cute. Dark hair, really nice arms. Strong, but not overly big. Nice backside too.* She giggled to herself. *I really love his eyes the most. And he dresses nice too. Even dressed down, he looks good. A tailored shirt with a starched collar; tucked into blue jeans; Gym shoes that got dirty after stepping into the dirt from that potted plant,.* Looking at his shoes crossed beneath his chair, she noticed something…a diamond shape, right in the middle of the shoe. *Why did that seem so familiar? Hmmm! That's so weird. I feel like I've seen that before,* she thought. As Sara approached Jason from behind, Jason turned and smiled.

"How'd you know I was behind you?"

"I could smell your wonderful fragrance," said Jason. "Ready to go?" he asked.

"Yes, yes, I am," smiled Sara. "Thanks for waiting."

Another crazy cab ride and they made it back home.

Walking down the hall together, Jason turned sideways as they approached Anna's door.

"It's okay, Jason," said Sara. She stopped and gently turned Jason's body so that she could see Anna's door. "I don't want to forget her," she said.

"I know," said Jason and then he walked down the hall to Sara's unit. "Call me if you need anything." Jason handed Sara his number on a napkin from the restaurant.

She folded it and put it in her purse. "Thanks again, Jason, I really had a wonderful time."

Jason started down toward his apartment and Sara reached up and inserted her key to unlock the door, but before she could turn the key, it creaked open.

"Oh my God! Oh my God!" shrieked Sara.

CHAPTER 4

Sara shrieked, turned and saw Jason put his key in the lock. Jason immediately ran down the hall toward her. "What's wrong?" he asked.

"My, my, my door wasn't locked," said Sara.

"Are you sure you locked it when you left?"

"Yeah! I ran back for my purse and I remember locking it when I came out because when I went to take the key out, I dropped it." Sara bent down toward the floor and stopped.

"Jason, there's another footprint," she said, pointing at the dirt. She backed up into him and Jason wrapped his arms around her and pulled her away from the door.

"Wait for me in my apartment, the key's in the door."

"What about you? I don't want you to get hurt," said Sara.

"I'm not gonna go in. I'm just gonna watch the door to make sure no one leaves without me seeing them. Now go. And Sara, call 911."

Sara backed down the hall to Jason's apartment. She used his key and stepped inside the door, closing it immediately and pulling out her cell phone.

"911, what's your emergency?" said the operator.

"Someone broke into my apartment," said Sara.

"What is your name and your address," asked the operator.

"My name is Sara Parkins and I live at Chicago Hi-Towers, 371 North Lake Shore Drive, suite 1414."

"Okay Sara, try to relax and tell me where you are in the apartment," asked the operator.

"I'm not, I'm not," said Sara.

"You're not what?" said the operator.

"I'm not in the apartment."

"Where are you?"

"I'm down the hall at a friend's." Sara opened the front door, glanced at the number and closed it again. "I'm in 1418."

"Okay, that's good, Sara. So, what makes you think there's someone in your apartment," asked the operator.

"My door was open. You need to send someone right away."

"Where is your friend?" asked the operator.

"He's in the hall, watching the door to my apartment in case they try to leave."

"Sara, this is very important. My name is Sam and I'm going to help you. Can you get your friend's attention without making any noise?"

"I think so," said Sara.

"Good, because you need to have him wait with you. The police are on the way, Sara. So I want you to open the front door of your friend's apartment and look into the hall and see if you can get your friend's attention without making any noise. Can you do that Sara?" asked Sam.

"Yes, I can do that, I can do that."

Sara opened the front door and looked around the corner. Jason wasn't there. She quickly closed the door again.

"Sam, Oh my God! Oh my God!"

"What is it Sara? Calm down and tell me what's wrong? Sara!"

"It's Jason. It's Jason."

"Is Jason your friend, Sara?"

"Yes, but he's not there. He's not in the hall."

"Alright, it's okay Sara. Go back into his apartment and wait there. The police will be there any minute," said Sam.

"But what about Jason? What if something's wrong?"

"Sara, take a deep breath. Everything will be fine."

"He must have gone in my apartment. What if something happened."

"Everything is gonna be fine. The police are coming up in the elevator now. Unlock the front door and go into an inside room in your friend's apartment, like the bathroom and lock the door until the police come for you, okay," said Sam.

"Okay!"

Wow! His apartment is layed out just like mine. Sara walked down to the bathroom. She pushed open the door, stepped inside, closed the door and locked it.

"I'm in the bathroom," said Sara.

"Good!" said Sam. "The police are in your apartment right now. After they've made sure no one is there, they'll come for you. Okay?"

Sara's hands shook and perspiration pooled on her forehead and around her neck, underneath her hair. "I need an Advil," she said.

Sara suddenly stood and opened the medicine cabinet. *Oh my God! What am I doing*, she thought. *This isn't my bathroom.* She began to push the mirrored cabinet closed, when a bottle fell off the first shelf. Without looking, she caught it and put it back in and sat down. Sara cocked her head to the right. She heard footsteps outside the door.

"It's the police ma'am. Can you open the door, please?"

"Sara, this is Sam. It is the police. You can go ahead and open the door."

Sara unlocked the bathroom door and opened it slightly. Blue, long sleeved shirts, shiny black shoes and badges waited on the other side. Two sets, side-by-side. She pulled the door open the rest of the way.

"Are you okay, Sara?" asked Sam.

"Yes, Sam, thank you."

"Okay! I'm going to hang up now. Everything will be fine. Give all of the information to the officers," said Sam

"Thank you, Sam. Goodbye."

"Miss, are you okay?" asked the officer to her left, who stood slightly in front of the other.

"Yes, what about Jason. Is he okay? Was there someone in there?" asked Sara.

"No one was in there and it doesn't look like anything was taken, but we'll need you to come with us and see. Are you up to doing that?" asked the officer.

"Yes, I am. Thank you."

The officers turned and Jason appeared at the front door. "Sara, are you okay?"

The larger officer immediately stepped between Jason and Sara. "Miss, do you know this man?"

"Yes officer, it's okay, this is his apartment," said Sara. Looking at Jason, Sara squinted her eyes. "Where were you? Did you go in my apartment?"

"No, I slipped into the stairwell so that I could keep an eye on your door without anyone seeing me. But I heard something a couple flights down when the police…" he nodded his head at the men in blue. " …arrived, so I went down to check it out. Just tenants."

Sara turned back to the police officers. "So, what do we do? Could you tell someone broke into my apartment?" said Sara.

"First things first…we'd like you to check and see if there's anything missing. If there is, you'll need to file a report for the stolen article. If not, we need to figure out what the intruder might have been looking for."

The second officer stepped forward. "I'm Officer Hyde and I did notice there was some kind of dirt in front of your door and going down the hall. I saw three distinct shoes in the dirt. One, I believe is yours and…" He turned toward Jason. "Can I see the bottom of your shoes?"

Jason pulled his right leg up, bent at the knee.

"That's one of the other ones," said Officer Hyde. "I actually found the third footprint in your bathroom too."

"Why! why would someone break into my apartment? I don't understand. I don't have any money in there. What do you think he wanted? Can we check for fingerprints or something? Or the footprint…can you match that to somebody?" asked Sara.

"Okay! Slow down, Miss. Unfortunately, it's not easy to match a footprint, unless it was the same footprint used in another crime. Now we do have a couple of questions we need to ask."

"Okay!" said Sara.

"Do you take any kind of heavy-duty prescription drugs?"

Sara's eyes opened wide and her mouth dropped.

"Sorry ma'am, but we have to ask," said Officer Hyde.

"No, I don't take any prescription medications at all," said Sara. "I have a brand new bottle of Advil, but that's it."

"Are you a new tenant?" asked the second officer.

"No. why?"

"Sometimes, people leave drugs behind…hidden in the toilet tank or underneath it," said the officer. "When they remember, they come back for it."

"No, I've lived here for over two years and I've done enough thorough cleaning to know there's nothing like that in my apartment."

"Okay, well, now we have to see if anything's missing then," said Officer Hyde.

Jason stepped in. "Why don't we all go to your apartment and take a look." He headed toward his front door.

Sara followed Jason and the officers followed Sara down the hall and into her apartment. After checking for missing articles and finding nothing gone, they filled out police reports for breaking and entering. After an hour, both officers got up to leave.

"Ma'am, if we can match a footprint to some other break in, we'll let you know. That's about all we can do for now - what with nothing missing." He walked toward the door to leave. "You might want to stay at a friend's house for tonight," he suggested.

As Officer Hyde stepped out into the dirt outside her front door, Sara's eyes opened wide and her jaw dropped.

"Wait! Officer Hyde. There was another break in, or at least we think there was. Just three doors down, my neighbor, Mrs. Anna McClusky..." Sara's head fell forward and she stopped.

Jason put his hand up. "We thought," said Jason. "Thought being the operative word, that there was a break in, but we didn't notice anything taken there either."

"No, but there was something else," said Sara looking at Jason. "I forgot to tell you. There was a set of footprints in the tub, as though someone stood behind the curtain. They weren't perfectly formed, and at first I thought Mrs. McClusky might have put an old pair of shoes in the tub to dry, but they definitely weren't hers. It was a set of footprints made by a man's shoe. I have the key, I can show you," said Sara.

"Is Mrs. McClusky home," asked Officer Hyde.

A quiet "no" escaped Sara's lips. "She passed away this morning. When I came home from getting her things at the hospital, Jason said he found the front door open. He asked me to check out the apartment because Mrs. McClusky was a friend of mine. So, I did. It was the same as here, nothing was taken that I could see, but I don't know all the little memorabilia she might have had," said Sara.

"Okay! Let's take a look," said Officer Hyde.

Jason trailing, Sara led the way to Anna's apartment and the two officers followed her in.

"In here, in the tub…" Sara began. She pulled back the shower curtain and pointed at the base of the tub, looking back at the officer.

The officer's eyes shifted from side to side. "I don't see anything ma'am. It's actually pretty clean."

The second officer rolled his eyes.

Sara's eyes shifted to the tub. "That's impossible!" Sara searched the tub, but the officer was right…there was nothing.

"I know what I saw. The same man must have broken in here again and cleaned up the footprints," said Sara. "Then he broke into my apartment. Maybe he's not sure what apartment he was supposed to break into to get what he's looking for. Maybe it was a friend who had the drugs and he lived on this floor and this guy's not sure which apartment."

"Ma'am," began the second officer. "When they say 'the crooks cleaned up,' they don't mean it literally."

"Hey, Jason," said Sara. "You've only lived here since last weekend. Maybe it's your apartment they're looking for." Her head swiveled from left to right, hands motioning in the air.

Jason gently took Sara's hands in his and looked into her eyes.

"Sara, I don't have any prescription drugs either."

"Ma'am," said Officer Hyde. "It sounds like you've been through a lot today. I think maybe you need some rest. If you come up with anything else tomorrow, you can give us a call." Officer Hyde handed Sara a business card.

Jason smiled at the officer. "I'll make sure she's okay."

The officers walked out into the hall to leave.

"Thank you," said Sara barely audible.

"Sara, it'll be okay. I promise," said Jason. "Are you nervous about staying in your apartment? Do you have another place to stay for the night?"

"No, I'll be fine. I'll double lock the door and put that stick thing up under the doorknob." She glanced up at Jason. "But I'll put your number on speed dial if you don't mind."

"Not at all," said Jason. Jason shifted his feet and bit into his bottom lip.

"Um, you know, if you're nervous, I'd be happy stay with you…on the couch, I mean. Well of course, I mean where else? Um! Anyway, I'm just trying to say, if you need anything, please don't hesitate to ask. Okay?"

Sara lifted up on her tiptoes and kissed Jason on the cheek.

"Thank you. I won't."

Stepping into the hall, Jason followed Sara. She turned and locked Anna's door and walked down the hall with Jason to her apartment. Looking at her door, she hesitated and looked at Jason.

"Want me to check one more time?" asked Jason.

"Yes, please."

"Wait here," said Jason. Sara could hear him opening and closing closet doors and making his way around the apartment and back to her.

"It's fine. Oh! And I checked under the bed too," he said smiling. "Sure you're okay?"

"Yes, thank you. Again."

Sara slowly closed the door. She double locked it and put the stick up underneath the handle.

Sara could see Jason through the peephole. He leaned his hand on the door and waited to hear her lock it. His eyes weary, but warm.

"Good night Jason."

"Good night Sara."

Jason turned and walked away.

***

"There's always tomorrow for dreams to come true" played and vibrated on the nightstand. "The time is now 10:13am," said a mechanical voice.

Sara reached for the phone and clicked the answer button.

"Hello."

"Did I wake you?" said the voice at the other end.

"No, I was just about to get up," said Sara. *Oh my God! It's Jason.* She stretched her arms above her head and looked at her phone for the time. *What time did it say? It's after 10...he must think I've lost it,* she thought.

"I can call you later," said Jason. I just wanted to make sure you were okay. It's been a couple of days and I wanted to know if you needed anything." His voice was sweet and caring. He hesitated and waited for a response.

"Thank you so-o-o much. I really do appreciate it. I guess my body needed to work some things out and sleep seemed to be just what the doctor ordered. Yesterday, I went through some old pictures of Anna and I actually filled three poster boards and dropped them off at the Funeral Home. Besides that, I was on the phone a good portion of the day with the doctor and the police and then running other errands," said Sara. "I don't think I fell asleep until after 1:30am."

"You said you talked to the police? Did they find out who might have broken into your apartment?"

"No! I called to apologize to them for rambling on and on the other night. They must have thought I was nuts," said Sara.

"I'm sure they didn't think that. Like the officer said, you'd been through a lot that day. Sometimes your mind plays tricks on you," said Jason.

Sara rolled on to her side. "No, I'm not second-guessing what I saw, but since the footprints were gone, I shouldn't have gone on like that to the police. But, I was thinking," continued Sara, "about asking you to help me."

Sara held her breath and pulled at the drawstrings of her sweats that she'd fallen asleep in last night.

"Help you what?"

"Help me find out whose footprints were in Anna's tub and if they were the same ones going into my apartment," said Sara. "Unless, you'd rather not?"

"No, I'll do what I can to help. I'm not sure where to start though."

"Well, I started making notes…" said Sara. She lay on her back, tied and untied the drawstring… "of everything that happened the day Anna passed away. I remember when I came back from the hospital there was a man in a long black coat who literally knocked me over when he came off the elevator. When I turned to apologize for being in his way, he was already gone. Now, I usually wait to see if anyone's getting off the elevator before I jump on, but I was a little off that day myself. But when I went back and thought about it, even if it was my fault…what guy would knock a woman over and not even say they were sorry or stop to help," said Sara. "Unless they were in a big hurry to get out of there."

"Did you see the man's face?" asked Jason.

"No, unfortunately, I wasn't looking up…I was thinking about Anna. But, I thought that maybe the security cameras would have a picture of him. And there was one thing I did notice. When his arm swung out and knocked into me, I do remember seeing a two inch scar between his thumb and forefinger, but that was it - Jason, I have to find out what's going on," said Sara.

"Well, I've got a few things to do this morning, but I'll be free at four o'clock. Maybe we could grab dinner and figure out where we can go from here?" said Jason.

"You're amazing," said Sara.

"What do you mean?"

"Well, we basically only met a few days ago and you're really listening to what I'm saying. And, you don't seem to think I'm nuts."

Jason chuckled. "No I definitely don't think you're nuts." He hesitated. "I'm really glad you asked for my help, Sara."

"Me too. Four o'clock it is," said Sara.

She hung up the phone and lay back down. *How could I possibly still be tired?* she thought. She stretched her arms over her head and yawned. Dragging her legs over the side of the bed, she reluctantly sat up once more. *I need to eat something,* she thought. With that, she slipped on a pair of fuzzy slippers and walked into the kitchen. She poured herself a glass of cranberry juice and popped an English muffin into the toaster. While that toasted, she peeled a banana, leaned against the counter and bit off one chunk at a time, taking a sip of juice in between. *I wonder if this is like a date tonight? I mean, I know he's helping me, but he did say over dinner. He could've said he'd look into it when he had time. Is he just being polite or was that a way to let me know it's a date? Oh! I hate it when I'm not sure. I really do like him.*

"Pop."

Sara plucked the muffin from the toaster and buttered it while it was hot, spread a little jam over the top, cut it in half and took a bite. *Now I have to figure out what I'm gonna wear for this "maybe" date.* She leaned against the counter, cocked her head to the right and finished the banana and muffin. *I know, my burgundy tunic with my jeans. It's not too sexy, but not like a prude either. It says I'm serious about getting something done, but soft enough to be feminine. Yeah! That's what I'll wear.*

Sara walked to the closet and selected her blue jeans and her burgundy tunic and hung them on the doorknob. The tunic was sleeveless with spaghetti straps and a boat neck. It curved in at the waist and flared out a little toward the hips with a slit on either side. She turned and selected a pair of simple blue denim drop earrings and a denim lace choker with a burgundy stone that hung down a quarter inch in the center.

CHAPTER 5

She heard the bell, checked the peep hole, and smiled. There stood Jason. He wore a gray and black lumberjack shirt with a gray t-shirt underneath. *I'm glad I decided on jeans,* she thought. She grabbed her keys and purse and opened the door.

"It's four o'clock on the dot," said Jason.

"Wow! You really are prompt."

"I never keep a beautiful woman waiting," he said. The left corner of his mouth pulled up and his eyes glistened. "What a beautiful outfit. I love that color."

"You look really nice too," said Sara.

Sara fumbled with her keys and Jason took them gently from her and locked the door. "There you go," said Jason. He held out his left arm and she wrapped her right arm tightly around it. Jason's scent sifted past Sara's nose.

"I love that scent…is that Paco Rabanne?" asked Sara.

Jason pulled her a little closer. "Yes it is."

The elevator door opened and they both got on. This time they stood on the same side, arm-in-arm.

This definitely feels like a date, thought Sara. *Yay!!!*

Jason pressed L and they took a non-stop route to the lobby, then made their way to the front door. Jason stepped in the revolving doors first to give it a push for Sara. Once Sara stepped outside, Jason took her arm again, pulled her close and looked down at her.

"What?" asked Sara, looking up at him.

"I think I've figured out that beautiful scent you're wearing," said Jason.

"I don't know. It's not one of the more popular ones," Sara mused.

"Could it be Charlie," he asked.

Sara pulled away, mouth gaping, lips turned up. "How in the world did you know that?"

"Well, I am a doctor of sorts and deal with a great many substances. I noticed that the molecular structure of certain scents carry a heavier…"

Sara's eyes stayed focused on Jason. Her mouth still open, her fingers reached for Jason's arm.

Jason rolled his head back and bellowed. "Oh! I just can't do it. I actually saw it on your table in the kitchen."

Sara gasped and slapped his arm. "You! You really had me going."

Jason raised his hand to flag a cab and laughed. "Well, I guess impressing you is out of the question now."

Sara chuckled through the long slender fingers of her right hand and leaned toward him. "I wouldn't say that," she replied.

Jason tilted his head down toward Sara. Sara's hand dropped and her eyes closed. She waited in anticipation.

"Beep, beep," a green and white checkered cab pulled in tight to the curb. Sara's eyes flew open, Jason cleared his throat, righted himself, and opened the door for Sara to step in.

"Good afternoon, Miss Sara," said Frank.

The corners of Sara's mouth rose. "Good afternoon, Frank."

Sara slid to the far end of the cab and then remembered.

"Oh my gosh! I almost forgot. I'm very sorry about your mother, Frank."

"Thank you, Miss Sara. I will definitely miss her. But I believe she is in a much better place now," said Frank smiling in the mirror.

Jason stepped in and sat right by the door. Sara and Jason barely looked at each other.

"Good afternoon to you too, Mr. Jason," said Frank.

Sara did a double take. "You know each other?" she asked.

"Yeah! He picked me up a couple of days ago," said Jason.

"Where can I take the two of you today?" asked Frank.

"There's always tomorrow…"

"Ooooh! I'm sorry, I have to get that." Sara leaned toward the left door and pushed the phone to her right ear. "Hello!" said Sara.

Frank turned toward Jason. "Thank you for the lovely flowers, Mr. Jason," he began.

"You're welcome!" mouthed Jason, shifting his eyes to Sara and back again.

"Oh!" said Frank. "Sorry!

"Just one minute, Frank. I'd like to see where Sara wants to go," said Jason.

"No problem, Mr. Jason.

The decibels of Sara's conversation rose. "That's wonderful! I'd be happy to. Tomorrow at 2 pm sounds great," said Sara. Sara glanced over her shoulder at Jason, eyes wide, face beaming, lips still pressed to the mouthpiece. "Thank you so much. You won't be sorry," said Sara.

Sara clicked the off button and threw her arms into the air. "I can't believe it! That was the agency. They chose me for the commercial. Oh! My! God! I can't believe it, a national commercial," said Sara. She threw her arms up and Jason leaned forward and gave her a congratulatory hug. She wrapped her arms around him and felt his rock hard abs against her.

"Ahem! Congratulations, Miss Sara," said Frank.

Sara quickly pulled back from Jason and slid a distance away.

"Thank you, Frank," said Sara as she tugged on the bottom of her tunic and fixed a strap that had fallen down.

"Am I going to get my autograph, Miss Sara?" smiled Frank.

"As many as you like," she mused. "I can't believe they chose me."

"And this surprises you why?" asked Jason.

"Because there were so many beautiful girls there and I thought they'd of called me by now, if I were the one. I thought they picked someone else." Sara took a deep breath. "I'm so-o-o excited."

Frank glanced in the rearview mirror at Jason. "Did you want to go back to Riggati's, Mr. Jason?"

"Riggati's?" said Sara. That's at six fourteen North Wabash?"

"Yes, Miss Sara. I took Mr. Jason to the same building that day. Two very nice people from the same building, going to the same place," Frank smiled.

Jason fidgeted in the seat. "I'd heard that Riggati's was the Chicago pizza place," said Jason. "I thought of trying a different place today, but we could go there if you like. It was really good."

"That's so weird," said Sara.

"What is?" asked Jason.

"That we went to the same address on the same day," Sara replied.

"Yeah! You're right…that is. Maybe it means we were destined to meet." Jason slid his left hand toward Sara's and intertwined his fingers. Sara immediately produced a row of pearly whites.

Glancing in the rearview mirror a few times, the corners of Frank's mouth rose.

Jason tilted his head toward Sara. "Sara, is there anything special you'd like to have for dinner?"

Sara gritted her teeth and pulled her chin downward.

"Um! I shouldn't but, I'm sort of in the mood for pork ribs. I know they're really messy, but I love 'em."

"A woman after my own heart," said Jason. "I heard there's a place called 'Mama's' that's pretty good."

On cue, Frank pulled away from the curb and headed down Ontario.

"Frank, is Mama's as good as they say? After all, this is a celebration. Since you know Chicago so well, can you help us out? Where's the best place for killer ribs?"

Frank's smile lit up his face and his eyes beamed. "Mama's is good, but I know of a much better place that other people don't know about, Mr. Jason. It's small, but the ribs are the best in Chicago. My regular fares told me of this place and they were right. It's called Mulaney's Pub."

Frank merged over three lanes of traffic and turned left in front of an oncoming bus. Horns blared, but Frank's smile never wavered. Sara lost her grip on the door and slid over into Jason's lap. This time Sara didn't attempt to return to her original spot. Eyes entranced by his, she leaned closer against his shoulder and Jason wrapped his left arm around her. The fingers of his right hand intertwined with hers. He dipped his head down and placed his lips against her ear.

"I'll keep you from sliding," he whispered.

Warm air caressed Sara's ear, goosebumps raised on her arm, and her face went flush. Eyelids fluttering, she uttered, "Thank you."

Frank peeked in the rearview mirror and smiled. Arriving at their destination, he leaned forward, turned off the meter and circled the block once more. Jason nodded his appreciation while Sara relaxed in his arm.

Coming back around, he pulled in slowly to the curb and put the car in park.

"We are here," he announced. "These are the best ribs in town. You will be talking about them for weeks." Frank noticed Sara's movement and turned toward them.

"You two have a fabulous dinner and give me a call when you are done. I would be happy to bring you home," he said.

Jason grabbed his wallet and slipped a twenty to Frank. Frank began to get change, but Jason narrowed his eyes. "We're good, Frank," said Jason.

"Thank you, Mr. Jason."

Jason opened the door and held Sara's hand as she stepped out.

Mulaney's pub was a quaint little establishment that you might miss if you were talking to a friend as you walked by, thought Sara. A brownish-red brick with an orange awning and a cozy look.

Jason opened the door for Sara and the smell of barbecue sauce rushed past their noses and into the street.

Jason took the lead, fingers intertwined with Sara's, and grabbed a little table in the corner in the back. He pulled out Sara's chair and sat down across from her.

"This is cozy. I like this place already," said Sara.

"Me too. It has character," said Jason.

An older waitress with gray hair, a sauce-stained apron over a crisp white shirt, and worn out gym shoes, approached the table. Her eyes glistened green and a wide smile emerged as she closed in on them.

"Hi there folks. I'm Gladys and I'll be your waitress for this evening. What can I getcha to drink?" she asked.

Jason held his right hand palm up and nodded toward Sara.

"Hmmm hmm hmm. Let me see. Do you have O'Doul's Amber here?" asked Sara.

"One O'Doul's Amber coming up." Gladys swiveled her head toward Jason. "And for you, sir! What'll ya be havin'?"

"Gladys, I think I'll have one of the richest beers around…" he began.

"A rootbeer?" said Gladys.

Jason smiled. "How did you know I was going to say that?"

"I'm seventy-two years old, honey. Been workin' here for thirty four years and I've heard 'em all. But I like you…you're cute." She reached over and pinched his cheek.

"Here are your menus folks. Be right back with your drinks," said Gladys.

Sara fidgeted in her chair and waited for Gladys to leave.

"Jason, you can have an alcoholic beverage if you want. I'm just watching my weight," said Sara.

Jason rubbed his cheek with the backside of his hand. "Well, truth be told, that's the reason I'm not having an alcoholic beverage," said Jason.

Sara scrunched her eyes and looked Jason up and down. "Because you're watching your weight?" said Sara. *There's no way. He looks and feels rock hard*, she thought, her mind drifting back to the cab.

Jason dipped his chin and raised his eyebrows. "No, because I'm watching yours. And, by the way, I don't want to miss anything by drinking." He reached for Sara's hand across the table and lay his hand on hers.

Sara giggled nervously and pulled her hand off the table. "I hate to disappoint you, but maybe you should have that drink," said Sara.

Jason's mouth became a gash and his eyebrows sloped down. "Oh! no I didn't mean. I would never. I mean I…I was doing my best and obviously fumbling miserably at giving you the highest compliment I could. I think you're a knock out…there I said it." Jason's face turned ashen and she noticed the perspiration from the palms of his hands on the plastic tablecloth.

Sara's face held a blank expression for all of ten seconds before she could hold it no longer and the corners of her mouth pulled up and she burst into laughter.

Jason's color returned, but his embarrassment remained. He waved his hands in front of him. "I know, I know, I'm an idiot," he said.

Sara grabbed both his hands in hers. "You're not an idiot. A little nervous maybe. But, I think you're sweet and you're thoughtful. I like that," she said. She brought his hands down on the table and rested hers on top.

Another patron dropped a few coins in the jukebox up by the front door. 'You Are So Beautiful,' by Billy Preston and Joe Cocker filled the room.

"There, see, if I'd waited sixty seconds, I could have said, they're playing your song," said Jason. "Would have saved me a lot of embarrassment."

Sara smiled and her eyes twinkled.

"One O'Doul's Amber and one root beer." Gladys doled out the drinks like cards.

Looking down, Jason gulped down half the glass of root beer without taking a breath.

"Have you folks decided what you'll be having to eat?" asked Gladys.

"Well, actually we came here specifically for the pork ribs. We heard they were the best. Would you recommend 'em?" asked Jason.

Gladys patted her stomach. "Are ya kiddin' me, honey? Where do ya think I got this? I have 'em almost every day. They're awesome."

"Just what we wanted to hear," said Jason. Gesturing with an open faced palm toward Sara, he continued. "This lovely young lady will have the pork ribs and so will I."

Gladys turned to Sara. "Full slab or half slab?"

"Half," said Sara.

"Baked, mashed, double baked or fries?" continued Gladys.

"Baked," said Sara.

"Soup or salad?" said Gladys. "The soup is minestrone."

"I'll have the dinner salad with no dressing," said Sara.

Gladys pivoted to start the process all over again. "Full…"

"I'll have the full slab, double baked and I'll have the Minestrone," said Jason.

Gladys grabbed a weaved basket from the tray behind her. "Hot bread and butter for ya and I'll have the soup and salad in a sec," said Gladys.

Gladys may be a tad overweight, thought Sara, *but she's light on her feet and a wonderful waitress. And the music, dim lighting, and small corner table make everything perfect.*

"Gladys, can I get a bunch of extra napkins please. Sometimes ribs can get a little messy for me," laughed Sara.

"No problem, honey. I'll getcha a stack," said Gladys and off she went.

"Wow! I think Gladys is the only waitress here. She has one…two…three…four tables by the door, one next to the bar and our table," said Sara. "But she never misses a beat."

No sooner did she say it, that Gladys returned.

"Here's your salad and your soup," said Gladys. She placed them down in front of each of them, scanned the table, and stopped at Jason. "Refills are free. Would you like one?"

"Yes. Thank you," said Jason.

Sara wrapped her hand around her frosty bottle of O'Doul's Amber and gently touched her lips to the mouth of it.

Jason downed the rest of his root beer.

Within thirty seconds, Gladys returned with a new glass of root beer and retrieved the empty glass. "How's everything so far folks?"

"Couldn't be better," said Jason.

"Very good," Sara chimed in.

Sara scooped up the last two croutons in her salad while Jason finished off the last spoonful of soup and started on a roll.

Gladys retrieved both empty bowls, turned on her heel and returned to the kitchen in seconds.

"She's amazing," said Sara. "She hasn't slowed down since we got here."

"I know. And she's seventy-two years old. She <u>is</u> amazing."

Jason leaned across the table. "So about this shoot tomorrow…That is what you call it, right?"

"Yes! I guess it is," said Sara.

"How does it work? Is it a whole day thing or what?"

"Well honestly, I'm not sure. This is my first national call back from an audition. It may take a few days to get it down just right. I'm really excited about it."

"Well, I'm not surprised at all that they chose you."

Sara blushed.

"No, I'm serious. You're beautiful. You have a great smile and I love your eyes. They seem to capture a mood and hold on to it."

Wow! This guy is too good to be true, thought Sara. "That's really sweet and I could definitely use all the support I can get. I am really excited, but I'm still a little nervous too," said Sara.

"Don't be. You'll be great. And, I'd be more than willing to come and watch how it's done and support you in person, anytime you like," said Jason. "Just say the word."

Gladys's right hand balanced a large silver tray above her head, while she dropped off drinks at the table near the bar. Continuing on, Gladys delivered Jason and Sara's food.

"Here ya go folks. Enjoy! And if you need a take home pack, just give me a holler. Oh! And here are the extra napkins."

Curls of heat rose from the pork and the smell of rich, sweet barbecue sauce wafted over their table. Potatoes done to perfection and tender broccoli filled their plate. Sara lifted her fork and placed it at the first section of ribs. Before she could even push down, the pork fell away from the bone.

"Wow, that's amazing," said Sara. "This is really tender." She slid the pork and barbecue sauce into her mouth and it melted its way down her throat.

Jason picked up the slab in thumb and forefinger at both ends and the pork fell off on to the plate. He collected the bones and set them to the side and ate with a fork.

"Mouth watering. This stuff is great," said Jason. He took care to fully swallow before talking.

Conversation subsided as Jason and Sara slid bite after bite into their mouths.

"Mmmmm mmmmm," said Sara.

"Mmmmm mmmmm," agreed Jason.

Jason finished first and sat back in his chair, resting his hands on his belt buckle. "Whew! I'm stuffed! Frank was right…they were awesome." Jason downed the second glass of root beer and exhaled.

Sara wasn't far behind. The last juicy bite went slowly into her mouth, tongue sweeping over her lips to be sure every bit was consumed. She too, sat back and rested her hands on her lap.

No sooner did they finish, Gladys swooped in and scooped up their plates, basket of bread and silverware.

"How did ya like those pork ribs?" asked Gladys. Gladys scanned the plates. "Looks like you both did pretty good. Can I get you two a dessert?"

"The ribs were fantastic Gladys. I feel like I'm gonna burst," said Sara. "Think I need some time to let my stomach digest before I decide on dessert."

"I'm with ya on that," said Jason.

"No problem folks. Those ribs'll fill ya up quick. Take all the time you need."

Jason pulled his chair in tight to the table and leaned forward. "Now that our stomachs are full, maybe we can continue our conversation from the other night. When did you move to the building? When did you first meet Mrs. McClusky?"

The sparkle in Sara's eyes disappeared.

"I'm sorry. I didn't mean to upset you," said Jason.

"No, it's not that. It's just that I feel bad. Here I am celebrating and having a nice time… when Mrs. McClusky died only a few days ago," said Sara.

"You know what? I really think Mrs. McClusky - Anna- would have wanted it that way. She wouldn't want you to suffer, or to be sad. She seemed like a really neat lady and I think she'd be happy that you're happy. And I know she'd be proud you got that commercial."

Sara smiled and tilted her head slightly. "You're right. She would. She's a…she was a wonderful person."

Jason reached his right hand over to Sara's left hand and gently caressed it.

"Did you ever find out what happened…I mean what the doctors found out caused Mrs. McClusky to pass away?" asked Jason.

"Well, when I talked to the doctor the next day, he sort of gave me the run-around. I mean, he said it was a mini heart attack or a stroke, but it didn't react normally," said Sara.

"What do you mean?"

"I don't know. She was fine one minute and then like someone threw a switch, she developed an abnormal arrhythmia and went into cardiac arrest, even though her tests came back fine minutes before." Sara stared at the table as she continued. "He said at first, he thought it was a virus, but that he'd never seen that before. I don't know, but like I said, her whole family was pretty healthy. I just don't get it."

"I know," said Jason. He squeezed her hand gently. "She was very lucky to have such a wonderful friend in you."

"Thank you," said Sara.

"Sara, did they give you her death certificate? I'm just wondering what they listed as the cause. I only ask," said Jason, "because if you want me to help, I'd need to know what they thought was the cause before I could check into it. Medical findings is sort of my expertise, especially if it had anything to do with medicines and interactions. We wanna make sure the hospital did their job and didn't give her something she shouldn't have had."

"Oh! sure. Yes, I have it. I can show you when we go home…I mean when I go home. I can show you then." Sara's lips rose slightly and her eyes glistened again.

"That sounds great. So, can I ask you a couple of questions?" said Jason.

"Of course."

"Did you know of anything else that she might be taking periodically or if she was allergic to any kind of medication? Even if she didn't say she was, do you ever remember her having a hard time breathing after taking a medication? Or did she ever mention a rash?"

"It's strange because – Anna- I mean Mrs. McClusky…" Sara hesitated.

"She's your friend. You should call her Anna," said Jason.

"You're right. I was going to say, it's funny because Anna really was very healthy. And I know I'm not helping, but I don't recall her ever having any problems. She never mentioned taking medications until she started with the Rilosac. But that didn't seem to bother her. She really didn't like taking anything, but she trusted doctors. Just like she trusts the police and priests…her generation I guess. Even though she felt healthy, if she was told to take something, she'd do it. That's why she got the flu shot."

"My Mom and Dad were a lot like that too," said Jason.

"Then of course, there's me," said Sara. I never figured anyone knew what was good for me except me." Sara chuckled. "Of course, the other day…"

As Sara was about to continue, she noticed Gladys smiling and moving across the pub towards Jason. But Gladys's stride slowed, her smile disappeared, her head dipped and she grabbed her stomach. Leaning against the bar, she reached for a stool.

Jason jumped up and grabbed her under the arms as she slid to the floor.

Sara was right behind him. "Gladys, are you okay? What happened?" asked Sara.

"Ooooh! my stomach. All a the sudden, started getting this nauseatin' feelin'," said Gladys.

Jason stooped down as he lowered Gladys to the floor. Once she made it to the floor softly, he removed his hands. "Gladys, do you want me to help you up to the stool?" he asked.

"No, I'd rather sit here for a spell," said Gladys. She exhaled in short spurts and pushed on her stomach with one hand and pushed on the floor behind her with the other. "This is nasty. All a the sudden, whew!"

"Gladys, did you take anything tonight…any medication?" asked Jason.

"Just a couple Sudafed. Had this nasty cold for two weeks. It's almost gone now though," said Gladys.

"Anything else," asked Jason.

"Well, I take Rilosac for reflux. That's it though."

"You had Rilosac tonight?" Jason's eyelids fell and his jaw tightened.

Sara's hand was on Jason's shoulder. "What is it?" she whispered.

"Nothing. It's okay." Jason turned back to Gladys. "How long have you been taking that stuff?"

"Honey, when you're my age and you eat ribs every other day, you need it every night. Been takin' it for a couple months now," said Gladys. She winced in pain. "This nausea is really bad though. I've never had anything like this before."

"I'm callin' 911," said the owner.

"Henry, don't be crazy. I'm fine," said Gladys.

"If you're fine, how come you're still sittin' on the floor. I ain't seen you sit down anywhere for more than thirty seconds ever."

Henry turned toward the phone. "I'm makin' the call."

"It's a good idea," said Jason. "I'd like to go to the hospital with you, if I could."

Sara looked at Jason with a confused look on her face.

"Like I said, sometimes a combination of things can cause a problem and maybe while I'm in the ambulance, she'll tell me about something else she took. A lot of doctors don't know about all the subtle interactions with different foods or medicines and what they can cause in different people. If I can, I can tell them what to give her," said Jason. "She reminds me of my Mother. I just want to help."

"That's really nice," said Sara. "I'll go with you."

"No, that's okay. I'll get you a cab and come by after. You've got that shoot tomorrow. I don't want you too tired. Would that be alright?" asked Jason.

"Sure, that'd be great," said Sara. "But I'm staying until the paramedics get here."

Sara leaned down and placed her lips softly on Jason's cheek and moved to his ear. "I had a wonderful dinner. Thank you."

Sirens got louder and louder and the red lights began bouncing off the front window.

"They're here, Gladys. Just relax and let them help you. And I'll be here too," said Jason.

"This is one lucky day. I got the best lookin' guy in the place to take care of me. Not bad," she smiled.

"What am I chopped liver?" asked Henry.

Henry was a slight man with a full head of silver hair. He stood five foot, seven inches tall.

"I'm only a year older than you, ya know. And I still got all my hair."

"I'm talking fantasy, Henry. Lemme have my fun," said Gladys. She blew a kiss at Henry as they hoisted her up on the stretcher.

"I'm comin' with," said Henry.

"Who's gonna watch the bar?" she asked.

"I can close down," he said. He rushed to the table by the door and started turning the chairs upside down on the top of the table.

"Henry!!!" Gladys brought her pitch as high as she could. "Stop it. I'll be fine."

Henry squinted so you could barely see his pupils and he gritted his teeth so hard his bridge popped up. "You're an ornery thing you are. Fine!"

Henry removed the chairs he'd placed upside down and put them on the floor again.

"You'd better take care a her…she's my main girl."

Gladys smiled. "Didn't know you cared."

"Yeah, well, who am I gonna get to work tomorrow's evening shift, if you're sick?" Henry countered. A single tear escaped his left eye. He turned and wiped his sleeve over it.

Sara lay her hand on Jason's shoulder. "Let me know how Gladys is," she said.

Jason turned and stood. "I'll get you a cab," he said, turning toward the door.

Sara gently grasped his arm and Jason turned toward her. "I'm okay. You take care of Gladys."

Jason leaned in to Sara and kissed her gently on the cheek. "Thank you. I'll talk to you later."

Sara looked over her shoulder. "You take care, Gladys. You were right about the ribs. And don't worry, 'cause you're in good hands."

Gladys proffered a half smile and lifted her right arm to attempt a wave. "You two are a cute couple," she yelled in return.

Sara heard Jason's faint response. "I hope so," as she flagged down a cab.

CHAPTER 6

"There's always tomorrow for dreams to come true" played and vibrated on the nightstand. "The time is now 7:13am," announced the cell phone.

With a towel partially draped around her, Sara ran dripping wet from the bathroom. She grabbed the phone and tucked the towel under her arm.

"Hello!" said Sara.

"I hope I didn't wake you," said Jason. "I wanted to tell you to break a leg."

"Oh, no! I just stepped out of the shower. How did everything go last night? When I didn't hear anything, I got worried," said Sara.

"I'm sorry. You know hospitals…it takes forever just to get someone to see you. It went fine," said Jason.

"You know how people say things always happen in three's," said Sara. "It's weird, first Anna, then Frank's mother…I was afraid Gladys was going to be number three."

"Everything is fine. I want you to go to that shoot and knock 'em dead…" Jason gritted his teeth. "Sorry! wrong choice of words, but you know what I mean," said Jason.

Sara nodded her head. Realizing she was on the phone, she said, "yes, I do."

"I've got to go," said Jason. "But I'd like to see you tonight, if you're available."

"I'd like that," said Sara. "I'll call you when I get home. You have a good day too and thanks for all your support. By the way, I thought it was really nice of you to go to the hospital with Gladys."

"Thanks," said Jason. "Call ya tonight."

Sara hung up the phone and ran back into the bathroom to return the towel. Glancing at herself in the mirror, she turned sideways, bent her left leg and put her hand on her hip. "I can do this. This is gonna be great. He's right," said Sara. "Heck, if I can look at myself naked, I can certainly deal with any outfit they want me to wear," she said aloud.

I wonder what I'll be wearing, she thought. *A wine commercial is usually very sophisticated and sexy. We'll see.*

A pair of dark gray sweats and a wine colored racer back tank top lay on Sara's bed. Wine trimmed Nike's lay on the floor.

After applying her hand cream and deodorant, she slipped into white panties and a bra and turned on the TV news in the living room. Applying only base makeup, Sara listened casually to the news in the next room.

Ooooh! I should call Frank, she thought. She grabbed her cell phone and dialed. "Hi Frank, this is Sara. Would there be any chance of you picking me up at 8:30am. I'm going for the first day of that Commercial Shoot," said Sara. She paused. "Thank you, Frank. I'm really excited. Okay! I'll see you at 8:30. Thank you. Bye!"

Sara glanced at the clock on her phone. Already 8:03am. Sara pulled on her sweatpants and threw her shirt over her head and tucked it in. She looked in the mirror and turned from one side to the other. *It's so different than the audition*, she thought. *No makeup or jewelry and wear loose fitting clothing.* "Hmm! Kind of nice to have all that done for you," she said aloud.

"Okay Sara," she said to herself. "You're ready to rock n' roll." She stepped into her Nike's, located her keys and purse, and headed for the door. She heard the TV on in the living room, something about a death. Sara didn't want to hear it, so she found the remote and clicked it off. She wanted to be happy today, to feel good about doing something she'd worked really hard for. Sara smiled and walked out the front door, locking it behind her.

A quick elevator ride and Sara walked out the door to where Frank waited for her. She opened the door and slid in past the rip in the seat.

"Hi, Frank. Thank you for picking me up."

"It is my pleasure, Miss Sara. Are you excited about today?"

"Yeah! I am. But, I'm also a little nervous. My last shoot was over a year ago and it was local. This is national. I just hope I do a good job, that's all."

Frank smiled and he pulled away from the curb. "Don't you worry, Miss Sara. Be yourself and you will be wonderful. Listen to me…I know what I am talking about."

Sara giggled. Sirens raced by and big metal machines pounded on cement, making it almost impossible to hear.

Sara leaned forward. "Chicago isn't Chicago without all the noise."

"Do you know when you will be finished, Miss Sara?" asked Frank.

"No. It'll depend on a lot of different things. The lighting, sound, costume flaws and how well I do. But I'll give you a call and see if you're around," said Sara.

"I look forward to hearing from you."

Another cabbie cut in front of Frank and Frank laid on his horn.

"I don't know how you do this every day," said Sara. "I think I'd be ready for the looney bin."

Frank winked in the rearview mirror and pulled up behind two black stretch limos in front of Six Fourteen North Wabash.

"This looks like a very important commercial," said Frank.

Sara bit her lip.

"Don't worry, Miss Sara. You will do great. Break a leg, Miss Sara."

Sara grabbed five dollars from her wallet and Frank put the palm of his hand up facing her.

"This one is on me, Miss Sara. A congratulations cab ride."

"Thank you, Frank." She stepped out of the cab and hurried up the cement steps.

Climbing to the second floor, Sara opened the door where the producer waited for her.

"I'm sorry! Am I late?" asked Sara, checking her watch.

"No, no, actually you're early, which is great! I'm Craig. Welcome to Momentum Productions. We've got a car waiting downstairs for you. The shoot is at the Wilmette Yacht Club. The makeup and wardrobe trailers are already there. I guess you just need to sign in here and we can be on our way."

A girl sat at the front desk with a nametag pinned to her shirt. 'Tandra'. She handed the clipboard to Sara.

Sara braced the board with her left hand and signed in at 8:37am. She handed it back to Tandra.

"Oh! don't forget to sign out on location," said Tandra. They'll let you know when you need to come back. Oh! and thanks for showing up early."

"No problem," said Sara.

Craig brought his left arm up and away from his body to usher Sara to the door. "I'm gonna be riding with you. I like to go over the feeling I want the commercial to convey. I want the mood to show up in the film," said Craig.

"That'd be great," said Sara.

They both took the steps at a rapid clip and reached the stretch limo in seconds. Sara slid all the way to the far side and Craig sat by the other door.

"First off, we're glad we got you. You've got the perfect look for this commercial," said Craig.

"Thank you," nodded Sara.

"The setting is you and your boyfriend on his yacht. It's romantic and sexy and the wine adds to that, of course," said Craig. "You'll be wearing a cross between a bikini and a nightgown. It's actually a white bra and panty with a burgundy/wine shaded see-through wrap. Four inch stiletto heels and you're good to go."

Craig noticed Sara swallow deeply as the car hit a pothole.

"Don't worry. It's gonna be very tasteful…very romantic," said Craig.

"It sounds fine," said Sara.

The car pulled into the lot and the driver exited to open the door for Sara and Craig. Craig extended a hand to help Sara out. Sara took it and stepped on to the pavement. Six trailers lined up like buses circled the parking lot. There were four white aluminum structured trailers and two silver structures, one for the Producer and one for the Director. Manned by two chefs, a fifty foot square white tent with long tables and chairs was set up next to the medium size food truck. The sun was already up, the sky a perfect blue with a light breeze out of the south. The smell of scrambled eggs and bacon drifted across the parking lot from the food truck along with coffee and hashbrowns.

Sara caught the scent and was immediately re-directed.

"Sara, this is the Director, Phil Staben," said Craig.

Phil, a tall balding man, mid-sixties, wearing jeans and a polo shirt stepped up.

"It's nice to meet you, Mr. Staben," said Sara.

"You can call me Phil. I'm gonna take you to the makeup trailer, so we can get you started."

"Sounds good to me," said Sara. "I'm really excited about being in this …."

"Excuse me…Phil, we've got a problem," interrupted Paul, one of the casting directors that Sara had auditioned for.

Phil turned away from Sara and rolled his eyes. "What is it now?"

"The guy we cast to be her boyfriend, Jim, was carjacked last night. He got banged up pretty bad," said Paul.

"That's just great! So, now what?" said Phil.

"Well, see that guy over there by the trailer," Paul began, "his name is Adam. He said he's here for the audition. I told him the auditions were held last week. He said he flew in from New York. Normally, I'd say, too bad. But since the other guy isn't coming…" He tilted his head toward his right shoulder and brought his hands up in front of him. "He belongs to a modeling agency out there. Got his resume and he does fit the bill."

"Did you run him through the lines you had at the auditions?" asked Phil.

"Yeah! He did really well, and he's got the body and attitude too," said Paul.

Phil ran his fingers through his close cropped hair. "All right, this is his lucky day. Get him ready," said Phil.

Phil turned toward Sara. "Sorry! There's always something."

Paul pivoted to leave, but stopped. "Oh! We also had to get a replacement for one of the grips."

"Yeah! Okay! Whatever!" said Phil. He waved his hand behind his head and turned toward Sara.

"Ready to go?" asked Phil.

"The guy who was playing my boyfriend was carjacked? Is he alright?" asked Sara.

"Yeah! I guess he got knocked around pretty bad, but he'll be okay. But we lucked out and we've got a replacement. So we better get going." Phil walked in long strides toward the makeup trailer and Sara did her best to keep up.

"Okay," said Phil, slowing down. "If you can step into the trailer here, they'll get your makeup and hair started."

Sara stepped up into the trailer and took a seat in the chair on the far right.

On the right, an array of makeup cases filled with facial bases, blushes, shadows, eyeliner, mascara and cover-up lined the countertop; next to that, brushes, combs, hairdryers, curling irons, straight irons and hairspray. Even hair pieces. Short crown pieces, ponytails and extensions in every color lying out on the nine foot counter, overshadowed only by the mirror that stretched to a ten foot ceiling. At the opposite end of the trailer, the exact same layout.

"Hello there!" came a voice from the back of the trailer. "I'm Babs and I'm gonna make you smokin' hot." She stopped and looked Sara up and down, then continued. "But that's only because you've already done most of the work."

With green eyes as wide as quarters and a head of lush red hair with a two inch green streak down the right side, Babs had a smile that took up most of her face. But when she turned away, Sara noted a two inch buzz cut just over her left ear. Sara remembered most hair stylists she came in contact with were a bit on the bizarre side, but always very nice.

"Hi Babs, "I'm Sara."

Babs wrapped a colorful drape over Sara's shoulders, snapped it in the back, and began to apply makeup.

"I'm always amazed," said Sara. "How much make-up artists remind me of painters. You're all so talented and precise."

"Thanks. A lot of people think it's not a talent at all. But, those are the ones who can't apply everyday makeup to save their life," laughed Babs.

Babs ran the eyeliner pencil with precision over and under each eye, then highlighter, shadow and mascara. She blended colors with her thumb and then brushed them lightly.

Babs twirled Sara around to look in the mirror. "What do you think?" asked Babs.

"I think you do great work," said Sara. "Thank you."

"Next on to the hair," said Babs. Babs held a curling brush, curling iron, brush and a comb all at the same time.

"Well, if you're ever short of work here, you could always be a juggler," laughed Sara. "Personally, I have difficulty holding a flattening iron without burning myself."

Adam climbed the steps into the trailer occupied by Sara and Babs.

"Hi! I'm Adam. Supposed to get hair and makeup done in here."

A whiff of a very strong cologne entered the trailer.

"Hi there handsome, I'm Travis," said a voice from two steps behind Adam. "My friends call me creampuff." Travis ran his hand across Adam's chest. "Why don't you take a seat right over there, sugar," said Travis.

Adam smirked. "I'm interested in women, just so you know."

Sara looked down and smiled.

"All the good ones are," snapped Travis. "At least I get to run my fingers through your hair for a little while."

Adam leaned toward Travis and whispered in his ear.

Travis pulled his eyes up and to the left and pointed his index finger at Sara. “Her? Yeah! She’s your girlfriend for the shoot. I guess she’s hot, if you like that sort of thing,” said Travis.

Adam’s eyes could have severed steel when he grabbed Travis’s arm and turned him around. “What the hell’s wrong with you,” he said through gritted teeth.

Travis waved his arm in front of Adam. “Oh honey! She could read it all over your face.”

Adam glanced around Travis at Sara. Sara immediately closed her eyes as Bab’s set the final touches with hairspray. But, her lips held a delicate smile.

“My, my, my, aren’t you the hunk?” said Travis. “Beautiful blue eyes, dark brown hair…” Travis walked around Adam licking his lips.

He took a small pair of scissors and ran his fingers through Adam’s hair with the scissors right behind. “Snip, snip, snip. Not much to do here, gorgeous.”

Travis wore gray and red plaid pants with white suspenders and a white skin-tight sleeveless t-shirt.

“You’re pretty buff. You sure you wouldn’t want to try a different road?” said Travis as he began brushing loose hair from Adam’s lap.

“Heh! Dude! I said I’m not interested.” Adam grabbed Travis’s hand.

Babs turned around and threw a makeup sponge across the room at Travis. “Hey! the guys not interested. “No means no.”

“Ya can’t blame a guy for trying,” said Travis. He flapped his right arm limp at the wrist and batted his eyes.

“Okay Sara, you’re done and you look gorgeous,” said Babs.

Sara caught Adam leaning on the arm of his chair to get a glimpse of her around Travis.

"You do look beautiful," said Adam.

"Thank you," said Sara. She took off the drape, folded it on the chair and walked to the door. Her eyes glanced at Travis and she smiled at Adam as she walked down the steps. She stopped on the first step to fix her shoe.

"Hey! What can you tell me about her?" said Adam.

Travis raised his left eyebrow, pursed his lips and fanned his own chest with the brush. "What's in it for me?" he asked.

Sara smiled and leaned back slightly to hear what Adam would say.

"I might be inclined to take off my shirt," said Adam.

Sara saw Travis's cheeks go flush as he applied Adam's base makeup and blush.

"She's twenty nine years old, 5'6", 127 lbs and she doesn't have a boyfriend…but," Travis paused. "She's a goodie goodie, so you're not gonna get anywhere with her." He cocked his head to the left and then the right. "Me on the other hand…"

Good! thought Sara. *I'd rather have someone thinking that, than something else.*

"Yeah! Yeah! Yeah," said Adam as he removed his shirt. Adam had a six pack and a deep tan. "If you find out what she likes and dislikes, we'll see what we can do," said Adam grazing Travis's chest with his hand.

Travis gritted his teeth and leaned on one hip. "You're such a tease, biatch."

Sara smiled and stepped quietly down on to the ground as Paul stepped up into the trailer. "Travis, what are you doing in here? We have to get Adam to wardrobe."

The wardrobe trailer was one trailer down from the hair and makeup trailer. Sara stepped up the three metal steps and turned left. Racks of clothes ran down both sides of the trailer, ending only two feet from a shower on either side. Above the racks hung shelves of shoes of every color, but from what she could see, only in her size. Sara found her name pinned to an outfit at the end of the first rack. Lifting up the outfit, she saw the sales receipt. "Whew!" Twelve hundred dollars. Two duplicate outfits hung together, totaling twenty four hundred dollars.

"Wow!" said Sara.

Sara retrieved a pair of shoes sitting directly above the outfits and placed them on the floor. She closed the trailer door, slipped out of her clothes and into the bikini with cover-up and four inch heels. Walking to the right of the trailer door, she checked herself out in the floor-to-ceiling mirror.

"Okay! Be confident and smile. You look great, Sara Ann Parkins," she said aloud.

There was a knock at the door and Sara opened it.

"Are you ready?" asked Phil.

"Yes, I am. This is a very beautiful outfit," said Sara.

"Yes it is, and you look great in it," said Phil. He offered his hand and she walked carefully down the metal stairs.

I know he only wants to make sure nothing happens to me or the shoes that would jeopardize the shoot, she thought.

The cameraman set up the lighting and hung the microphone booms overhead. The yacht was safely secured fifty feet away from the dock and a motorized walkway went out to the bow of the yacht when needed. *A perfect day*, thought Sara. *Eighty degrees with a slight breeze. Of course, the lights'll heat things up quite a bit too.*

Sara took her place on the stern of the beige, seventy-five foot yacht. She wore a white bikini/panty with three white pearls forming a v at the top and a white lace bikini/bra top with three pearls along each cup and one dangling between them. Over that, she wore a three-quarter sleeve chiffon, see-through cover-up in shades of burgundy, pink and mauve. Her colors had been coordinated with the yacht's cream colored, burgundy trimmed sails.

Sara saw that the producer sat beside the director to ensure everything looked perfect.

"Where's our runner?" asked Phil.

"Right here," said a perky 5'4", 140lb blonde. "My name's Clare."

"Okay! Clare, Stay with the grips and…" Phil began.

"Phil, she's okay. She's worked with us before," said Craig.

"Okay then, let's get started. Get that fan positioned to the left of Sara. We want the wrap to flow away from her. We don't want it all wound up around her. And use the small round table for the bottle of wine and glasses," said Phil.

The grips angled the fan and Clare placed the table as requested and returned to the bow. Both Babs and Travis stayed in the back by the grips.

"Sara, honey, pick up the glass of wine and hold it in your left hand and rest your right arm on the railing on the port side," said Phil.

Sara's eyes searched left, then right as she pivoted.

"That's to your right, the left side of the yacht," said Phil. "Don't worry, it can be confusing. The wind is perfect now, so let's get some shots in."

The motorized walkway cranked toward the yacht with Adam on it. He wore torn blue jeans with the top snap undone. No shirt and no shoes.

Adam stepped over the railing, smiled at Sara, and took his place with a glass of wine in one hand and the bottle in the other.

"Take One," said Phil. "Action."

Adam moved close to Sara and wrapped his hand with the glass of wine underneath the chiffon cover-up and around her waist. With the other hand, he poured a bit of wine into Sara's glass.

"You're beautiful," said Adam. "To us."

The two lifted their glasses by the stem and took a long sip and Adam pulled her in and gently kissed her. She smiled and gently kissed him back.

Sara raised her eyebrows and pouted her lips. "More please," said Sara.

Adam glanced at the bottle of wine and then at her and smiled. He filled her glass. Sara smiled.

"Cue tagline," said Phil.

You're good people and you deserve the good things in life. Chateau Martinat – "Epicurea - Cotes de Bourg. With scents of raspberry and dark cherry, this wine exhibits ripe elegant fruit merged with a robust body and fullness. Allow the ripe silky tannins to flow over your palate as hints of chocolate and warm cedar melt into your tongue. It will keep your passion surging.

"Cut! Run it on the right alongside Sara and Adam enjoying the wine. Okay! That was good, but Adam, when you put your arm around her, be careful not to get caught in the chiffon cover-up," said Phil. "We want people to compare her body to the bottle of wine. And hold the bottle above the label and make sure it's turned out toward the camera," said Phil. "Take Two, Action!"

Adam took his original spot and Sara did the same.

Adam moved in close to Sara and wrapped his arm around Sara's waist. The wind blew her chiffon cover-up over the top of the glass.

"Cut," said Phil. "Places…take three. Action."

"You're beautiful," said Adam. They raised their glasses. "To us," he said

The two took a long sip and Adam pulled her in and gently kissed her. She smiled and gently kissed him back.

Sara raised her eyebrows and pouted her lips. "More please," she said.

Adam glanced at the bottle of wine and then at her and smiled. He filled her glass.

"Cut," called Phil. "Don't fill the glass so high. We don't want her to look like a lush. Grips, get a new bottle."

The grips replaced the bottle and fixed her wrap. They lowered the boom mike and Babs fixed Sara's hair.

"Sara," said Phil. "After Adam fills your glass at the end before you smile…lick your lips and add the line, mmmm, a hint of chocolate. We'll see if it works or not."

Sara nodded her head and took her place.

"Take four," said Phil. "Action!"

Adam moved close to Sara and wrapped his hand with the glass of wine underneath the chiffon cover-up and around her waist. With the other hand, he poured a bit of wine into Sara's glass.

"You're beautiful," said Adam. "To us."

A wave hit the yacht and Sara lost her balance. She caught herself, but it ruined the take.

Thirty three takes later, the lighting seemed right, the sound approved and Adam began.

Adam moved close to Sara and wrapped his hand with the glass of wine underneath the chiffon cover-up and around her waist. With the other hand, he poured a bit of wine into Sara's glass.

"You're beautiful," said Adam. "To us."

The two took a long sip and Adam pulled her in and gently kissed her. She smiled, pressed her lips to his, then rolled her head back.

Bringing her focus back to Adam, Sara raised her eyebrows and pouted her lips. "More please," said Sara.

Adam glanced at the bottle of wine and then at her and smiled. He pulled her closer and filled her glass.

Sara smiled.

"Mmm-mmm," Sara ran her tongue over the lip of her glass. "A hint of chocolate."

The tagline played: *You're good people and you deserve good things in life. Boudenae can keep your passion surging.*

"It's a wrap people. That was great Sara. I loved the adlib. Better idea, licking the lip of the glass. Good job. You too, Adam. I liked the way you pulled her in and the bottle was right next to her waist. Perfect," said Phil. "Get the talent off the yacht before you start breaking it down."

"We can play with the tagline later. See if it looks better underneath or to the side," said Phil.

Adam lifted his right leg to step over the side and something caught his foot.

A snap and the wind blew hard.

"The jig sheet, it's loose," yelled the main grip. "Sara, look out!"

No sooner did he yell, then the jig swung right for Sara. She leaned her body back as the jig came toward her. The bottom pole hit her head hard, knocking her off balance and sending her into the waters of Lake Michigan. Her chiffon wrap got caught on the rope and slowed her descent until the wrap pulled free and floated to the surface.

CHAPTER 7

Sara sank fast. Phil and Paul rushed to the walkway while Adam and the grips ran to the side. The main grip jumped in.

"Get her out," yelled Phil. "There's a strong undercurrent today."

Paul jumped over the side; dove down beneath Sara; and helped the first grip pull her to the surface.

Phil and Adam reached over the edge and lifted Sara onto the yacht.

Sara's face was pale and her eyes closed. Phil turned her head and pushed on her chest and Sara's body jumped. She coughed, turned her head again and water spurted out. A trickle of blood ran down her forehead, her eyes hazy.

"Are you okay?" asked Phil, wrapping a large beach towel around Sara.

Turning further on her side, Sara expelled the water from her lungs. She leaned on her left arm, pushed her wet hair straight back off her face and rubbed at the graze on her forehead. “Yeah! I’m okay,” she said, sputtering. “Couldn’t get out of the way fast enough,” said Sara.

“Let’s get you in a chair,” said Paul.

“Kind of like to get on dry land, if you don’t mind,” said Sara. She forced a smile and Phil and Paul helped her down the plank to a chair on the beach.

“We need to get you to the hospital? I’ll call 911,” said Phil, taking out his cell phone.

“No, it just grazed me. I don’t like hospitals. I’m fine really.” said Sara. “I think it just really shook me up.”

“Alright, but if something starts to bother you later, just give me a call,” said Phil.

Phil handed Sara his business card with his cell phone number on it.

“Sit down for awhile until you feel okay,” said Phil as he rested his hand on her shoulder.

Adam got her a hot chocolate, but Sara’s hands shook uncontrollably, unable to hold the cup.

“Sorry!” said Sara. “It really scared me,” she said quietly.

“We’re really glad you moved so quickly. If you hadn’t, I’m afraid to think about what could have happened,” said Phil. Phil looked at the grips. “What the hell happened anyway? Isn’t all that stuff checked?”

“I think Adam tripped over the jib sheet, you know the line that holds the sail. It came loose, I guess,” said one of the grips.

“I barely tripped on it,” said Adam. Look at my ankle.” No bruise, no burn, nothing. “It would have taken a heavy burn to undo a rope,” said Adam.

"It was tied tight this morning," said the First grip. "You must have pulled the rope and it untied."

"I tripped over it, I didn't loosen it," said Adam. He held his teeth tight, planted his feet on the ground and stared into the eyes of the first grip. "At the very least, I'd have a burn, if I'd pushed and pulled so hard that it loosened, don't you think?" Adam pointed an index finger at his ankle. "And by the way, isn't it your job to make sure these things are secure?"

"I'd like to change and go home," said Sara quietly. Everyone stopped talking and turned toward her.

"I'll walk you to your trailer," said Phil.

Phil looked at the grips, his stare, hard and deliberate. "It wasn't Adam's fault. Tripping over the jib sheet, shouldn't have caused it to come loose. Making sure that doesn't happen falls on you." He turned away, wrapped an arm around Sara and helped her to the Wardrobe Trailer.

"If you need any help, just holler. I'll be right outside," said Clare.

"Thank you," said Sara in a whisper.

She slipped out of her outfit and stepped into the shower at the back of the trailer. She lay her head on her forearm against the shower wall, while the hot water beat down on her. After about five minutes, she slowly stepped out and dried off. Sara grabbed her clothes and slipped them back on and opened the trailer door. Phil, Paul, Adam and Clare stood outside the trailer door, waiting for her.

"Sara, would you like some food to take home. You haven't eaten all day. It's already 6:30pm," said Phil. He motioned with his hands toward the food truck. "They've got steak and potatoes or lasagna, even salads. There's a bunch of desserts. You did a great job, you deserve it."

Phil clasped and unclasped his hands. He turned toward Clare, the runner.

"Clare, can you get a few different entrees for Sara to take home. Get her one of each, would ya?" said Phil.

"Sure, no problem!" Clare took off toward the food truck.

"That's not necessary I…" began Sara.

"It'll just go to waste if you don't take it," smiled Phil. "I mean, I feel terrible. I've got to do something for you."

"Okay! Thank you," smiled Sara.

"Oh! And the limo will take you back to your home, not the agency, okay!" said Phil.

"Thank you. That would be great," said Sara.

Phil looked at Paul. "Make sure she gets home alright, will ya?"

"Sure, no problem."

Sara suddenly looked up, eyes wide.

"Is something wrong?" asked Paul.

"I haven't even thanked you for pulling me out of the water," said Sara.
I'm so sorry! Thank you so much."

"I'm glad I could help," said Paul, who she noticed was soaked to the skin.

"Yeah, me too," said the main grip.

Clare walked as quickly as she could with four containers still steaming hot and an empty bag over one arm with a small bag in the other. She put the bags on the ground in front of Sara and one by one put the dinners into the bag. "I got filet mignon and a baked potato," said Clare. She whispered in Sara's ear. "That's usually just for the producer and the director." Stepping back she continued, "I also got the lasagna and a Chicken Caesar Salad with four steaming hot dinner rolls."

Sara raised her hands in front of her and waved them from side to side. "Oh! My heavens, that's way too much."

Clare scrunched up one side of her face and glanced around. "They can afford it. Don't worry about it. Save it for dinner for tomorrow night - and the next. Oh! And I put in two huge pieces of double chocolate cake."

"Thanks Clare. I appreciate it," said Sara.

Clare placed the bags inside the stretch limo on the floor and Sara stepped in the other side and relaxed in the fresh smelling leather.

"I gave Bill, the driver, your address. It shouldn't take more than twenty minutes," said Paul. "I'll check on you tomorrow."

Once the door closed, the aroma of fresh cheese and meat sauce coupled with hot bread, filled the back seat. Sara leaned her head back and closed her eyes.

A hand grasped Sara's shoulder from behind and Sara jumped. She grabbed for something familiar, but found nothing there.

The hand gripped tighter and another hand gripped her other shoulder.

Sara's heart raced and her palms began to perspire. Her eyes darted from one side to the other. She was unable to speak, to breathe. She tried to get away, but the grip was too strong.

"Miss Parkins, we're here," said Bill. He gently shook her shoulders and she opened her eyes. "You must have fallen asleep," said Bill. "I didn't mean to frighten you. I called your name, but you didn't answer."

Sitting in front of her building, it took a moment for Sara to focus. She noticed her arms folded tightly across her chest and unfolded them.

"I'm so sorry," she said. "I didn't remember where I was." Sara leaned on her left arm to move closer to the door. Bill extended his hand and helped Sara from the limo.

"You must be exhausted. I think you fell asleep as soon as the door closed," said Bill.

Sara looked into his eyes. "Thank you."

"Oh wait! Don't forget your food. It's still hot." He lifted the bags from the floor and handed them to her.

Sara raised her lips slightly and took the bags. "Thank you."

"Are you sure you're okay. The boss wanted me to make sure you were alright."

"I'm fine. Just a little drained, I guess," said Sara.

Sara waved as she walked through the revolving door. She passed up 'Garden Pure' and 'Pizza Heaven' and went straight to the open door of the elevator. Sara pressed fourteen and leaned back on the wall. *What a day*, she thought.

The elevator climbed directly to fourteen and the door opened. Sara stepped out to find Jason walking down the hall.

The corners of Sara's lips pulled up, but her eyes remained at half mast.

Jason hurried to meet her. "How did it go? Am I allowed to talk to you, now that you're a star?" Jason smiled and gave Sara a hug. Sara wrapped her free arm around Jason and rested her head on his chest.

"Wow! What a day," she sighed. "Amazing, exciting and terrifying all at the same time."

"Terrifying? You weren't nervous about the shoot were you?"

"No…well a little, but that wasn't it," said Sara.

She took a deep breath and exhaled slowly, continuing to walk. "I kind of…fell off the yacht,"

"Whoa! You fell off the yacht!" Jason turned her toward him. "Are you alright?"

Sara looked up at him and Jason saw a small scrape with a welt forming on her forehead.

"Yeah! A little shaken up, but I'm okay!" said Sara.

"How did that happen?" he asked.

Sara stared into space. "My mind isn't going very fast. I think I just need to sit down for awhile."

"Of course," said Jason. "Let me get you some ice for that." He glanced down at her bags. "Smells like pasta. I'll take care of that for you," said Jason. "Do you want some now?"

"No, I think I'll save it for later."

Jason took the bags from Sara and wrapped an arm around her shoulders.

Sara laid her head on Jason's chest and held his arm as they walked toward her apartment. She dropped her keys in his open hand. He unlocked the door and walked her into the kitchen.

"Listen! You get comfortable on the couch. I'll get you some ice and I'll put this stuff away for you. Then you can tell me what happened. Does that sound like a plan?"

Sara lifted her head, her eyes still at half mast. “Yes, it sounds perfect. Thank you.”

Jason put the bags on the counter while Sara walked into the living room. He returned with an icepack and lay it on her forehead.

“I’ll be right back.”

She layed down on the couch, propped her head on a throw pillow, and waited for Jason.

“This looks like really good stuff. But, it looks like you haven’t eaten any of it,” said Jason. He put the meals into plastic containers he found in the cupboards and stacked them in the refrigerator. “I sure hope you had something to eat.”

Finishing with the food, Jason walked into the living room where Sara lay barely awake. He lifted her head, slid beneath her and cradled her in his arms. Sara could smell the Paco Rabanne drifting under her nose.

“Here you go, just relax and tell me all about your fascinating day,” said Jason.

Sara sighed, “It was a long day…” she yawned.

Jason ran his fingers through her hair and Sara fell asleep.

The phone in the kitchen was ringing, or *was it a dream*, thought Sara. She opened her eyes and heard Jason talking in the kitchen. She noticed the sun coming through the curtains in the living room and glanced at her phone.

“Oh my God!” said Sara. She jumped up from the couch. “It’s 6:25am.”

“She doesn’t know yet,” said Jason in the kitchen. “I’ll call you later.” Jason darted into the living room. “Sara, are you okay?” he asked.

Sara stared in disbelief, her mouth open.

"Do you feel okay" repeated Jason.

"Were you here all night," asked Sara.

Jason smiled. "Yes, I wanted to make sure you were okay. Two guys, Adam and Phil, called shortly after you fell asleep to see if you were okay. They said they were from the shoot. I wasn't going to answer it, but I was afraid it was gonna wake you up. I hope you don't mind."

"No, no, that's fine," said Sara. "I couldn't help but overhear you on the phone, you said, she doesn't know yet. Were you talking about me?"

Jason squinted his eyes and tilted his head. "What did I say?" said Jason.

"You said, 'she doesn't know yet'."

Jason opened his mouth and rolled his head back. "Oh! yes, I was…I was telling that guy from the shoot that you didn't know he had called last night. Because you were asleep, of course," said Jason.

"Oh yeah! Thank you."

"Well, they said you were amazing yesterday. But then they explained how you were knocked off the yacht. That must've been so scary. I checked on you all night long to make sure you didn't stop breathing. It's no wonder you were so tired. Anyway, they wanted to make sure you didn't have a concussion. I told them last night that I'd stay with you and keep watch."

Sara ran her fingers through her hair. "I must look a mess," said Sara. She looked down at the floor. "Thank you so much for staying with me. Did I fall asleep right away?"

"Right after I lay your head on my lap…on top of the small pillow of course," said Jason.

Sara's eyes pulled to the left and then down. "I'm so sorry! Did you get any sleep at all," asked Sara.

"Not really! But I'm not complaining. I had a beautiful view."

Jason held out his arms and she walked into them. They hugged for a while and then Jason pulled back to look into her eyes.

"Are you feeling okay this morning? Any headaches, dizziness?"

"No, I'm good. I think the sleep really helped. Of course my own personal Guardian Angel didn't hurt either." She smiled and hugged him again.

Jason hugged her back. "Okay! Well, I'd love to stay, but I think I should probably get a little sleep myself. Mainly because I was hoping you'd have dinner with me tonight at my place. I'm a pretty good cook. What do ya say?"

"I'd love to." Her cheeks flushed and she felt goose bumps rising on her arms.

Jason kissed Sara on the cheek. "I'll see you tonight then," said Jason. "Say six-ish?"

"Sounds great! Thank you again," said Sara. Before he could turn, Sara placed her lips on his cheek and gently kissed him too. "See you tonight...at six-ish," she said.

CHAPTER 8

Sara heard the phone in the kitchen ringing. "Front Desk," it announced. Sara picked up.

"We have a package for Sara Ann Parkins. Would you like it brought up? It's from Momentum Productions," said the voice on the other end.

"Yes, thank you," said Sara.

Within five minutes Sara heard knocking at her front door. She checked the peephole and saw the big toothy grin of Harry, the night manager. *Even at seventy-two years old and over 200 lbs, Harry was a jolly fellow,* thought Sara. She unlocked and opened the door.

"Here you go, Miss Parkins, and there's a note too," said Harry, his voice monotone.

Sara took the package and placed it on the table in the hall.

"Thank you," said Sara. "You seem a little quiet. Is everything alright?"

"My wife passed away the other day. Guess I'm kinda lonely."

Sara opened the door a little further. "I'm so sorry, I didn't know she'd passed away," said Sara. "When did it happen?"

"It's odd because Elizabeth passed away the day before Mrs. McClusky did. My wife had a massive heart attack." Harry stood frozen until Sara touched his arm. "She was a good woman, my wife. I really miss her."

Sara stepped forward and wrapped her arms around him, then pulled back. "I'm so sorry. When is the wake?" asked Sara.

"Tomorrow at Morley & Sons Funeral Home," said Harry. "It was going to be Wednesday, but some of her relatives are from out of state."

"Oh, my gosh! You're kidding. Mrs. McClusky's wake is there tomorrow too," said Sara. "I'll definitely stop by your room."

"Thank you, Sara. I know you were close to Mrs. McClusky. I'm sorry for your loss too." He squeezed her hands and turned to leave.

Sara closed the door and brought the package into the kitchen. *Wow! There's my three, she thought. Three people I know passed away in a very short period of time. I was afraid it would be Gladys.*

She got a pair of scissors from the drawer and cut open one end of the package. *I wonder what they sent me.*

Sara's eyes expanded and her mouth dropped. She pulled the items from the box one by one. The bikini/panty, bra and chiffon cover up she wore for the shoot. Sara opened the letter.

Sara,

I hope you're feeling okay! The commercial looks great! You mentioned how much you loved this outfit, so since we had a spare, I thought I'd send it as a small token. Thanks again.

Phil

"Wow! I can't believe they gave this to me. Well, now at least I know what I'm wearing underneath my outfit tonight. Of course it's worth more than five of my outfits put together."

Sara walked back into the bedroom, dropped the robe to the floor and slipped off her everyday panty and bra and slipped into the very expensive bikini/panty and bra and looked in the mirror. "I feel so good in this," she said. Sara glanced at her phone on the nightstand. It said 5:30pm. "I've already tried on a million different outfits and I can't decide," said Sara aloud. "What is my problem?"

A stack of skirts, pants and dresses lay strewn across the bed. Sara picked up each piece and put it in one of three separate piles. Definitely no, maybe, and I really like this one. She had already spent the past two hours stepping into and out of dresses, skirts and pants and remained undecided. Sara caught another glimpse of herself in the mirror and turned face forward. "I want to look sexy, but not too sexy. I want to be comfortable, but I don't want to look blah."

Sara walked to the bed and took the 'no' pile and hung everything back in the closet. Then she went to the 'maybe' pile again, and one by one, began hanging those back up too. Either too sexy, too comfy, or just not right for how she felt today.

She walked to the third pile and spread the seven outfits out on the bed. "Okay!" she said. "It's just down the hall, so I can wear higher heels and kick them off, if they start to bother me. I want to look sexy in a subtle way," she told herself.

Sara reached over and grabbed a red plunging sundress and hung it up in the closet. "Too sexy," she said.

Next she ran her hand across a short chiffon black dress with a drape over one side. "No, this is too dressy." Sara's mouth dropped. "Oh my God! I wasn't even thinking about what he's gonna wear. It's dinner at his house. I doubt he's gonna get dressed to the nines. Okay!" said Sara. She picked up a black and white chiffon sundress that had ruffles for straps and wasn't super tight. It hung loose, but tapered in toward her waist to show off all her curves. A chiffon black and white flowered drape lay over a black satin slip. The drape fell between her knees and her ankles on the left side and went up on an angle to above her knees on the right. The neckline swooped down in a v in front and a half circle in the back. "It's subtle, sexy and feminine. This is it," said Sara.

She stepped to the dresser, pulled open a drawer and found a pair of tan thigh highs with a two inch lace border. Sitting on the bed, Sara scrunched up one leg, slipped in her foot and slowly pulled them up, so as not to cause a run. She repeated the procedure for the second leg. She stood, picked up the dress and dropped it over her head. It fell gracefully about her body.

The shoes were a much easier decision. She looked on the shelf above her clothes and grabbed a pair of four inch stilettos. The heels were clear and opaque, depending on the angle in which you looked at them, and the straps were clear with a black border. They crossed low on her foot in an x and once around her heel.

Sara grabbed a little black bag and quickly transferred everything from her everyday purse. She noticed her phone said 5:58pm and she stepped quickly to the dresser, picked up her bottle of Charlie and sprayed it generously around her. She returned the bottle and began waving her hands around herself and walking quickly about the room, so that the cologne wouldn't be too terribly strong.

Sara stepped in front of the mirror again and smiled at her choice.

"Okay! Sara Ann Parkins. Have fun," she told herself.

She grabbed her keys and stepped out the door. She turned, double locked it, and double checked to be sure.

Sara walked slowly down to Jason's apartment. She ran the palms of her hands on the front of the dress to make sure it hung properly. She lifted her nose in the air, sniffing about to be sure her cologne wasn't overwhelming. She finally stopped outside Jason's door and took a deep breath while using the door knocker to announce her arrival.

The door opened and a wonderful aroma filled the hallway.

"Well, hello there!" said Jason. "You look beautiful," he said as he leaned forward and kissed her on the cheek. He took her hand and walked her inside.

Jason wore a pair of dark gray Dockers and a light gray and black button down shirt with a smoky gray t-shirt beneath it.

"Thank you. You look very nice yourself," said Sara. "It looks like you got the memo," Sara teased.

Jason's eyes narrowed and he looked at Sara. The light went on in his eyes and his jaw promptly dropped. "Oh! the black and gray thing," he said. "I'm a little slow."

"That's okay. Sometimes slow is good," she smiled.

"Make yourself comfortable in the living room and I'll be right there," said Jason.

"Everything smells amazing," said Sara.

"We're gonna have baby back ribs and double baked potatoes and fresh asparagus. I know I'm taking a chance, cuz I know you love ribs, but I decided to go for it," said Jason.

Sara smiled as she sat down on a brown overstuffed sofa. "I'm already impressed. I'm impressed you can make baby back ribs. I wouldn't even know where to start. So, you don't have to worry," she laughed.

"Well, we'll see."

With oven mitts on, Jason came around the corner into the living room.

"I'm putting in the dinner rolls, so it shouldn't be more than five minutes."

He disappeared back into the kitchen where she heard the oven door closing and the timer going off for something else.

"Do you need any help?" asked Sara.

"No, no, I'm good. You just relax," said Jason.

A beautiful song played overhead and the canister lighting was set to low. Sara glanced over to the dining area where she saw two long white candles, two rose colored plates with folded napkins to the side and three pieces of silverware for each setting. Two crystal wine glasses sat by a bottle of Chardonnay in a crystal bucket of ice.

Wow! that's beautiful, thought Sara. *He's too good to be true. He's romantic, great looking and sensitive...and a cook. I'll leave my judgment of his cooking until after we've eaten.*

"Ding! Okay! It's ready," said Jason. He carried an elegant serving tray with four half slabs of baby back ribs, a smaller tray with four double baked potatoes and a rose china bowl of fresh steamed asparagus. After setting those down on a cart near the table, he returned to the kitchen for the rolls, which he wrapped in a towel and put in a basket.

Jason took off the oven mitts and pulled out Sara's chair for her. "Miss," he said.

Sara smiled and sat down.

"Let me move you in a smudge," said Jason, gently pushing her chair forward.

"Thank you. Everything looks and smells wonderful," said Sara. "Only one problem!"

"What did I forget?" said Jason.

"No, it's not that. But, now I'm never gonna be able to have you to dinner. No way it'd look this good," she laughed.

Jason bit his lip. "You haven't even tasted it yet. And, if you want to leave it at that, that's okay with me too," he smiled. "And as for having dinner at your house, believe me, I wouldn't be lookin at the food."

Sara's face flushed and she glanced down at the table. "You're sweet." She then quickly picked up her fork. "I know it's going to be just as good to eat as it looks. Cocking her head to the right, she looked at Jason. "What's that song that's playing?" asked Sara.

"It's called 'My Heart Will Go On' by Celine Dion. It's the theme song from the movie, 'The Titanic.' I thought it might be appropriate in case this meal goes under as well," said Jason. The left corner of his mouth slid up as he pulled out his own chair.

"I don't know about under, but mines definitely going down," she laughed as she lifted her fork.

"Ooooh! I almost forgot. The candles," said Jason. He stepped to the kitchen and found the long plastic handled lighter, returned and carefully lit each candle.

"There, now we're ready," he smiled.

With silver tongs, Jason picked up a half slab of ribs and placed it on Sara's plate. He lifted a doubled baked potato with a smaller set of tongs and placed that next to the ribs. The fresh steamed asparagus sat in a bowl in front of Sara's plate.

"Help yourself. Take as much or as little as you want," said Jason.

Sara lifted the serving spoon and put a small helping on her plate. *There's barely enough room for much else,* she thought.

Jason filled his plate, poured the wine and held his glass high to toast. Sara held her glass up and gently touched his.

"To our first real date," said Jason.

Sara smiled and clinked her glass with his. "To wonderful beginnings."

Jason clinked his glass with hers. "Yes, indeed."

Placing a napkin on her lap, Sara lifted the knife to help cut apart the ribs.

"Wow! This is really tender. It's sliding off the bone," said Sara. *I could've used a spoon,* she thought.

Jason peered over the candles, waiting for Sara to take the first bite.

Sara picked up a fork full of pork and placed it on her tongue. "Mmmmmm," she said. Sara rolled her eyes and her eyelids fell shut. She shook her head back and forth from the left to the right.

Jason waited patiently tapping his fingers on the table.

"I have never tasted sauce this good before, and the meat is melting on my tongue. How in the world did you ever learn to cook like this?" said Sara.

Jason let out a sigh of relief. "Whew! I was worried for a minute there. So you like it?"

Sara tilted the left side of her face toward him and squinted her eyes. "No, I don't like it…I love it. This is absolutely delicious."

Sara lifted fork after fork full to her mouth. Every third or fourth bite, she would take a bite of the double baked potato and a small portion of asparagus.

Jason offered the basket of rolls. "Don't forget a roll while they're still hot," he said.

Sara took two rolls and put them on a side plate and immediately began to cut and butter them. Jason beamed.

Sara looked up from eating only to see that Jason had barely touched his food.

"Aren't you going to eat," she asked.

"Oh! Yes, yes, of course," he said, lifting his fork to his mouth. "Sorry! I'm just so thrilled that you like the food that much."

Sara put her fork down. "Oh! my God, am I eating too much? Look at me, I haven't stopped since I started…"

Jason reached his hand across the table and touched Sara's hand. "I couldn't be happier. Seriously, the more you eat, the happier I am," said Jason. Sara looked into his eyes and smiled.

"Well then you must be very happy," she said.

"I am."

Mouth full of food, Sara shook her head up and down. "Ummmmmm!"

Jason caught up to Sara rather quickly, finishing off his first half slab and moving on to a second.

Sara finished her half slab of ribs, a double baked potato, two rolls and a cup of steamed asparagus. Taking a sip of wine, she leaned back in her chair and placed her hands on her stomach.

"Whew! I don't think I've eaten like that in a long time," she said. "How long have you been able to cook like that?" she asked.

"I learned to cook from my Dad. He always loved to be in the kitchen. My Mom would try to help, but Dad would always tell her to sit down and relax while he took care of the cooking. I think I was about seven when he first let me really help. I really enjoy it."

"Well it sure shows. That's for sure," said Sara.

"My other passion is baking…I love chocolate and I've found lots of different things to make with it. Are you a chocolate fan?" asked Jason.

"The question should really be, 'should I be a chocolate fan?' I love chocolate, but I try not to eat too much. If I could decide where it goes, I'd be fine with it, but my body and I are not really in agreement with the outcome." Sara laughed.

Jason stood and placed his napkin across the back of the chair and began removing the rest of the food.

"Why don't you take a seat in the living room and I'll be back in a minute. I have dessert, but I thought we might wait a while," said Jason. He patted his stomach and moved his hand up and down. "I'll need a little time to digest," he said.

Sara stood, placed her napkin over the back of the chair, stacked both plates and grabbed them in her right hand.

Another Celine Dion song played in the background. When Jason noticed what Sara was doing, he raised an eyebrow and opened his mouth, but before he could say a word, Sara stood inches from his face.

"You, spent hours in the kitchen," she said, pushing her index finger into his chest. "for I don't know how long," she continued, "to make this entire meal, which was exquisite by the way, and I'm not about to sit here and let you clean up by yourself. End of sentence," she smiled.

Jason raised his index finger and Sara grabbed it and kissed it. "Where would you like these plates?" she asked.

"Alright then. Thank you. I usually rinse off the plates and they go in the dishwasher and I have plastic bags in the left cabinet over the stove for the leftovers," said Jason.

The same size and layout as Sara's kitchen with a walk through, plenty of room for one person, but with two people, it got tight.

Jason began wrapping the extra half slab of ribs in tinfoil, while the hot water ran on the platter. Sara stacked plates to the right of the sink. She grabbed a plastic bowl and cover from the cabinet and emptied the dish of asparagus into it.

"Here's the asparagus. Is there any room in there?" asked Sara.

As Jason placed the ribs on the bottom shelf, he leaned in further to rearrange some items on the top shelf to make room for the asparagus. Sara smiled as she stood behind him and enjoyed the view.

Nice bottom, she thought.

The food smells had dissipated and Sara's senses took in Jason's cologne once again. She turned to finish washing the serving platter and handed it to Jason.

"I didn't think this would fit in the dishwasher," she said.

"It wouldn't. Thanks!"

Sara opened the dishwasher, bent over and stacked the other dishes inside. Jason grazed Sara's hip and she saw him smile.

"Careful," warned Jason. He had opened the cupboard directly above Sara's head before she stood up. She came up fast and Jason threw his right arm out, attempting to hold the bottom of the door and protect Sara's head from the cabinet. His arm promptly smacked into the edge instead.

Sara knew instantly what had happened.

"Oh! my gosh, thank you so much. I'm so sorry." Sara grabbed his wrist, turned it over and saw a six-inch welt rise on Jason's forearm. Pulling it toward her, she placed her lips on his skin. Kissing gently up and down, then looked up. "Is it feeling better?" she asked.

Jason stood frozen with his arm extended away from his body. He gazed into her blue eyes and smiled.

Sara tilted her head and kissed his arm again. "How about now?" she asked.

Jason took a step backwards and leaned against the refrigerator.

"I'm sorry! I think my body just went to heaven. I didn't hear what you were saying."

Sara took her index finger and ran it from his wrist to his elbow, kissing every couple of inches. At his shoulder, she lifted his sleeve and ran her lips as far up as she could. Then she slid across his chest and pushed his collar out of the way and ran her lips up the left side of his neck to his earlobe.

"Can you hear me now?" whispered Sara.

She pulled his earlobe carefully between her lips and nibbled gently, while breathing into his ear.

Jason's head tilted back against the refrigerator and his body went limp.

"God, you smell great," said Jason. He slowly retrieved his right hand and ran his fingers along her neck and up through her hair. He turned his left arm and placed it on the small of her back and pulled her close to him. She purred in his arms. He tilted her head back and pressed his lips to hers, releasing his passion.

They stood still for a moment, then Jason slid his hand down to Sara's wrist and pulled her toward the center of the living room and stopped abruptly.

"Don't move," said Jason.

He stepped quickly to the DVD player and chose a disc and hit play. 'I Hope You Dance' by Lee Ann Womack filled the room. He turned and stepped up to Sara, taking her right hand in his left, and wrapping his right arm around her waist.

The candles still burned in the distance and the smell of Charlie and Paco Rabanne intermingled. *He's amazing*, thought Sara. *He even dances like a dream.*

Jason pulled her close and moved gracefully about the living room. Sara laid her head on Jason's chest and Jason smelled the delicate fragrance of her hair. She moved her chin up and gently kissed his neck. She nibbled playfully and soon their bodies drew closer. Jason bent his chin toward her and kissed her forehead and then her cheek.

"You smell wonderful," said Jason, as he buried his head in her neck.

Sara's hands found his chest. *I'm still hungry, but it's for something other than food,* thought Sara. Her head swirled and she lifted her right arm up and placed it around his neck, pulling herself even closer. Raising her right leg, she hooked it around his hip, ran her fingers through his hair from the neck up and kissed him hard.

Jason bent and lifted Sara in his arms. He maneuvered around the cart in the dining room, carried her into the bedroom and lay her on the bed.

"Don't go away," he said. Sara heard him rushing around the corner and back again. 'Then' by Brad Paisley filled the air and Jason began kissing Sara's shoulders and running his hands beneath the ruffled straps. Sara reached up and slowly unbuttoned his shirt, then grabbed his t-shirt from the bottom and lifted it off, over his head.

She ran her fingers across his chest. *Solid as a rock, tan and beautifully smooth*, she thought. She lifted herself up to kiss his naval and run her tongue up to his neck, all the while she kept her right leg wrapped around one of his.

Using his left hand, Jason glided his finger tips up her right calf past her knee and hovered there. Sara laid her hand on his and moved it slowly up her outer thigh. Kissing her passionately, he caressed every inch of her. Their bodies glistened together. Sliding his hand around to the front, he found the pearls on her bikini. He slid his thumb and forefinger around the band and slowly slipped in to grasp her bottom.

Sara was in ecstasy. She undid the snap and lowered the zipper of his khakis, sliding her hand inside the top band, and all the way around.

Jason brought his lips close to Sara's ear. "Are you okay with this?" he whispered.

"I'm definitely okay with this," she responded.

With that, Jason stood up and dropped his pants and shorts to the floor. He grasped her sundress and lifted it up and over her head, tossing it on the chair across from the bed.

"What a beautiful bra and panty," he said. He played with the pearls on the panty with his index finger while running his tongue around the pearls hanging down from the bra. Gently wrapping his arms around her back, he unclasped the bikini top and pulled it forward and off of her. Milky white skin with breasts standing proud. He kissed them gently and caressed them in his hands as he scooted down on the bed and separated her legs. Positioning himself at her feet, he moved both hands up and down her calves. His lips and tongue ran over her thigh-highs to the lace at the top and then to the bare skin of her inner thigh. Sara's hands intertwined in Jason's hair, her body glistening, as she brought her left leg up and wrapped it around him.

Jason's eyes opened a window to his soul as he moved up and held Sara's face in his hands. He ran his tongue gently around her lips and she rolled her tongue around his. Her hands caressed his face and slid back through his hair. Turning his body slightly, Jason ran his tongue down the center of her body to her navel where he sucked gently. Once again stepping between Sara's legs, he knelt and with thumb and forefinger gently slid her bikini/panty slowly down to her knees, running his tongue at the top of her thigh. Then he pulled her panty down past her calves and over her feet. He tossed them off the bed onto the chair.

Jason caressed Sara's breasts with his hands and pushed his lips against hers as he lowered himself on top of her. Sara's body slowly rose to meet his.

"God! You're beautiful," said Jason. "I love the smell and feel of you."

"Oooooh! Kiss me," said Sara. And Jason did.

He kissed her passionately and moved carefully, but confidently in. Sara's breath came in gasps, their hearts racing side by side in a marathon. A rhythmic motion began, their breaths quickened, and passion ensued. Sara slid her hands up and around Jason's waist and then dropped them to his bottom and pulled him in tight. She wrapped her legs around him and he slid his hands under her and nestled her bottom in the palm of his hands. Jason groaned, pushing forward. Sara responded passionately, bodies and souls undulating together. Sara purred until, until…a long shrill scream and a low grunt and Jason's body collapsed and Sara's body relaxed.

Sweat ran between them. They lay in contented silence as the background music played on.

Several minutes passed before Jason rolled onto his back and pulled Sara to his chest. He wrapped his left arm around her and she kept her left leg wrapped over him. Their eyelids fell, their arms lay still, their hearts slowed and they slept.

***

In the darkness of the night, Sara awoke. She slid out from under the covers and found a lumberjack shirt that Jason had draped over a chair. Making her way to the bathroom, she quietly closed the door before turning on the light. Her eyes adjusted to the glare as she glanced at herself in the mirror. She immediately touched her finger to the soap pump and dabbed it beneath her eyes and used a tissue to wipe off the excess mascara. *I love when mascara says waterproof,* she thought. *It isn't even sleep proof.*

Sara rolled her neck slowly and it twinged. *Must've pulled something,* she told herself. She smiled, "it was worth it." *Maybe he has an Advil or an aspirin.* Sara opened the cabinet and moved half a dozen bottles, but there was no Advil. There was extra-strength Fahrer aspirin. She removed the cover and spilled two into her hand. Tossing them back down her throat, she filled the palm of her hand with water and poured it into her mouth.

Putting the aspirin back in the cabinet, a razor fell out and slid into the tub.

Sara cringed, hoping not to wake Jason. She peeked into the tub and saw the razor laying up against a pair of old gym shoes. She grabbed the razor and returned it to the cabinet.

I hope I didn't wake him, she thought.

She rubbed her neck, turned out the light and returned to bed. Quietly slipping out of his shirt and draping it over the chair, she slid under the covers, nuzzling up close to Jason.

It seemed like only moments later when Sara heard something and opened her eyes once more. The clock said 4:30am. She turned and Jason was gone. She could hear him talking in the kitchen.

Why would he be on the phone at 4:30am? she thought. Sara threw on her bikini panty and the lumberjack shirt, and walked to the hall, where she stopped.

"No, she doesn't know anything about my past. She has no idea," said Jason. "I really want to tell her, but I don't think she'll understand. It's too much to take in. Sometimes lying is the best option." Jason hesitated and shrugged his shoulders. "Well, I guess if she finds out, I'll have to kill her too," said Jason.

Sara froze, standing in the hall in Jason's shirt. She listened more intently.

"I drugged Mrs. McClusky. I know my medicine, no one would ever suspect foul play. Yeah! I took the pills from her apartment, so no one would know that's what killed her. Yeah! It was easy, I put some of the tainted ones in the box when I brought her that piece of cake." He hesitated. "No, I hid in the tub, so they didn't see me. Don't worry, she's not gonna find out."

Sara turned and the floor board squeaked. She gasped.

"Sara? Is that you?" said Jason quietly.

Sara didn't answer. She stepped quietly back into the bedroom and slid under the sheets.

"I gotta go," said Jason. Jason hung up the phone and walked into the bedroom.

Sara lay still, eyes closed, heart pounding. *Please God! Please God! Let him think I'm sleeping,* she thought.

"Sara," Jason whispered. "Are you awake?"

Sara didn't move.

Jason slid behind her and wrapped an arm around her waist, resting his hand on her chest.

Slow down, slow down, slow down. Sara tried to will her heart to relax, but it got faster and faster.

Jason sat up abruptly. "You're awake," he said. "What did you hear?" he yelled.

Sara's eyes pulled open and she clasped her chest. "What? What's wrong?"

"Why were you up? And what did you hear?"

Sara tried to scramble from the bed, but Jason grabbed her shoulders and pinned her down.

"I don't know what you're talking about," Sara cried. She scrunched up her eyes and turned her head. Tears ran down her face.

"It's too late for that. I really didn't want to do this, but I have to go," said Jason.

Sara kicked her legs and struggled to get free, but she couldn't. "No!" she yelled. "No!"

"Sara look at me," said Jason. "I didn't want to do this, but I have to go. I'm sorry."

In one last attempt, Sara threw her knee forward, hitting him in the chest and her hands were free. She pushed herself up and yelled. "No!"

Sara's eyes opened and Jason sat on the bed next to her, eyebrows pitched.

"Sara, Sara, are you okay?" "I'm sorry, I didn't mean to wake you, but I have to go. I've got a job this morning, but I didn't want to just leave." He rubbed her shoulder and arm. "I think you were having a bad dream."

Sara glanced at the clock. It said, 7:37am. She looked at Jason, who seemed confused.

"I'm sorry! I did. I had a bad dream. Wow! That was weird. Maybe it was the aspirin. I don't usually have bad dreams," said Sara.

"A time-release aspirin?" said Jason. "I didn't remember you taking anything."

"Oh! I don't know. It was about 12:30 and I went into the bathroom. I think I pulled something in my neck, so…" Sara hesitated. "I hope you don't mind, but I looked in your medicine cabinet for an Advil or something. I saw the aspirin, so I took two."

Jason's eyes bulged and he leaned toward her. "How are you feeling?" he asked.

"Oh! I'm fine now. I think it just gave me nightmares."

"I thought you didn't like medicine," said Jason quickly.

Sara raised her eyebrows, her mouth closed.

"Sorry!" said Jason.

"I usually don't," said Sara. "But after Anna passed away, the day I ran all those errands, I got to thinking that maybe there is something to medicine. Heck, I even got a flu shot. And, I figured if you take aspirin, it can't be all that bad," she said smiling.

"What? Oh! Yeah!" said Jason. His face blank. He took her hands and looked into her eyes. "I want you to stay here, okay! I have to do a few things this morning, but I would really like it if you could wait here for me."

Sara squinted her eyes. "How long will it be before you come back?" she asked.

"About two hours, that's all. I promise. And then I'll explain everything."

"I'm really confused," said Sara. "Is there something wrong?"

Jason's face softened, his eyes were warm again and he held her face in his hands. "Everything's fine. I just need to talk to you about some things. Can you wait for me?"

"Okay! I'll wait for you," she said softly.

Jason kissed Sara gently on the lips. "I had the most marvelous evening last night. Thank you." He grabbed his wallet and keys and left.

Sara heard him lock the door from the outside. She sat on the bed for awhile, thinking about what he said. *He seemed upset and worried, so what does he want to tell me?*

"Okay! Sara, get a grip. He's a wonderful man with so many amazing talents and gifts, I can't even count them all." She crossed her legs under the covers. "What could possibly be the problem?" she said aloud. She stretched her arms above her head and jerked them back suddenly, holding them across her chest.

"Oh God, I hope he's not married."

Sara got out of bed, threw on Jason's lumberjack shirt and walked into the hall.

Oh my God, that would really suck, if he was married. Sara walked around the living room and back into the bedroom, her eyes searching the top of the dresser and nightstands for any pictures. There were none.

Sara, do you really think he'd have a picture of his wife on a nightstand next to the bed he brought someone else to? she asked herself. *Maybe he's separated and the divorce process isn't quite finished yet. That's possible. Courts can be very slow,* she nodded.

Sara passed by the mirror and caught a glimpse of herself. "What are you looking so glum about? He said he'd tell you everything when he got back?' *But what if it's something I don't wanna hear? I really, really like him. I want this to work out. And now this. I hate waiting for information. He could have just told me right then and there...then I could decide what to do next.*

Sara paced about the apartment, running her hand over his bed and then over the recliner in the living room. *Dear God, please let it not be a bad thing. I hope I'm not just another notch on his belt.*

Sara stopped in her tracks. *Okay, Sara, pull yourself together. Don't make stuff up. Do something to take your mind off of it.*

I know, I can exercise for a while. That always makes me feel better, she thought.

It's so quiet and lonely, being in a place that's not your own. Maybe he's got some dance music. He had nice music on last night. Sara smiled and bit her lip.

She walked to the CD player and looked for a good dancing song.

"Ooooh, 'Dancing from the 70's'…sounds promising." She put it in and hit play. It started with 'YMCA' by the Village People, then 'Fire' by the Ohio Players and 'Ladies Night' by Kool and the Gang. Sara danced and moved about the living room, lip synching to all the oldies for over forty five minutes before noticing a tape labeled Best Released.

"These must be his favorites," she said aloud. She put it in and got ready to gyrate. No music. Sara pushed rewind and then play. Someone began talking… Jason. .

"I never wanted to hurt anyone," said Jason. But, how many women are dead because of what I did…"

Sara's face went pale. Her heart stopped and her mouth dropped.

"I didn't mean for any of this to happen," he continued.

Sara heard a noise at the door and leapt for the tape player, glancing at the door and hitting eject at the same time. Her heart racing, her mind in overdrive. The tape was stuck, so she pulled it out and the plastic broke allowing a stream of ribbon to slip from the cassette.

"Oh my God!" muttered Sara.

CHAPTER 9

She took a deep breath and stood paralyzed, waiting for Jason to walk back in. *He's going to ask why I have his tape in my hand and why the ribbon is streaming out of it. Then he'll realize which tape it is and...Stop Sara, no one is coming in. It was probably the paper delivery.* She took another deep breath and did her best to wind the tape back up. She pushed the tape back in and hit play. It's my business…blbb lb blb blb. I did …bllblblb…I'm paid to blbb lb blb blb, rrrrrrrrr.

"Oh crap!" *What did I do? I can't hear it now. I need to hear more to know what he's talking about. The women that died because of him?* Sara's mind raced. She began to remember things she'd seen or heard that seemed odd. *Jason was in Anna's apartment; he knew Frank even though he'd just moved here; he went to the hospital with Gladys. Did he kill Anna and Frank's wife, and the night manager, Henry's wife? Is that what he's saying?*

Sara paced around the room. "Am I crazy? Did he really do that?" *What else would he be talking about?* She stopped in her tracks, seeing her reflection in the TV. She ran her hands down the front of the shirt she wore…Jason's shirt.

"Oh my God! I slept with him."

She remembered last night, going into Jason's medicine cabinet.

When we went to Mulaney's Pub, I remember he said he didn't take medicine of any kind. Sara ran into the bathroom and pulled open the cabinet. *One, two, three, four bottles*. She turned them toward her. They were bottles of Rilosac. She hadn't looked at the label last night because she knew they weren't Advil. She looked closer. Her face went flush as she read the label of each one. *Anna McClusky, Izzy Delmar, Elizabeth Truman and…* Sara dropped the bottle in the sink. Her hands began to shake. The fourth bottle had the name, Gladys Murray, on it.

"Oh my God." *Maybe she's still okay, but maybe not for long. I've got to see her.*

What else has been strange, thought Sara. *The footprints…* Sara's head jerked to the right and pulled the shower curtain open. She reached down and picked up the gym shoes and there it was, the diamond shape she had seen in Anna's tub.

It was Jason. I've gotta get outta here. I've got to tell someone, but I've gotta have proof.

Sara grabbed an empty plastic grocery bag from one of the kitchen cabinets and threw the four bottles of Rilosac in it. She then remembered the Fahrer aspirin that Anna had on her living room end table. She hadn't seen it since.

"Oh my God!" *That's what I took last night. It could have been hers.* Sara ran into the bathroom, retrieved the aspirin and tossed that in the bag too. She threw on her sundress and shoes and dashed for the front door. Sara stopped suddenly. *Think Sara..okay, I live three doors down. It's not like he wouldn't know how to find me. I need to leave a note and act as though nothing has happened. I don't want him to think that I know anything...not yet, not before I've gone to the police.* She picked up a scrap of paper and wrote.

Jason,

I had a wonderful time last night.

I got a call about the wake tonight. I had to go and take care of it. I'll talk to you later.

Sara

She taped it to the wall, just inside the front door.

Okay Sara, think for a second, what do you really know about Jason? she asked herself. *He was nice to Anna. He brought her cake that he made.* She hesitated. *But, she died that next morning. And Frank, how did he get to know Frank so quickly. He just moved into town. And, how is it we happened to be at that little bar when Gladys ended up with nausea. Is he drugging them or what? He went with her to the hospital and he said she was alright, so how did he get her bottle of Rilosac. It has to be hers.* "A finger print." *I need to get something with his fingerprints on it...just in case.*

Sara ran back into the bathroom and snagged his toothbrush and put it into a plastic bag and into the grocery bag. Grocery bag in her left hand, her purse over her left shoulder, she headed for the front door.

She stopped, took a deep breath and looked up. *Please let me get to my apartment without him coming home,* she prayed silently. She opened the front door, stepped into the hall and closed the door tight. Sara ran down to her apartment and searched through her purse for the keys.

"Damn it." *I should have gotten them out*, she thought. She found them under her checkbook, pulled them out and put them into the lock. The elevator door sounded and she heard the doors open. She stepped inside just as someone stepped out. Heart beating rapidly, she leaned up against her front door and peered out the peephole to see if it was him. She heard heavy footsteps that stopped just before her door. Sara stopped breathing.

"Smack…"

The newspaper hit the bottom of the door. She got a different paper than Jason did. She got the Daily Prime Time, which apparently got delivered after the Chicago Lake News.

Sara let out a long breath and stared down at the bag. *I have to put it somewhere no one else will find it.* She walked through the hallway to the bathroom, opening cabinets, and then to the bedroom where she checked drawers. *No, that would be too obvious,* she thought. She walked to the living room and back in the kitchen.

Where can I put these? She said, looking left and right. *I don't know. Maybe I should just throw them out.* "That's it." *I'll put them in the garbage…well not so much in the garbage as in the garbage can underneath the garbage bag.*

Sara removed the garbage bag from the plastic container under the sink. She put the plastic grocery bag at the bottom and placed the garbage bag back on top. *Brilliant! That was a great idea, she told herself. Now, what next?*

Opening her purse, she retrieved Frank's card. She looked at his last name. It was Delmar. Sara wasn't surprised. Izzy Delmar was his Mother. She pulled her cell phone out and dialed him.

"Hi, Frank. This is Sara. Is there any way you could pick me up in about fifteen minutes? I need a ride to Mulaney's Pub." She waited. "Oh! That's wonderful. Thank you so much. I'll be waiting."

Sara stepped out of her sundress and stripped off the thigh highs and bra and panty. Using Vaseline, she wiped off her makeup, jumped in the shower and quickly washed. Five minutes later, she stepped out, dried off and rubbed in body lotion. The adrenalin pumping fast, Sara threw on a pair of jeans and a tank top, snagged her purse and keys with three minutes to spare.

She went to her front door, opened it slowly…she looked up and down… no one in the hall. She closed the door and locked it and ran for the elevator. Standing at the elevator, she began shaking. *What if the door opened and …? Or I got to the first floor and…* Sara made a beeline for the stairs. *Fourteen flights isn't that bad,* she thought. *And going down would be a lot easier than climbing up*, she told herself.

Taking two steps at a time, she made it in four minutes. She opened the door and stepped into the hall. *The stairs are around the corner from the elevator bay, so I should be able to get to the door unnoticed. But once outside, who knows?* Looking to the left and the right, she moved quickly past Italian Heaven and Garden Pure. *Please don't let Mr. Adashi see me,* she thought. "Keep going, keep going, keep going," she repeated in a whisper to herself.

She made it to the revolving doors and pushed forward. The fresh air hit her in the face and the smell of the lake and the noise of construction across the street filled her senses.

Frank waited at the curb. Sara walked swiftly to the cab, opened the door, her eyes darting, and lowered herself inside, closing the door. She breathed a sigh of relief and turned toward Frank.

"Thanks, Frank," said Sara. Her eyes wide and her speech fast.

"Is something wrong, Miss Sara? You seem very nervous. Are you alright?" His eyes wide and warm, he smiled at her.

"Yes and no. I just need to go to Mulaney's Pub," said Sara.

"Yes, of course, Miss Sara. Are you meeting Mr. Jason there?" he asked.

"No," she answered sharply.

Frank's smile disappeared, his mouth a mere gash in his face. "Oh, I am sorry if I have said something wrong," said Frank.

"No, Frank, it's me. I'm sorry! I uh! I need to ask you some things, if that's okay?" said Sara. Sara leaned forward and rested her right arm between the back of the front seats.

"Yes, of course, Miss Sara. What is wrong?"

"The day you took Jason to Riggati's at Six Fourteen North Wabash, was that the first day you met him?" asked Sara.

"Yes, Miss Sara, it was. Why?"

"If you could just bear with me for a minute. Has Jason ever been to your mother's house?"

Frank's eyes squinted and his eyebrows raised as he pulled away from the curb and glanced at Sara in the rearview mirror.

"My mother lived with me and, yes, he visited my house on the day of my mother's wake. He is a good man. He brought flowers and talked to me for a very long time." said Frank.

"I know this is gonna sound strange," said Sara, "but did he take anything from your house?" asked Sara.

Frank pulled in front of Mulaney's Pub. He put the cab in park and turned toward Sara.

"I don't understand, Miss Sara. What would Mr. Jason want to take from my house? He is a good friend. If there was something he wanted, I would give it to him," said Frank.

"Yes, yes, I know. I'm sorry. You probably think I'm crazy. There are just some things I need to figure out. Can you wait for me?" asked Sara.

"Are you going to be at least thirty minutes, Miss Sara" asked Frank.

"Yes, but I'll pay you for the time you're waiting."

Frank lay his hand on Sara's. "That is not my concern. I have a fare that called just after you. It is someone like you, that I take places when I can. It will be about thirty minutes and I'll be back here, if that is okay?" said Frank.

"Absolutely, Frank. You're a sweetheart. I really appreciate it. Should I pay you at the end or now?" asked Sara.

"After I come back will be fine," said Frank. Frank squeezed Sara's hand. "Things aren't always as they seem, Miss Sara."

Sara smiled, opened the door to step out and turned toward Frank. “I’m sorry about all the questions, please forgive me for prying,” she said.

“It is not a problem, Miss Sara. It is forgotten.”

Sara stepped out of the cab and strode to the front door of Mulaney’s Pub. She grasped the door knob when she realized it was only 9:45am. *What am I doing? The pub doesn’t open until 4pm., she thought.* About to release the handle, she noticed a light on inside. The door moved forward. She hesitated, pushed the door open and stepped inside.

“Hello! Is anyone here?” she yelled.

Sara thought she heard something in the back and she walked slowly toward the other end of the bar.

“Hello! Is anyone here,” she yelled again. Nothing!

Sara turned toward the tables in the back and continued into the kitchen. *This is so weird, she thought. Why would the front door be open?*

“Is anyone here? Hello!”

Sara walked around the cutting counter, staring at the knives hanging there. Half afraid to go on and half afraid not to, she circled the kitchen and walked to the women’s bathroom. Placing her palm on the door, she pushed it open and flipped on the light as fast as she could. Her heart was beating faster and faster. No one in sight. “Whew!” Sara bent down and looked underneath each of the stalls and pushed each door open with her foot, jumping backward each time.

“I’m being paranoid. Henry probably forgot to lock up after Gladys got sick and went to the hospital.” She wiped her hands on her pants and continued searching.

After she was sure the bathroom was empty, she stepped out and flipped the light switch off. She walked to the Men's bathroom, took a deep breath and pushed the door open hard with her foot and flipped on the light. The door hit the wall and she turned quickly from side to side to be sure she was alone. She didn't see anyone. She then proceeded to check beneath each stall as she did in the women's bathroom. Once she was satisfied, she pulled the door open and shut off the light. Sara turned to the left and froze in her tracks.

Jason sat at a table in the dining area.

"Hi Sara!" said Jason. "I think we need to talk."

Sara turned and lost her balance. She knocked over a chair and scrambled to stand up to get to the door. "Help!" she whimpered. Her voice got lost and she attempted to scream again.

Jason stood over her now with his hand extended.

"Please, Sara, I need to explain. Please, give me a chance. There are things I need to tell you," said Jason, his eyes red and saddened.

There's a fear in him, thought Sara. *A fear of what he might do*.

Jason bent down and offered his hand to her. "Let me help you up," said Jason. "I know you're afraid, but I can explain everything."

"You mean how you killed those women. Where is Gladys? Did you kill her too?" shouted Sara. She cowered on the floor.

"Sara, I didn't kill anyone. Gladys died of a massive heart attack," said Jason.

"Oh! My God! You lied to me. You said she was fine," said Sara.

Sara began pushing herself back to the side wall, half way to the door.

"I didn't tell you because I wanted you to have a good shoot. And after I found out you were almost killed, I didn't think it was the right time to tell you then either. There was nothing you could do," said Jason. "Besides, I needed to know if I could trust you."

"Trust me? You didn't know if you could trust me?" she yelled. "You mean you didn't know if you could trust me to keep your secret. Well, you can't," said Sara.

"I know it looks bad, but it's not what you think. After last night, I knew I could trust you." Jason lifted both hands, palms out. "Not to keep the secret you think, though."

"Are you crazy? They were your footprints in Anna's tub," yelled Sara. "You took all those bottles of medicine from each of the women you killed." Tears ran down Sara's face as she continued. "The first time I met you, you had a newspaper with a heading about two women dying of massive heart attacks. That wasn't a paper from here, was it? You're a mass murderer aren't you? Why haven't you killed me yet?" she screamed.

Tears streamed down his face. His head fell. He shook it from side to side and Sara saw her chance. She pushed up off the ground and ran for the door. Opening the door, she saw Frank standing on the other side.

"Is everything alright?" asked Frank.

"Frank, thank God! Call the police. Jason's a mass murderer," said Sara. Sara attempted to push Frank out the door, but he wouldn't budge. She looked up into his face and Frank stared at her.

"He is a good man, Miss Sara, a good man."

"Oh my God, you knew! You knew he was here. You're in it together. Help! Help!" screamed Sara.

I really didn't want to do this," said Jason. He reached up with a cloth and put it over her nose and mouth. Sara's hearing became faint and distorted. The racing in Sara's mind stopped and her heart slowed and she fell.

CHAPTER 10

The room spun and a pungent odor hung in the air. Seated on a chair, Sara couldn't move. Her arms secured to her sides, her head hung down, too heavy to lift. She opened and closed her eyes several times before objects became clearer. Floor boards, legs of the chair. She lifted her head slightly and saw a figure. She focused - Jason.

Jason knelt in front of her, tears in his eyes.

"Sara, please forgive me. I am so sorry for all of this. But, I couldn't let you tell anyone…not yet. I didn't want you to get hurt."

Sara's eyes drilled through him.

"You didn't want me to get hurt!" she screamed, as loud as her throat allowed. "So, I guess knocking me out and tying me up is your way of saying 'I care'. Why don't you just kill me like you killed Anna, you bastard!"

"Sara, it's not like that." He moved closer and reached out to touch her face.

Sara jerked her head back, almost knocking the chair over. "Don't you touch me! I'd rather be dead! You killed Anna and…."

"Sara," said a voice from behind her. Sara stopped and turned her head quickly. It was Frank.

"Miss Sara, please listen to him. Please…he has hurt no one. He is trying to help," said Frank.

"So, he's got you on his side, huh? What about your mother, Frank? He has a bottle of Rilosac with your Mom's name on it. How do you suppose he got that?" asked Sara.

Frank walked slowly, dragging his left foot. He stopped and looked down at her. "I gave it to him, Miss Sara. He is going to find out who killed my mother," said Frank.

Sara struggled with the ropes, trying her best to squirm out of them.

"He killed her, Frank. I don't know what he did, but he gave her something. He's a medical researcher…he knows drugs and what they can do to your body. When we first met, he told me that. He was in your house and he was in Anna's apartment the day she died."

"I know," said Frank. "I know. But, he didn't do it. Please let him explain, Miss Sara, please."

Sara's eyes were slits in her face, the corners of her mouth pulled down.

"Fine!" said Sara, with a deep resonance to her voice. "Not that I have much of a choice."

Jason bowed his head. "Sara, I'll explain everything from the beginning. And if you have any questions, I'll do my best to answer them." He shifted his feet and walked around his chair over to a white board. "Frank picked this up for me, so I could explain a little better." Jason walked toward Sara again. "But first of all, I just wanna say, I know I've done some things that weren't very smart, and believe me, I'm learning my lesson the hard way."

Jason began to pace and swallowed hard. "Okay, this is what happened," he said.

Sara's eyes stared blankly at Jason, her body rigid, her teeth clenched. She shot a glance of displeasure at Frank.

"After I explain," said Jason. "If you want to go, you can. I promise."

Jason pulled up a chair in front of Sara and began again.

"Six years ago, I graduated from Harvard Medical…one of the top three students in my class. And like any kid, I was really excited about the differences I thought I was gonna make in the world. Then I started getting offers from all over the place."

Sara rolled her eyes and moved her jaw to the right.

"I'll admit I got a bit cocky about all the opportunities and I lost my perspective. And in the midst of that, I got a call from a cutting edge company in New York. They said they were looking for a Director of Medical Research…a hands-on type of guy, who wasn't afraid of new possibilities. They said they wanted to cure cancer and they said with me on their team, they could do it. Even the guy that was number one in my school didn't get called about this job. So, I thought I'd made it. I should've realized then, something wasn't right. But I was so impressed with myself, that I accepted the position. I really wanted this job because of what I'd be doing." Jason twisted his jaw. "And before ya say it…yeah! it definitely came with a very hefty salary and sign-on bonus. They explained to me that I'd be working on things that weren't FDA approved, but then again that's what research is all about. That was even more exciting to me."

Sara scrunched her eyes and twitched her mouth. The fire in her eyes died down.

"Anyway, the first two years were pretty ordinary for a guy in my position. I tested enzymes, molecules and worked with bacteria and drugs to see how the human body dealt with them. But four years ago, my boss called me into his office and told me about a top secret program. He said I couldn't know all the details, but it was gonna be a breakthrough for the health of all Americans. I was ecstatic to be asked to join the team and I said, 'yes'. I started testing time released medications and their durations. Then within six months they had me working on a second project that they said was totally separate, but just as important."

Frank held a glass of water to Sara's mouth. She took a sip and licked her lips. Her focus fixed on Jason.

"And exactly what project was that?" said Sara.

Jason's jaw relaxed. "The project included studying the interaction between time released formulas, broken down to the most minuscule of particles. I was so interested in working at that level, that I wasn't seeing the big picture. I mean, I knew what I was doing, but I didn't know what they were doing." said Jason.

A sadness overtook Jason's face.

"I didn't know, Sara. You've got to believe me, I didn't know." Tears streamed down his cheeks.

"You didn't know what? You didn't know you'd be killing people!" asked Sara.

"No!" he said, pounding his fists on the chair. "I didn't know they'd be killing people with my research."

Sara's face softened, her body relaxed and Jason continued.

"I hate it that something I created helped these sick bastards! When I found out, I was physically sick every night for weeks. And, the reason I didn't tell you is because I couldn't take a chance…not yet. I didn't know what to say. It was still too confusing to me. I needed some kind of evidence.

Anyway, the first time I found out that something wasn't right, was one night, six months ago. I'll never forget," he said, shaking his head. "I was working late, no one else was there, and I was getting frustrated with a theory, and I threw my notebook. It knocked a fax off my bosses desk, Larz, who I thought was my friend." Jason hesitated and then looked directly at Sara.

Sara, I picked up the memo and it was from a company I'd never heard of. When I read that memo, I got sick."

"Why? What did it say," asked Sara, struggling to get comfortable.

"It was on the letterhead of another country. I mean, we've dealt with other countries before…like France and Canada, but this was a third world country. It talked about the H1N1 flu shot and stated that they wanted to be sure the time release factor would be tested within the year.

I tried to make sense of it. I kept asking myself why was information about the H1N1 serum being shared with a third world country and what did they mean when they said it would be tested within the year? The H1N1 vaccine already had the time release factor in it and our company supplied the bulk of it."

Jason stood, arms folded in front of him, and stared at nothing. "The discoveries I'd made on coupling releases…they hadn't been approved yet, even though I'd sent my reports in months before. I hadn't been given any date of when they might be used. I was still testing possible side effects."

Jason circled his chair. "Sara, I was the only one working on the time release factor and I didn't know anything about this. I couldn't figure out why they weren't sharing it with me. My mind started going crazy. Because now, it wasn't about my work, it was about who else could be using my work…and for what?"

Jason stopped pacing and sat on the edge of his chair. "That's how this all started. I had to know more. Every night after everybody left, I started going through faxes, emails, letters, everything on Larz's desk. But there was no mention of this company, or this country again…until three weeks later. I looked through a folder marked "dead files" that I'd looked through before. It only had four dead projects in it. But this particular day, there was something else. It was another fax."

"What did it say," asked Sara. She knew he was going to tell her, but she couldn't seem to wait until he said it. She attempted to lean forward, but couldn't.

"I'm sorry," said Jason. "Let me cut the ropes first."

Jason got out his knife and cut the ropes. He had put padding underneath, so it wouldn't leave a mark.

"I'm sorry Sara. I never meant to get you involved. You have to believe me. I should have stayed away, but I needed information about Anna. And, I had no idea that I was going to…" His gaze fell to the floor. "Fall in love with you."

Sara's eyes opened wide. She rubbed her arms and stretched them out and to the side, as her focus turned inward.

"I'm sorry," he said.

"So-o, what did this second fax say?" she asked.

"It was from the same country, and it was an update, letting Larz know that everything was on schedule. But this time Larz wrote a name on it…Mujahdeen Jihad. I checked him out right away on the internet."

"And…" said Sara.

Jason sat on the edge of the chair and leaned toward Sara. "And…" He took a deep breath. "Mujahdeen Jihad is a terrorist. I got hold of an underground newspaper that listed some of the work it said he's doing. Sara, it was mine, my work, my research." Jason took another deep breath. "Everything I'd worked on and sent in months ago thru Larz was written as his work. I didn't know what to think. Was the whole company in on this or was Larz an insider? Larz is my boss - and I thought my friend. I didn't know who to talk to or what I'd say. I should've gone with my first instincts," said Jason.

"What do ya mean?" asked Sara.

"When I first met Larz, I thought it was strange he was my boss. I don't know…not to sound cocky, but he didn't seem to know very much. It bothered me a lot at first. I guess I didn't like the idea of someone who didn't understand what I was doing giving me work. But then, all the assignments he gave me were really important, so I stopped worrying about it. Now I know the real reason they chose me. Yeah! I was smart, but I was any easy mark too."

Jason sat back in his chair. "I had to find out what they were planning to do, so I kept looking in that dead file …until I found newspaper articles starting to crop up about women having massive heart attacks. When it made the front page, I knew I had to do something. That's when I lucked out and found a database. It listed all of the people in Chicago who'd gotten the H1N1 vaccine. But there was a second column. It listed who got prescriptions for Rilosac."

"Why would it list that?" asked Sara.

"I didn't know. But I knew it was my link to an answer. So, I focused on one name on the list, someone who lived close to the others, and I got an apartment nearby." Jason looked down.

"Was it Mrs. McClusky's name?" asked Sara.

"Yes, it was. I called and found a vacant apartment on the same floor and I took it. I was hoping to get the information I needed before anything happened. I'm sorry! I didn't know exactly what was gonna happen. And after Mrs. McClusky died...that's when I realized... my work has been helping this animal find ways to kill people," said Jason.

"But how? Not everyone that took the flu shot is gonna die...are they?" asked Sara.

"No, they had to make sure it worked first. And they didn't want anyone to be able to track it back to them. I'm afraid Anna was part of a test run. That's why they had me working on time releases.

Jason got up and walked to the white board. "Let me use the board. It'll be easier to understand." Jason drew the following table:

H1N1= time release+bacteria = Reflux
H1N1 + Rilosac = Heart Arrhythmia + secondary time release in Rilosac = Stop Arrhythmia after 1 hour.

Rilosac w/extra time releases + any other time release medication = Death

"I'm gonna explain it as simply as possible. If you get confused, just stop me," said Jason. He took a deep breath and continued.

"I developed a time release for the H1N1 vaccine and it was approved by the FDA. A time release allows a medication to be dispersed periodically instead of all at once.

So here's what's happening. The H1N1 vaccine had a bacteria and an extra time release mechanism put in it. The bacteria caused reflux and ingesting Rilosec triggered the extra time release to work. Once someone did that - took Rilosac - within thirty six hours after ingesting it, the extra time release would cause a heart arrhythmia. An hour after that, a second time release from the Rilosac would stop the arrhythmia." Jason shook his head.

"The terrorist wanted the results recorded before moving ahead with the final plan. I'm pretty sure they didn't realize that other time release medications – like aspirin - taken with 36 hours of the Rilosac would cause the arrhythmia to begin again – and this time it meant death." Jason sat on the chair in front of Sara.

"I'm afraid this pushed up their timeline because people actually died.

Sara tilted her head slightly. "So it wasn't about giving people reflux, it was about hiding their tracks?" asked Sara.

"Exactly," said Jason.

Sara stared at the board for a while. "So, they weren't actually figuring on killing Anna…Oh my God! Oh my God!" Sara jumped up.

"I killed her. I killed her. Jason, I gave Anna the aspirin. It was the third time release medication," she said, pointing at the white board. "The paramedics told me to and I gave it to her."

Sara collapsed back onto the chair, covered her face with her hands and began sobbing.

Jason pulled her hands away and knelt in front of her. "Sara, it's not your fault. You didn't do anything wrong."

"I killed her," said Sara. Her head dropped to her hands again. "I killed my friend."

"I know how you feel," said Jason. "That's how I've felt for weeks now."

Sara stood and circled the chair. "It's not the same. She was my friend. She trusted me," sobbed Sara.

Jason remained kneeling. "Sara, I know I wasn't her friend, but I felt for her and for you when she died. And you're right, it's not the same. You gave her an aspirin because she was having a heart attack," he said, standing. "I developed a time release that's being used to kill good people like Anna and millions of others like Frank's Mom. But, I can't focus on that. I have to focus on finding a drug to stop it from happening again."

Jason cupped her head in his hands. "I was physically sick when I found that memo, Sara. I didn't want to know any more because I didn't know if I could handle it. But when I found that list for recipients of the H1N1 vaccine in Chicago, I knew I had to move here immediately. I had to. I didn't have proof of what I knew except that I was the one that developed it. And I had to stop it. And if I told anyone, I'd be implicating myself and wouldn't be able to find a cure in time to help anyone else." He gazed deep into her eyes.

"I need your help, Sara. We need to focus. This was a pre-cursor to the real thing - a worldwide strike. It worked a lot better than they thought. They're going to try and take away a few steps now."

"Oh my God! I just realized…the reason you had all their medications…" said Sara.

Jason raised a finger, "I…"

"Wait, I know, you needed to test each one to see if they had those extra time releases in them and test them with other drugs to find a cure," said Sara calmly.

Jason smiled for the first time in a while. "Yes, you catch on very quickly. I've been able to get a few hours in at a lab here in Chicago," said Jason. He nodded his head toward Frank. "Frank set me up with a friend of his. Unfortunately, I still need more time to see if there is a way to unarm the release factor in the H1N1 serum. I worked for three years to make it do exactly what it's doing, but not for the same reason. It's supposed to combat disease, illness and bacteria by releasing when it comes in contact with them."

Sara sat staring at Jason, nodding periodically.

Jason stood again and started waving his hands in the air.

"This monster has taken the development of the time release theory and is using it to harm people!" Jason placed his hands behind his neck and threw back his head. "I can't believe how stupid I've been! I was so proud of myself. It never occurred to me that someone would use them like this. I guess that's pretty naïve."

Jason held his left hand out, palm up toward Frank. "Thank God for Frank. He knows so many people and they know to be discrete. I don't know what I would have done without your help."

"You are helping me to discover who killed my mother. I am very grateful for that, Mr. Jason," said Frank.

"What's the worse case scenario here," asked Sara.

"That's a very good question," said Jason. "There may be an actual time release factor that doesn't require a third component, to release…or a second one, for that matter," said Jason. I did manage to get two test tubes with the H1N1 flu shot. It was from two different test periods. I'm hoping to get to a lab and test them to see if they're different. Hopefully, they haven't put a new one into production yet. As I said, I only found out about the connection to Rilosac after coming to Chicago."

Sara scrunched her mouth to the side, "hmmm," she said, looking down.

"What is it?" asked Jason.

"It's really not important, but, I was just wondering about the tub," said Sara. "Why were you standing in the tub?"

Sara gulped her water now and Jason retrieved a glass of water from the bar too.

"This is where I got scared," said Jason. "I'm the one that broke into Anna's apartment, because I had to get the medication and get some proof. But, while I was in there, someone else broke in too."

"That's why you were so nervous," said Sara.

"Yes."

"So, you hid in the tub?" asked Sara, eyes narrowing toward the bridge of her nose.

"It was the only thing I could think to do. I had the medication, so I stepped in the shower, pulled the curtain and prayed. This guy went through the medicine cabinet and the drawers and everywhere else. But he was very neat.

He didn't upset anything. I thanked God a million times that he didn't pull back the curtain.

I think he broke into your apartment too. I found out that someone had asked the night manager if Mrs. McClusky had any friends. And when you told me that Anna's brother called, but you knew that her brother was dead, I knew something was up. I'm sorry to say, I had to be sure you didn't work for them too. I've got to tell you, I'm so glad you don't," said Jason.

"So, when did you realize that I wasn't working for them?" asked Sara.

"The day you called and asked for my help. Only then, I didn't know how to answer you. You wanted to know about the footprints, but they were mine. I needed to have more information before I dropped all of this on you. I was afraid you might not believe me," said Jason, looking down.

"So, were they looking for the medication too?" asked Sara.

"Yes, apparently they don't want any physical evidence left behind. And they may already know something's going on with me too. I told Larz I needed to take a month off for personal reasons. I still have an apartment in NewYork, Sara."

Sara looked down and to the side. "You're not married, are you?" she asked.

Jason lifted her head. "No, I'm not. I never wanted to get married, but now I think it would be really nice."

The corners of Sara's mouth rose high and her face flushed.

"So now that they didn't find the medication, they won't come back, right?" asked Sara.

Jason's expression changed again. Lines appeared in his forehead and deepened. "When I left you this morning, I had a friend working with me to find more information. He found out that the accident on the yacht, wasn't an accident at all. Sara, was there someone, anyone that worked on the shoot that shouldn't have been?"

"Well, I don't know. The guy who was supposed to play my boyfriend in the shoot didn't make it."

"Did they say why?" asked Jason.

"The Casting Director said that the original guy was carjacked the night before and got pretty beat up. So, when another guy showed up the day of the shoot…Oh my God! Do you think he…"

Jason nodded his head. "He was a plant. Someone loosened the rope to the jig on that yacht and my guess is, it was him. They wanted to hurt you Sara," said Jason. His voice lowered. "And it's all because of me."

"Why do they want to hurt me? I didn't have anything to do with it," said Sara.

"You started asking questions at the hospital and then with the police. You were bringing too much attention to Anna's death."

"This whole thing is like a movie. The weird thing is," said Sara. "That guy, Adam, looked really shocked when they accused him of loosening the rope. He kept saying he only tripped over it. So, you think it was all an act?"

"Yeah! I know, it's really scary. You think you can trust people and then you find out you can't," said Jason.

"Yeah! I know about that…" Sara started. "I know of the feeling…I know now it wasn't the case."

"Thank you," said Jason.

"So, what should we do?" asked Sara. "Do you think it's safe to go home? Maybe we should call the police or the FBI."

"I've wanted to do that from the beginning, but I need more evidence of who's doing what. Right now, if I tried to convince them, they'd either think I was crazy, or they'd look into it and find out that I'm the one who's been working on it all along," said Jason. "I'm such an idiot."

"Trusting people doesn't make you stupid," said Sara. "But once you find out that they can't be trusted, you get away from them…you did that. And, you're doing what you can to make things right."

Jason circled the floor. "I know, but it's not enough. I've got to stop them."

"So where does that leave us?" said Sara. If we can't call the police or the FBI until we have more evidence, and we can't go home, where do we go?"

Frank stood and limped toward Sara. "That is why I am here, Miss Sara. Jason explained all of this to me and I want to help. These people killed my mother and your Anna. We can't give up. We have to do what we can. So until you are safe again, I have a small one bedroom condo, where my mother lived up until three months ago. She was having a hard time, so she moved in with me and my wife. There's not much there except furniture and a few dishes and silverware. The two of you can stay there for as long as you need," said Frank.

Sara glanced at Jason and back to Frank again.

"I'm sorry I do not have a two bedroom, but there is a very comfortable lounge chair and a couch," said Frank.

Jason leaned an arm on the bar and rested his hip on the stool. "I want you someplace safe. As for me, I can stay at my place. I'll barricade the door and come over to the condo during the day. It'll be fine."

"No it won't be," said Sara. "We both need to be safe."

Jason walked toward Sara, reaching for her hand. "Are you sure you're okay with that?"

The corner of Sara's mouth rose. "I'll admit it's a bit of a jump, but life is all about change. And if this is for the better, I'm okay with it."

Sara reached for Frank's arm. "Frank, you must think I'm terrible. To think Jason or you could have hurt anyone," said Sara.

Frank lay his hand on Sara's shoulder. "I know that you are a good person, Miss Sara and I know that Mr. Jason is a good person too," replied Frank. "There was a lot you did not know and as Mr. Jason said, there are a lot of people you cannot trust. Together you and Mr. Jason are going to find out who did this and bring them to justice. I will help in any way that I can."

Sara didn't let go of Frank's arm. "Frank, what happened to your leg?" asked Sara.

"It is nothing Miss Sara. I have had a bum leg since before I moved to this country. But it is not my driving foot," smiled Frank. "I am very fortunate to be as healthy as I am."

"You're amazing. You're so upbeat and positive. I had no idea you had any physical problems at all," said Sara. She looked down at the ground. "I'm sorry, Frank."

"Everything is good, Miss Sara. And everything is going to get better."

Jason grabbed Frank's shoulder, pulled him in and hugged him. "Thanks, Frank. I'm gonna get the proof we need."

Frank wiped off the board, tucked it under his arm and turned toward the door. "I will be in my cab waiting for you. Take all the time you need," said Frank.

"Thanks," said Jason.

Jason turned and gently grasped Sara's arm. "Can I ask you something?"

"Of course, what is it?"

"What made you start to think I had killed someone?" said Jason. His head swung down.

"Well," Sara cleared her throat. "This morning when you left, I was worried, but not in the way you think. I didn't want to think about what you said, because the only thing I could come up with, was that you were married," said Sara.

Jason lifted his head, the corners of his mouth ticked upward.

"So I needed a distraction," continued Sara. "I love to dance and I remembered all the wonderful music you played that night, so I decided to find some dance music." She looked down sheepishly. "That's my favorite exercise, dancing. So I found a music cd from the 70's - and I danced to that for a while. Then I found a tape marked, 'Best Released' and since it was hand labeled, I figured it had your favorite songs on it, so I put it in…"

"Oh my God!" said Jason.

"Yeah!" agreed Sara.

Jason squinted. "But, I explained why I did it, and…"

Sara interrupted. "It was at the end of the recording when I put it in, so I rewound just a little to see what kind of music it was. When I hit play, I heard your voice and you said, 'I never wanted to hurt anyone, but, how many women are dead because of what I did.' Then I heard a noise at the front door and I thought it was you. I was scared to death," said Sara.

"Oh my God," said Jason. He cupped his hand over his mouth. "I'm so sorry."

"Anyway, I leapt for the recorder and I hit eject. I guess I pulled it out too fast, because the plastic broke and the ribbon came out. I was so afraid you'd come in and see me and then…I don't know."

Jason's gaze fell to the floor as he chewed on his lip. "You thought I'd kill you, didn't you?" said Jason.

"I don't know. Nothing was making sense. I was scared and I didn't know why you said those things. And when I put the tape back in to listen to the rest to make sense of it, it was all garbled and the ribbon fell out again. That's when I remembered the bottles of medicine in the cabinet in the bathroom. I ran in and I turned them around and found Anna's name and the names of the other women who had died."

Jason wrapped Sara in his arms. "What a nightmare for you. I was trying to leave a tape explaining everything from the beginning, in case something happened to me."

"I know that now, but at the time, it had me putting all kinds of things together. All the times you didn't tell me the truth or you hid something from me."

Sara stopped, reached out and lifted Jason's face in her hands. "I know now," she said. She kissed him gently. "It's all behind us now." She held up an index finger and dipped her head, eyes raised slightly toward Jason. "Just promise me one thing,"

"Anything, anything at all," said Jason, shaking his head.

"No more secrets." She kissed her index finger and touched Jason's lips.

Jason grabbed her finger and kissed it. "I promise. No more secrets."

"Well, Frank is waiting, we should probably get going," said Sara, walking toward the front door.

Jason gently grasped Sara's arm and turned her toward him once more. "I have one more thing to apologize for. I am so-o-o sorry for all that you've been through because of me. I'm…I'm really sorry about the rope and…" Jason choked up and couldn't finish.

Sara lifted Jason's chin with her thumb and forefinger. "Hey, you! You never know if someone's into bondage until you try," she smiled.

Jason tilted his head and scrunched his mouth to the left.

"I'm not by the way," said Sara.

Jason took Sara in his arms and hugged her hard. He pulled her back, looked into her eyes and kissed her. "I love you Sara," said Jason.

"I know," she said and she kissed him back.

Jason glanced around the bar. "Ooooh! Almost forgot."

He ran back and put the chairs upside down on the table, grabbed the rope and cloth and threw them in the dumpster out back. Returning to the bar, he wrapped an arm around Sara and walked her outside to Frank's cab.

"How did you get in the pub," asked Sara.

Frank's good friends with Henry, the owner," said Jason as he opened the cab door for Sara.

Sara slid in, careful not to sit on the rip. Jason sat next to her. The cab's cigarette smell had vanished. Sara's senses turned to sound and sight. She glanced at the seat to the left of her…where there was a stack of mail addressed to her.

"Frank, is this mine?" asked Sara. How did you get it?"

Jason put his hand up. "I asked Frank to pick it up for you," he said.

"You wanted to double check that I wasn't getting any international mail?" asked Sara.

"It was my idea, Miss Sara. I wanted to protect Mr. Jason and I wanted to be 100% sure. I am sorry," said Frank. "You see it was not just you who had doubts."

"Let's call it even," said Sara. She noted that the envelopes were all slit open. What's the big one?" asked Sara.

"I believe they are pictures from your commercial shoot. They are very good," said Frank. "There is a dvd also."

"Thank you," said Sara.

Jason turned Sara toward him. "We're gonna need to go back to our apartments, pack a few things and leave as quickly as possible. It's not safe to stay there now," said Jason. "So, grab anything you think you'll need."

Sara bit her lip. "How long do you think it'll be?" she asked.

"I wish I could say. I don't know. But, I do know I want to make sure you're safe," said Jason.

"Wow! It's scary how easy it was for someone to get into my apartment?" said Sara.

"Yes. It is," agreed Jason.

Sara's eyes widened and she grasped Jason's wrist. "What about Phil and Adam? Aren't they going to expect me to call them back? After all, they sent me the outfit, called twice, the day of the accident, the next morning and now I'll have disappeared?"

"Yes, you should call. We'll have to come up with a story to tell them in case they ask where you are," said Jason. "And since you brought it up, I want to tell you something. Phil and Adam only called once. In the morning when you woke up, I was talking to Frank, not them. He was asking if I'd told you yet. Obviously, I hadn't. I just wanted you to know the truth," said Jason. He put his hand on Sara's. "If you have any other questions about anything, I've said or I've done, just ask me, and I'll tell you the truth."

Sara laid her head on Jason's shoulder and he wrapped his arm around her.

"I trust you," said Sara.

Jason sniffed the air above Sara's head. "Hmmmm! Charlie cologne," he said kissing her gently on the head.

Frank took them directly to Chicago Hi-Towers.

"I'll be back in twenty minutes, Mr. Jason. Is that enough time?" asked Frank.

Jason pushed back from Sara. "Can you get what you need in twenty minutes?" he asked.

"Sure. No problem!" said Sara.

"Okay! Let's go," said Jason.

Jason stepped quickly from the cab and helped Sara out. They made their way through the revolving doors and straight to the elevator. Sara nervously looked at Jason as they stood apart, waiting. A man in a long black overcoat stepped behind Sara. Sara saw his reflection in the trim around the door. Her eyes found Jason's and they darted from Jason to the man behind her.

Jason glanced back as he looked at his watch. The doors opened and the three of them stepped inside. "Fourteen please," said Sara. Jason stood on one side and hit fourteen and Sara stood on the other side and nodded. The man in the long black overcoat hit fifteen and stood in the middle at the back.

Sara began to perspire, her mind racing. She remembered the man in the long black overcoat who knocked her down by the elevator a few days ago. He had a scar between his thumb and forefinger. She strained to look, but she couldn't see. He carried his suit coat over his arm and it draped over his hand.

Is he carrying a gun under his coat? thought Sara.

The elevator hummed and Sara's heart raced. Jason's eyes focused on the man's suitcoat as he wiped the perspiration on his hands to his pants. The elevator approached fourteen. It stopped and suddenly dropped an inch. The man fell forward, he dropped his coat and something black and shiny stuck out from underneath it. Sara let out a small scream and Jason retrieved the item. A cell phone.

"Here you go sir," said Jason. He handed the cell phone and coat to the stranger.

"I'm sorry," said Sara. "Elevators always make me nervous."

The man smiled softly, accepted his cell phone and leaned on the back wall. Jason and Sara exited.

The doors closed and Sara grabbed Jason's arm. "Whew!"

"Are you okay?" asked Jason.

"Yes, I'm fine," replied Sara.

"I'm gonna check your place out first and then I'll go to mine. I'll knock on the door when I'm done. Alright?"

Sara unlocked her door and let Jason go in first. He circled the apartment, looking in closets and under the bed.

"It looks okay. Pack as fast as you can and I'll be right back," said Jason.

Sara stepped in front of him, held his face in her hands and kissed him. "I love you too," she said.

The corners of Jason's mouth pulled up and his eyes twinkled. "I needed that." He kissed her back and stepped out the door.

Sara locked the door and ran to the bedroom. She got out the biggest suitcase she had and packed everything she thought she might need. Since she travelled quite a bit, she already had a makeup kit and all the hair care essentials in a small bag, ready to go. She grabbed a pile of clothes and threw them into her suitcase. *Should be enough for a week*, she thought. She closed the suitcase and heard a knock at the door. Reaching the front door, Sara leaned toward the peep hole. Jason.

She opened the front door, ran back for her suitcase and rolled it into the hall.

"Oh wait, I forgot," said Sara. She ran into the kitchen and removed the garbage can from under the sink and pulled out the grocery bag at the bottom.

"Here. I took these from your apartment this morning. You might need them."

"Thanks Sara, you go down first and get in the cab and tell Frank I'll meet you around the corner. I'll go out the side door in case anyone is watching," said Jason.

Sara squinted a little and she swallowed hard.

Jason grabbed both her shoulders and looked into her eyes. "It's gonna be okay. I promise," said Jason. "Really!"

Sara smiled a meek smile. "I know, I know."

She wheeled her suitcase to the elevator and stepped in. Holding her breath, she hit L. It went straight to the lobby. The doors opened and Sara exhaled. She glanced around while moving quickly forward toward the revolving doors.

"Sara, I haven't seen you for a very long time," said Mr. Adashi, walking toward her from Garden Pure. "How have you been doing," he asked.

Not now, not now, thought Sara. "I'm fine, and you?"

Mr. Adashi stopped right in front of her.

"I'm good. Business is pretty good too, considering the economy," said Mr. Adashi.

Sara moved to the right to continue on and Mr. Adashi moved with her.

"Are you going out of town?" he asked.

Why is he asking me? thought Sara. *You idiot, you're pulling a suitcase*, she told herself. "Just for a week or so. Visiting a friend. It'll be nice to get away," said Sara. She smiled and looked away.

"Is everything alright," he asked.

"Oh yes, I'm fine. Thank you so much for asking," said Sara.

"So, how did that shoot go?" asked Mr. Adashi.

"It went really well. Finished in a day," she said. Sara began to walk again and Mr. Adashi stepped in front of her.

"How can you go out of town? Isn't Mrs. McClusky's wake tonight and the funeral on Saturday," he asked.

Sara shifted her weight from one foot to the other.

"Sara," came a voice from behind her. "Thanks so much for saying you'd babysit my friend's dogs for a couple days before going out of town. I really appreciate it, and I know he does too," said Jason.

"Oh! yeah! sure, no problem," said Sara.

"Well I've gotta get going. Do you wanna share a cab?" asked Jason.

"Yes. That's a good idea," said Sara. She turned to Mr. Adashi. "I'll see you at the wake."

Jason raised his arm and waved it palm up in front of him. "After you," he said.

Sara walked as fast as she could without looking too obvious. Jason followed directly behind her. Stretching his arm out in front of him, he pushed open the door and held it as Sara walked through. The air hit Sara in the face and she took a deep breath. As if on cue, Frank pulled up. Sara relaxed her shoulders as Jason waved to him.

They walked to the cab, Jason grabbed her bag, Sara got in, and Frank stepped out and popped the trunk. After placing both bags in the trunk, Jason got in the backseat beside Sara.

As Frank pulled away from the curb, Sara squeezed Jason's arm.

"Oh my God! Jason, the wake for Anna is tonight from 7 until 9. I have to go," said Sara.

"Of course you do," said Jason.

"I will pick you up at 6:30, Miss Sara, and bring you back after 9. Is that alright?" asked Frank.

"Yes, that's fine," said Sara.

Frank circled the Loop once and then, just in case someone followed, took a few back streets to get to the condo he owned.

Head tilted, staring at Jason, Sara was motionless. "It must have been really awful to keep up a front with so many people," said Sara. She gently ran her hand over his. "Not knowing who you could really trust. I'm freaking out after less than a day. I'm glad you trusted me enough to tell me."

"Me too!" said Jason. He squeezed her hand as Frank pulled into the curb.

CHAPTER 11

Jason stepped out and gave Sara his hand. Then, Frank popped the trunk and Jason removed one large suitcase and one medium size.

The day had changed so dramatically thought Sara. *One minute I'm falling in love with Jason and the next I wanted to strangle him with my bare hands...and the next, I'm falling in love again.*

The sun still shone and the noise of the city rustled on the wind in the distance.

"Thanks, Frank. We'll be in touch," said Jason.

Jason and Sara walked into the two story stone building, using their key to get through the first door. They walked to the back of the building and took the elevator to the 2nd floor. Unit #213, one unit from the end. Stepping into a small foyer, Jason placed the key on a wooden table. Sara took a right through a large kitchen with a dining area at the other end. Taking another left, she found a spacious living room with three bay windows.

This is a large condo for a single person, thought Sara. *And, there's that musty smell that's usually connected with older people. I guess even though almost all of her things are gone, that smell lingers. The furniture really has a quaint charm to it though.* All the wood in the furniture held an intricately carved pattern, while the material on the couch and chair boasted a brown and cream colored floral design.

Walking into the center of the living room, Jason extended an arm and index finger toward the wall.

"That picture over the couch," said Jason. "Frank said that's a picture of his Mom, Dad and himself, when he was a boy. He hadn't the heart to take it down yet. And his wife is still looking for a place to hang it in their home."

Sara tossed her mail on the kitchen counter, walked into the living room and leaned over the couch, resting her hand on the back. "I never knew Africa was so beautiful," said Sara. "It's amazing how he ended up here."

Jason nodded, walked to the hall and grabbed the handles of both suitcases. He pulled them down a long hallway, left of the kitchen, into the bedroom with Sara close behind him.

What a beautiful Victorian queen size bed. With a nightstand to match. Very romantic, thought Sara. She turned to the left. *A matching dresser...oooh! Four enormous drawers...that should work.*

"This should do," said Jason. "An over-stuffed lounger and he left blankets and sheets too."

Sara scrunched her mouth. *Wouldn't be so terrible if he slept in the bed,* thought Sara. *But I can't say anything. He's being a gentleman.* She glanced about the room. A cream colored clock radio sat alone on the nightstand. Sara opened a door a couple feet left of the nightstand – a walk-in closet with the smell of cedar. Stepping inside, she found a full length cheval mirror sat at the back of the closet. Walking out, she glanced back at the bed and at Jason.

Jason took Sara's arm. "Sara, you'll sleep in the bed, and if it's okay, I'll sleep on the recliner."

"Are you sure?" said Sara. "Do you think it'll be comfortable enough?"

"Absolutely," replied Jason. "Besides, it's gotta be really hard for you. Someone you thought you liked and trusted...and all of the sudden, you're tied up and…" Jason shook his head. "I want you to be at ease. I want you to take the time you need to feel comfortable with me again. Hopefully it won't take too much time." He smiled a sad smile.

Sara smiled and lifted her arm to look at her watch.

"You've got plenty of time to get ready," said Jason.

"Times Up," said Sara.

"I'm sorry!"

Sara wrapped her arms around his neck and pulled him close. "Times up! I'm comfortable with you…in fact I'm down right happy."

Jason picked her up and swung her around. He put her down and kissed her passionately. Tears ran from his face to hers and Sara stepped back.

"Are you okay?" she asked.

"Yeah! I am now. I really thought I'd messed it all up and I'd never get you back. Thank you for giving me another chance." He kissed her hard again.

Sara smiled coyly. "I'd better start putting my stuff away. I don't want to give you the impression I'm not neat." She giggled.

She took the top two drawers of the dresser and Jason took the bottom two. Hanging her dress up in the closet, she turned and bumped into Jason as he hung up his suit.

Their eyes met and Jason's hand brushed her bottom as she exited the closet.

"I should take a shower," said Sara, rounding the corner into the bathroom. "Wow, this is a nice size…" Turning around quickly, she accidentally bumped into Jason. "Oh my God! I'm sorry, I didn't mean to…"

"I'd rather you said that, then, 'Whoa! that's kind of small.'" smiled Jason.

Sara's face turned bright red and she turned to survey the rest of the bathroom.

One sink with a full countertop, a white porcelain tub with legs, and a nice size shower.

"I bet she had the bathroom redone," said Sara. "This tub is really cool."

"Yeah! It looks like she kept some of the retro look, but brought in some of the new," said Jason. "I like it. It's quaint, but it's works."

Running her hand along the edge of the tub, Sara found a small packet. "Ooooh! bubble bath. That's promising," said Sara.

Jason stepped into the glass enclosed shower. He could almost extend his arms.

"Let me try," said Sara. She stepped in facing Jason and extended her arms. Once again their eyes locked. "Rain, I think," he said.

"Rain?" said Sara.

"The pattern on the glass…I think it's rain."

"Oh! It's nice."

Jason turned to step out and Sara thrust her arm out in front of him.

She slid her hand up his chest, grasping his collar and pulled him close for a kiss.

Jason's arm extended against the shower wall above Sara. His right hand found the back of her head and he kissed her passionately.

Pulling back, Sara glanced into Jason's eyes again. "You're too serious. Everything's okay. Really! As a matter of fact…you know that shower I was talking about?" With that, Sara flipped on the shower, full force.

"Hey!!!" he screamed, as a rush of water hit the top of her head and bounced off his chest. Why you little vixen…" Jason attempted to turn the water off, but Sara placed her hand against his chest. Her fingers began unbuttoning his shirt, slowly moving down to the snaps on his jeans. He leaned down, took her face in his hands and kissed her. She unsnapped and unzipped his jeans and pulled his shirt out. Sliding his back down the opposite wall, Jason reached the top of Sara's jeans. He unsnapped, unzipped and slowly pulled them down. The soaked jeans stuck to her skin, so he turned her around to face the wall. Her fingers gripped the top of the shower stall as Jason freed her from the denim plastered against her legs.

"Nice view," said Jason.

Sara quickly faced him again and he tilted his mouth at the inside of her knee to catch the water as it came rushing down. Sara giggled and pushed his wet hair off his forehead.

"Let me help you out of these wet things," said Jason. He reached up, slid his two middle fingers over the top of the elastic band on both sides and pulled down her soaking wet panties.

Sara placed one foot on his chest to make it easier.

"I think I like it down here," said Jason, raising an eyebrow.

Sara giggled. "Come here you," she said coyly.

Sliding his hands up the outside of her thighs, he stood. He immediately pulled his jeans and shorts off and pressed up against Sara.

"I love you Sara," said Jason.

"I love you too, Jason."

Their bodies glistened as the hot water ran between them. Resting his head on her shoulder, he sensually sucked Sara's earlobe and nuzzled her neck. While using his left hand to cup her bottom, he slid his right hand under her shirt and ran his thumb back and forth across her nipple.

Sara hooked a leg around Jason while sliding her hand down his belly and wrapping her long tapered fingers completely around him, to reach the angle desired. Sara gasped…stood on her tiptoes and settled down to her heels. She ran her hands through his hair and pushed against him hard. He unbuttoned her shirt and wrapped his mouth around her left breast. Moving his hips in a circular motion, he glided all the way in. Again…up on her tiptoes and down. Sara felt Jason's right hand glide down her tummy. With the heel of his hand remaining on her pelvis, he moved his fingers rhythmically. With each timed movement beneath the rush of water, Sara gasped again and again and again.

As her body succumbed to a vacuum within, leaving her light headed, he ignited a fire that hit every sensitive nerve in her body.

"Oh God! Oh God! Oh God!" gasped Sara. Throwing her head back while arching her spine and tensing her calves, she let out the final high pitched squeal.

"Yes!" said Jason with several low grunts, a moan and then a release. He pushed against Sara, holding her tight and leaning on the glass door. "I love making love to you."

"I love it too," said Sara, barely audible. They held each other for what seemed like hours, nestled in each others arms, when Sara's eyes opened wide. She turned off the water.

"Oh my God! I forgot towels." They both looked at the linen closet door with a grimaced expression on their faces.

Sara opened the door and leaned forward.

"I'll hold on so you don't fall," said Jason smiling. He wrapped his hands around her hips as she extended her arm to pull the door open.

"I hope, I hope, I hope," she said. Jason crossed his fingers and the door swung open.

"Alright! Frank came through again," said Jason.

"Blankets, towels, bubblebath. I don't know if there's anything he didn't think of," said Sara as she pulled two towels off the shelf. She wrapped a mauve towel around herself and handed a teal towel to Jason.

"I wonder if there's anything he didn't think of…"

Jason and Sara immediately turned toward each other, their faces lit up.

"Food!!!" they said together.

They scampered off to the kitchen laughing. Jason got there a step ahead and pulled open the refrigerator. Sara secured the towel around Jason's waist, and jumped up on his back to look over his shoulder.

"God bless him," said Sara.

She slid down and Jason turned around.

"God bless us all," said Jason. "We should probably get you something to eat."

Sara grabbed a pan marked 'mostaccioli,' wrapped in tin foil and pulled back the corner.

"Ooooh! It looks really good."

Jason grabbed another package marked 'Homemade bread,' opened one end and slid out one of three loaves, cut off four thick slices and placed the remainder back in the refrigerator. Jason glanced at Sara. "Are two pieces enough for you?" he asked.

"More than enough," said Sara. She cut two squares of mostaccioli, one twice as big as the other, put them on separate plates, covered the pan, and put it back in the refrigerator.

"Thank God for microwaves," said Sara. "Three minutes for mine and…" Sara began.

"And five for mine," said Jason. "I'm guessing you remember how much I eat."

"Better you than me," said Sara.

Jason retrieved the butter and the napkins and Sara clasped the glasses and the silverware in-between her fingers. The smell of hot mostaccioli soon filled the kitchen. The microwave buzzed and Sara removed the plates and wrapped the bread in paper towels and put them in the microwave to warm. Jason poured bottled water for Sara and himself and took a container of mozzarella out of the refrigerator and placed it on the table. He pulled out Sara's chair and then sat across from her. They both stared at each other in their respective towels until Jason stretched both hands across the table and held Sara's hands in his.

"Thank you for being you," he said.

"This is so weird in such a nice way," said Sara.

"I know what you mean," said Jason. He bowed his head. "God, please help Sara and Frank and me to get through this in one piece and help us to uncover the truth. Amen!"

Sara bowed her head "Amen!"

After eating a plate of the mostaccioli and homemade bread prepared by Frank's wife, Jason and Sara began cleaning up. Jason glanced at his watch.

"It's already after six. You need to get ready for the wake," said Jason. He turned Sara toward him. "Sara, you know I'd go with, but I don't want anyone putting us together. And most people didn't know that I knew her. I think she'll understand."

"I'm sure she would. That's fine," said Sara. She kissed him on the mouth and walked into the bedroom and closed the door. Within twenty minutes, she emerged with makeup applied, hair dried and swept back behind one ear. She wore black stiletto heels, a long black handkerchief skirt and a sleeveless black silk shell.

"I know you're going to a wake, but you look gorgeous," said Jason.

Sara smiled and looked directly at him. "I wonder if she can see me now? I hope she knows I would have stayed with her that night at the hospital. I would have done anything for her," said Sara. Her eyes welled up and she lowered her head.

Jason hugged her close and rested his chin on her head. "She knows you inside out, Sara. And, I believe she's with you right now. She couldn't have asked for a better friend," said Jason.

"Thank you," said Sara.

Jason pulled back and locked eyes with Sara. "Listen to me very carefully, Sara. Frank will be waiting for you right outside the front door of the funeral home at 9:10pm. Don't walk outside and wait. Stay inside until you see him, okay! Promise me."

Sara swallowed hard. "I promise." Trying to change the subject, she picked up the packet from the shoot. "Hey! Wanna see some of my pictures. I haven't even seen them yet, myself," she giggled. Tilting the envelope, the pictures slid out.

Jason scooped up one of Sara standing on the yacht, sipping wine. "Who's this guy with his arm around your waist?" asked Jason.

"That would be my boyfriend for the shoot," said Sara.

Jason made a low growling noise and held his fist in the air. "I'm jealous," he said.

Sara smiled as she flipped through the rest of the pictures. She stopped on a picture where the grips adjusted the sail. The hand of a grip stood out in the forefront of the picture.

"Oh! my God! There it is, the two inch scar," said Sara.

"The what?" asked Jason.

"The guy with the two inch scar, the guy that knocked me over when he rushed out of the elevator. That's the only thing I saw."

"Are you sure?" asked Jason.

"I'm positive," said Sara.

"Well, now we know it wasn't an accident," said Jason. "Listen Sara, you'll be okay. There'll be a lot of people at the Funeral Home. If you don't go, they'll know something's up. But it's possible that this guy may be the same guy who went through your apartment. So, he might be at the wake too. I don't know, maybe I should go with."

Sara placed her palms on Jason's chest. "No! You said it yourself. There's gonna be a lot of people there. And, there's too much at stake for you to come."

She glanced out the window and saw Frank's cab. "Okay! I won't go anywhere until Frank gets there. Find out what you can while I'm gone, okay!"

"Okay!" said Jason. He kissed her. "I really do love you, ya know."

"I really do love you too," said Sara.

Hand resting delicately in Jason's, she turned toward the door.

"I should go," she said. She took the elevator down and walked out to Frank's cab. She opened the door and stepped in.

"Hello, Frank. How are you doing?" asked Sara.

"I am doing well, Miss Sara. And you?" said Frank.

"I'm tired, very tired, but I'm glad to have been able to do this for Anna. Thank you so much for taking me and picking me up."

"I am totally at the disposal of you and Mr. Jason at no charge until you find who is doing this terrible thing and stop it. It is my pleasure to be able to help in some small way."

"Oh, Frank, I almost forgot. Please tell your wife, Della, that her mostaccioli was out of this world. Thank you so much."

In the rearview mirror, Sara could see Frank's eyes glisten. "You are quite welcome. She will be very pleased that you liked it."

Sara leaned back in the seat and glanced out the window. She began to replay all the events of the day in her mind. She was so engrossed in thought, that she didn't even notice how light the traffic was, or how quickly they arrived at Morley & Sons Funeral Home. Frank pulled next to the curb and turned toward her.

"I am very sorry for your loss," he said. "I know it is very difficult."

"And yours too, but we're gonna make this right."

Sara opened the door and stepped onto the pavement. The sun was still out and it was a beautiful evening. A zephyr wafted from the south. Sara leaned in the passenger window toward Frank. "I'll see you at 9:10pm, right?"

"Yes, Miss Sara. Do not worry, I will be here."

Sara opened the front door and walked in as Frank pulled away from the curb.

"May I help you," said a man in a black suit.

"Yes, I'm Sara Parkins. And you are?"

"I'm Mr. Morley, the Funeral Director." He was a tall lean man with a chiseled face and soft brown eyes. *Probably in his fifties*, thought Sara.

"We spoke on the phone the other day," he said. He extended his hand and Sara shook it. "Everything is set up. It's an open casket and the flowers and holy cards arrived this morning. If there is anything else I can do, please don't hesitate to let me know. I'm very sorry for your loss."

"I really appreciate your professionalism and the guidance you provided. I've never had to arrange a wake before. I don't know what I would have done without your help."

"We're happy to be of service," he responded. He extended his arm, palm up toward a sign that read, 'Anna McClusky'.

Sara walked into the room and up the long aisle to the front where Anna was laid out. The smell of flowers permeated the air, but there was still a subtle smell of formaldehyde…of death. She knelt down next to the open bier and tears trickled down her face. She rested her head in her hands. "Anna, I'm so sorry. This should never have happened. You should still be here with me." Sara ran her hands over the mahogany casket. "I wish I'd been there with you. I know I couldn't have saved you, but I could have been with you, so you weren't afraid." Sara lifted her head and looked up. "I know you're okay now, but I'm not. I miss you so much. And Anna, I want you to know that we're gonna stop them. We won't let what happened to you happen to anyone else. At least we're gonna do our best. So, if you have any pull up there, we could use your help." Sara glanced at Anna, looking peaceful in her favorite orange dress and perfectly coiffed hair. "Love you Anna." Sara blessed herself and stood.

The wake will be open to the public in ten minutes, thought Sara. She went about checking the flowers and the holy cards to make sure they were correct. The funeral home had put the poster boards up on easels along the left side of the room. *It really looks very nice,* she thought. Sara signed the guest book and then walked around the room to be sure nothing was forgotten. She then took her place at the front of the hall to greet the guests.

Fifteen minutes past the hour and no one had come. *I sure hope someone shows up, thought Sara. But then again,*

I don't know who she knew. Twenty five after and still no one had arrived. Sara sat down on a chair in the front row.

"Anna, I'm so sorry. I didn't know who to call. I don't know who you would have wanted here," she whispered. *I did put an ad in the obituary column, but I don't know who saw it.* At seven thirty, Sara got up and walked up and down the aisles. She thought about the first time Anna and she had met and how Anna welcomed her immediately. *Such an amazing woman, thought Sara. Where are her friends?* Sara heard people as they walked into the Funeral Home talking, but no one stopped in to visit Anna.

"Oh, my gosh! I forgot Harry, the night manager, is having his wife's wake in the next room," remembered Sara. *I may as well stop by there now.*

Sara walked next door to Elizabeth Truman's wake, where there were about twelve people, people she'd seen in her building. She walked up to the front, knelt down and folded her hands.

"I'm sorry you had to leave like this, Mrs. Truman. I didn't know you, but Harry is a very nice man, so I'm sure you were a wonderful person, as well. And, by the way, I'm pretty sure I know what happened," she whispered. Sara paused, took a deep breath and looked around to make sure no one was close by. "Anyway, if you can hear me, a friend of mine and me are looking into what happened and we're going to get it all sorted out."

Sara got up and went over to Harry.

"Harry, how are you holding up?" asked Sara.

"Oh! about as well as can be expected. I do miss her though," said Harry.

"I know you do," said Sara, grasping his arm.

Harry wrung his hands as he talked. "It's just so strange, because she was as healthy as a horse until this happened. I guess what they say is true…you never know." Lips tight together, he pulled the corners up.

"Thanks for stopping by, Sara. I really appreciate it."

Sara hugged Harry and turned to leave. She made it to the back of Anna's room at the same time that the people from Elizabeth's room drifted over. Sara took her place at the front and greeted each of them. *How odd, she thought. I was in the other room with them and they didn't even say hi, but now they're all talking to me. I guess we are all, indeed, in our own little world,* thought Sara.

As Sara greeted each individual, she could see more people coming in and signing the guest book and making their way to the front.

Sara extended her hand. "How did you know Mrs. McClusky?" she asked. She usually got the same answer. "I knew her from the building or I ran into her when she got her mail"…and "she was a wonderfully warm woman."

"Hello,

Sara, how are you holding up?" said the next voice.

"Mr. Adashi. Thank you so much for coming. I'm good. I was afraid people wouldn't show because they didn't know about it."

"She was a wonderful woman and so are you. I'm glad to have made it." He kissed Sara on the cheek and made his way to the casket.

At 8:30, a short muscular man with jet black hair, tanned skin, wearing a dark suit, reached the front of the line and extended his hand.

Sara's mouth dropped, her eyes stared blankly at the man's hand. A two inch scar stretched between his thumb and forefinger.

"I'm sorry for your loss," he said as he cupped his other hand over hers.

"Thank you! I'm, I'm sure she would appreciate your coming," said Sara. She swallowed and looked up at him. "I'm sorry, you are?"

"Doug Anderson," he replied.

"How did you know Mrs. McClusky," asked Sara.

"I saw her at the bus stop one day and we had a nice long chat. She said I was like the son she never had. Mrs. McClusky was a lovely woman," said Doug. "I happened to be reading the obituaries," he hesitated and tilted his head to the right. "I have a lot of elderly clients and I saw her name."

"Do you set up estates?" asked Sara.

"Something like that," he said. His lips ticked upward. "Like I said, she was a lovely woman and I wanted to pay my respects."

"Thank you, I'm sure she appreciates it," said Sara.

"If you don't mind my asking, how did she die," Doug asked.

"She had a massive heart attack," said Sara. "I've known Mrs. McClusky for a few years, but I didn't realize she had heart issues in her family history. At least it was quick," Sara added, nodding her head.

"Yes. Quick. That is always the best way," said Doug.

Doug walked to the kneeler to pay his respects, then walked around to view the posters.

He was the last person in line. The others sat in chairs talking, so Sara took the opportunity to slip out of the room. She went into the ladies room and when the last woman had left, she flipped open her phone and dialed Jason.

"Jason, that man is here," said Sara. "The man that knocked me over by the elevator." Sara nodded her head. "Yes, I'm sure. He has the two inch scar between his thumb and forefinger. And, he said he met Anna at the bus stop. Jason, Anna has never taken a bus in her life. Yes, and he said she told him he was like the son she'd never had. If that was true, she would have told him to call her Anna. He's lying and I don't trust him."

Breathing heavily, Sara listened to Jason. "I'm fine. I just don't know what to do," said Sara. "Okay! I won't. I'll wait for Frank. No, I don't want you to come here. If he sees us together, he'll know something's up. I'll be fine. I'll stay with the Funeral Director until Frank gets here. Okay! Bye."

Sara exited the bathroom and stopped suddenly. There was Doug with a toothpick protruding from his mouth, leaning against the opposite wall. Pushing away, he flicked the toothpick into a nearby trash can.

"Sara, I've been waiting for you. I was wondering if you might help me with something. Mrs. McClusky said her favorite color was orange, so I had an arrangement specially made for her," said Doug. He rolled his eyes. "She sort of touched my heart, so I kind of went big, and it's a little awkward to carry by myself. Would you mind helping me get it out of my car?" The corners of Doug's mouth pulled way up and his eyes glistened as he placed another toothpick between his incisors.

"Sure," said Sara. *Oh God ! Oh God! What should I do? I can't go with him, he's too dangerous. . . but how do I say no?* she thought. *I'm only a couple of rooms away from the door, how do I get out of this? I know. . . I know . . . I'll have to pass by the Director's office. If I can get his attention, I could ask him to help. Then it won't look weird. God, I hope he's there.*

Doug walked by her side as they approached the front door.

Sara glanced toward the Director's Office. Mr. Morley wasn't there. Her mind racing, her hands perspiring, her eyes looking left to right for a way out, Doug placed his hand at the small of her back and pushed open the front door.

"Mr. Morley! It's you," said Sara as the funeral director walked through the door that Doug had just opened.

"I'm sorry. I stepped out for some night air," said Mr. Morley. "Is there something I can help you with?" he asked.

Sara stepped toward Mr. Morley and placed her hand on his arm. "As a matter of fact, this gentleman has a bouquet for Mrs. McClusky and needs help carrying it in. Would you be able to help with that? I hate to leave Mrs. McClusky's guests."

Doug's facial expression changed drastically. The glisten in his eyes disappeared. They became dark and hardened.

"I'd be more than happy to, Miss Parkins," said Mr. Morley.

Doug shuffled his weight from one foot to the other. "Why don't I pull my car up to the front door. That way, we won't have to carry it too far," said Doug. Without waiting for an answer, he pushed through the front door and out to the parking lot.

Sara and Mr. Morley waited by the front door. Five minutes passed and Doug's car never showed.

"That's odd," said Mr. Morley.

"Yes, well, I'll be back with Mrs. McClusky's guests," said Sara. "Thank you very much." Sara turned away and turned back again. "Mr. Morley, would you be able to walk me out to my cab when it gets here?" asked Sara.

"It's a very safe neighborhood, but yes, of course, I'd be happy to," said Mr. Morley.

Sara checked her watch every five minutes. Finally, it was 9:05pm. She closed the sign-in book, collected the posters, and walked to Mr. Morley's office. She peeked out the window and saw that Frank's cab was there.

"I trust everything went well," said Mr. Morley.

"Yes, thank you so much," said Sara. She extended her hand and Mr. Morley met her in the middle. *He has a firm, yet warm handshake that seems very sincere,* thought Sara.

"Mr. Morley, the flowers and um, Mrs. McClusky, will be at the church tomorrow morning, right?"

"Yes Miss Parkins. We'll take care of everything." Mr. Morley took the posters and the book from Sara and held open the cab door. After she slid in, Mr. Morley handed her things back to her. Sara clasped his hand in hers.

"You are a wonderfully warm man, Mr. Morley. Thank you for all that you do for people."

His eyes twinkled and a smile spread across his face. "Thank you. That means a lot." Mr. Morley closed the door and the cab pulled away from the curb.

"Frank, I'm so happy to see you," said Sara, before looking up. "I don't think I've ever gotten in on this side of the cab before," she said.

Frank didn't answer.

"Frank, is everything. . . " Sara leaned between the seats. Her mouth dropped as she pulled herself back.

Doug was in the driver's seat.

"Where's Frank? Who are you and what do you want?" yelled Sara.

"Well Sara, you're just a little too clever for me, aren't you?" said Doug.

"What are you talking about? I don't know what you're talking about," screamed Sara. She grabbed the door handle and all four doors locked. She frantically tried to unlock them, but nothing worked.

"You're not going anywhere. So, you may as well relax so I can tell you why I'm here," said Doug. "Your friend, Mrs. McClueless or whatever her name is…or should I say was."

"Her name was Mrs. McClusky," yelled Sara.

"Yeah! Whatever. She's one person and she was old anyway. Unfortunately, people die, that's just the way it goes Sara. And, because you're so determined to make waves, it looks like there may be another unfortunate death. Do you understand what I'm saying? Do you understand?"

Sara's hands shook. "Yes, I understand," she said. She reached for her lipstick and stopped herself.

"Well I hope so, because I want to make this as pleasant as I can."

Sara sat back behind Doug and he watched her through the rear-view mirror. *Think Sara, think,* she thought. Looking ahead, she carefully took her cell phone from her pocket, placed her index finger on the redial and held the phone up behind his seat.

"Who are you and what do you want with me?" said Sara.

"We've been watching you and we don't like that you've been asking questions about things that you know nothing about," said Doug.

"Who's been watching me? And where are you taking me?" asked Sara. She looked out the window as Doug turned onto the Edens Expressway going East.

Doug's smiled gloomed off the rearview mirror at Sara. "It doesn't matter, because no one's gonna find you, not for a long time. People drown every day. It certainly wouldn't be the first time some young thing goes skinny dipping off of Navy Pier,"

Doug weaved in and out of traffic.

I don't have anything to lose, thought Sara. *I need to find out as much as I can.*

"Why are you killing people? What did they do to you?" she said.

"You're so naïve. You think they care about getting rid of you as an individual. Typical self-absorbed model."

"What's that supposed to mean?" said Sara.

"It means you think the world revolves around you. This is so much bigger than you, than this city, this state…you have no idea," said Doug.

Sara bit her lip and leaned back. *Okay! I'm gonna have to pull myself together,* she thought. *I need to act like he doesn't scare me.* Sara crossed her legs toward the middle section of the car, continuing to hold the phone up at the back of the seat.

"Well, if you're gonna kill me anyway, why don't you tell me what's really going on, you know, what this big deal is all about? Unless, you're afraid of me and what I might do?"

Doug laughed a hearty laugh. "I don't think a fly would be afraid of you, sugar."

"So prove it. Tell me what I'm too dense to know, and then you can kill me," said Sara.

"Well, you've got more chutzpah than I thought. I'll give ya that. But, don't worry, I'm not going to kill you. It's gonna sort of happen…you know, naturally," said Doug.

"I'm not going to jump off of any pier," said Sara.

"So you're saying you might need a push? That can certainly be arranged."

Sara glanced out the window and noticed he'd turned on New Orleans and now onto Lower Wacker Drive.

"If you were as smart as you say, you'd know that Lower Wacker Drive isn't a direct route to Navy Pier," said Sara, eyes piercing, one arm folded. And, why are we slowing down? Adams? What's at Adams…no water, that's for sure," said Sara. Sara shot him a look of disgust in the rearview mirror. Doug stopped the car and turned toward her.

"Fine, you wanna know what's going on?" said Doug. "The end of the world, that's what. This is beyond the scope of anything you can imagine in that pretty little head of yours. And your friend, she was just phase I. It worked even better than they thought, so now they're already into phase II. If that goes well, then it hits the big time…and I do mean big time." He extended his palm face up with a time release aspirin in it.

"Take it, now," he said.

"You didn't tell me why? And who's doing this? Is it another country or the government, who?" Sara picked up the tablet and turned it over. "It's just an aspirin."

"I've told you enough. Take the pill," said Doug.

"So, you're afraid of me?" said Sara.

"No, but I do find you intriguing, which is more than I can say for most people."

"So, Doug is it, or is that a bogus name?" asked Sara.

"You been watching a lot of spy movies, huh!" Okay, my real first name is Carlo, but that's all you're getting. So, now that you know my name, do you feel better about dying? Take the damn pill."

"Why? Why do I have to take the pill?"

"Because if you don't take it, I'll have to kill you and I'd hate to have to leave you here to die with the rats. No, I think we're gonna go for that swim," said Carlo. "They won't find you for at least a week and by then, they'll say it was a heart attack."

"I'm not gonna take it," said Sara.

"Okay! I'm not playing games anymore. Take the damn aspirin!" said Carlo.

"No!"

Carlo unlocked his door and Sara's and stepped out. Sara placed her phone under the front seat, still on. The back door opened and Carlo extended his hand again, "Last chance to take it on your own," said Carlo.

Sara looked him in the eye. "You don't scare me. I'm not taking it."

Carlo grabbed her by the hair and pushed the aspirin into her mouth. "Swallow it, bitch," he yelled, gritting his teeth. She kicked him in the legs and scratched at his face, but he wouldn't let go. "Swallow it." He pushed her head into the door and yelled at her again. "Swallow it."

One well aimed kick and she could get him to let go. She kicked and connected one inch too low, embedding her nails in his neck at the same time. Now, blocking himself below the waist, he grabbed her wrists. She pierced his shin with the stiletto heel of her left shoe.

"You bitch," yelled Carlo as he pulled her from the car and dragged her behind a pole. She tried to stand, but the heel of her right shoe broke. Pushing her to the ground, he held the right side of her face against the pavement. Gravel and dirt pushed into her skin and sifted through her hair. Scratches and bruises welled up on her arms and legs.

"What's it gonna be bitch? Swallow it alive or die here?"

The saliva had already developed in Sara's mouth and the shove to her head broke open the capsule. Her body stopped struggling and she swallowed. He pulled her mouth open to be sure it was gone.

"Now, how hard was that?" said Carlo.

Sara's face was bruised and her body weak. He yanked her up from the ground, dragged her back to the car, pushed her into the back seat and slammed the door. The noise brought out some of the street people. An old man in a cardboard box started spouting jibberish as he walked toward them. Another bum in an old pair of jeans and a ripped shirt with a ski cap pulled down over half of his face limped over to the car with a rag in his hand.

"Washa winder?" said the bum.

"Get outta here," said Carlo.

"I jis wanna washa winder," repeated the bum. He placed the rag on the windshield and started dragging it around.

Carlo stepped out around the door and reached forward to grab the bum's forearm, when a taser connected with Carlo's chest. Carlo shook violently and fell to the ground. The bum dropped the taser and jumped on Carlo's chest. Sara watched from inside the cab as the bum pummeled Carlo until he didn't move. Then he walked toward the cab. Sara slid to the other side of the cab, bracing herself. He opened the door and pulled off his ski cap.

"Jason! Oh my God! Jason!" she cried. Sara wrapped her arms around him and wouldn't let go.

"Sara, I'm so sorry I didn't go with you. I thought you'd be okay," said Jason. "I don't know what I would've done if anything happened to you."

Sara stretched her mouth out to loosen her jaw. Her left cheek was swollen. She hugged Jason even harder.

"Sara, I've gotta get him in the trunk before anybody comes by," said Jason.

Sara nodded.

Jason jumped out and grabbed Carlo under the shoulders and dragged him to the back of the cab. Sara took off her shoes and stepped out to help.

"I'll grab his feet," she said.

"Okay! Thanks," said Jason. Jason took the bulk of his weight and heaved him into the trunk. He ran to a support beam nearby and grabbed a bag.

"What's that?" asked Sara.

"Some rope and tape, just in case. I snatched it from a construction site on the way over. And Frank gave me the taser the first day we met. Apparently folks leave a lot of strange things in his cab."

He raised his eyebrows. "Thank God, cuz it really came in handy."

Jason got the rope out and tied Carlo's feet together, then tied his hands behind his back. Carlo was still out cold. Jason took a long piece of tape and put it over Carlo's mouth and dropped the excess rope and tape in the trunk and slammed it shut. Jason turned and picked Sara up and put her carefully in the back seat.

"We'll be home in no time, right after we pick up Frank," said Jason. "He's waiting at a gas station."

Jason jumped in the driver's seat and pulled away.

"Is Frank okay?" asked Sara.

"Yeah! I got a call from him right after you called. I saw it was Frank and switched over. I thought he might know where this asshole was taking you. He said when he was filling up, this guy hit in the head, jumped in the cab and took off. I let him know I was listening to you, so I had to go. He told me what station he was at and I said we'd come back for him. He sounds okay, but he feels really bad."

"Thank God he's alright," said Sara.

Sara saw Frank pacing in the small parking lot as Jason pulled in. Jason stopped the car, jumped out, walked to Frank and gave him a hug. Sara couldn't make out what they said, but Frank looked very upset. Jason got in the back seat and Frank took the wheel.

"Oh Sara," said Jason as he ran his fingers gently over her bruised face. "I should've killed that bastard."

"I thought you did," said Sara. She attempted to smile, but a sharp pain shot up toward her eye. "Maybe he was right. I guess I didn't handle it that well," said Sara. Her gaze fell to her lap.

Gently, Jason held her face in his hands and lifted her head to look in her eyes. "Sara, what that asshole said was so far from the truth, it's not funny. You are the most un-self-centered person I know. That was brilliant of you to call me and lead me to where you were. Every time I'd hope you'd give me a clue as to what was going on, you did. And, you found out his first name too. I'll get the rest out of him. And if he still doesn't talk, we at least have his name, thanks to you."

Sara tilted her head and saw Frank's face in the rearview mirror as he turned away. She reached her right arm over the seat and touched Frank's shoulder and he glanced toward her.

"Oh my God," said Sara. "Look at your head…it's bleeding. I can see it in the mirror." You need to get to the hospital."

"I am fine, Miss Sara."

"No, you're not."

Frank pulled into the curb in front of his Mom's condo. He put the car in park and his head dropped.

"I am so sorry, Miss Sara. You were almost killed because of me. I can never forgive myself. I-I…" began Frank.

Sara leaned over the seat and lifted his chin. "Frank, listen to me, this wasn't your fault. I shouldn't have gotten in without seeing you. I was so happy the Director walked me to the door, I didn't notice that the cab pulled in the wrong way. You did nothing wrong. As a matter of fact, if it weren't for you, we wouldn't have a chance of stopping these people at all. You're the one with all the contacts.

You've gotten us everything we need." She leaned forward and kissed Frank's forehead.

Frank grabbed her hands and kissed them. "Thank you, thank you," he said. "I will not let you or Mr. Jason down again."

"What about your head?"

"I will take care of it, Miss Sara. I will be fine."

Jason stepped out of the car, grabbed the poster boards and sign-in book and offered his free hand to Sara. With broken shoes in her right hand, and purse under her arm, she grasped his hand and lifted herself out.

Jason leaned toward Frank. "I'm gonna get her settled and then I'll be back down and we can take him to that warehouse. You alright?"

"Yes, I will make the call and I will wait here for you," said Frank.

Jason helped Sara into the building and they rode the elevator in each other's arms.

Sara forced her legs to move, one in front of the other. Her eyes half closed, she barely made it to the couch before she collapsed. Jason was right beside her.

"Sara, Frank and I need to take that guy to a warehouse and question him. Are you going to be okay?"

Sara nodded.

I'll call you every hour, okay?" said Jason. "No one knows you're here, so you should be fine. I wouldn't go, but we're not gonna be able to keep this guy forever."

"I know. You should go. I'm fine. I don't want my getting beat up to be for nothing." The left side of her mouth lifted and her eyes sparkled.

"You're amazing, ya know," said Jason.

Her eyelids kept dipping down, opening wide and dipping down again.

"Stay there, I'll be right back," said Jason.

"He disappeared into the bathroom and didn't return for about five minutes.

"I think I have just the thing," he said.

"I don't know what's wrong with me. I'm so exhausted," said Sara.

"Sara, you've been through hell and back, I'm surprised you're standing at all. That's why I've started a bubble bath for you. It's aloe, so it should help with the bruising. So, why don't you go in and relax."

"Really? That would be awesome."

"I've gotta start somewhere to make all of this up to you."

"We're good," said Sara, dragging her body into the bathroom.

She turned the corner to find three cinnamon scented candles glowing in the darkness. One on the sink, one sitting on the floor of the shower stall, and the last one on a windowsill at the foot of the tub. A towel and washcloth were neatly folded on the toilet seat cover.

Jason popped around the corner with an icepack and kissed her gently on the cheek.

"I'll lock the outside door with the key and you lock the bathroom door," said Jason. Sara barely heard him, as she closed the bathroom door, locked it and slipped out of her clothes. Holding on to the sink, she picked up her right foot and stuck her big toe into the tub to test the water. It was perfect. She stepped in and sat down. *This is heaven.* The tub had an old fashioned feel to it, yet more comfortable. It slanted out at both ends, which was perfect for relaxing, and it was wider than most. Holding the icepack to her right cheek, she stared at the candle on the windowsill, as it sparkled off the glass. To the right and barely in front of her, was the shower. The candle sat directly in the center. *It looks like a prism,* she thought. *Like a light from above, where any minute an angel would appear within the doors and walk out to greet me.* "Hey! As long as you guys watch over me through this whole mess, I'm good," said Sara in a whisper.

Sara yawned and closed her eyes. The closed door blocked out any noise from the furnace and the smell of the candles wafted through the air.

***

Knock! Knock! Knock! Knock! Knock! Knock*! Sara heard something far away like someone hanging a picture or chopping celery. She couldn't quite make it out. Or maybe the TV was on and there was someone at the door, but no one answered it. Why wasn't someone answering the door?*

"Knock! Knock! Knock! Knock! Knock! Knock! Knock! Knock! Knock! Sara?" said a voice in the distance. *Who would be calling me,* she thought. She heard a jiggling noise and then **'thud'** and the bathroom door flew open.

CHAPTER 12

Sara's eyes bolted open and she jumped up, grabbed the candle and hurled it toward the door. Standing there dripping wet, eyes still not focused, unaware of who she'd hit, she screamed.

Two arms wrapped around her as she struggled to get free. A hand dropped to the small of her back and pulled her close. Lips pressed close to her ear as he held her still. "Sara, wake up! It's me," said Jason.

Sara pulled her head back, her eyes focused, her mind cleared and her body relaxed. Sara looked in Jason's eyes as he held her. A welt had already appeared above his left eye.

"Oh my God! Did I do that?" she asked, touching it gently.

"No big deal. Don't worry," said Jason. "We need to get some sleep."

Sara's eyes widened. *Oh my God! I can't believe I threw that at him.*

Jason picked up the towel and wrapped it around her.

"I'm sorry," said Jason. I called your phone three or four times and you didn't answer, so I got nervous. When you didn't answer when I knocked and called your name, I had to break in."

Sara's heart raced. "I, I, I must have fallen asleep. I was so-o-o tired and the bath felt so good. I thought I was dreaming when I heard knocking." She smiled at Jason. "I was wondering why no one answered the door. I was really out of it. Sorry!"

Jason swooped Sara up in his arms, blowing a few bubble clusters from her shoulders. "Do you want to rinse off in the shower?" he asked.

"Yes, that's probably a good idea," said Sara.

Jason set Sara down inside the shower stall and turned around. He put his hand behind him. "Hand me the towel and I won't turn back around until you've taken the towel again," said Jason.

"That's very gentlemanly of you," said Sara.

Placing the towel over Jason's outstretched arm, she noticed the corners of his mouth pull upward. Sara picked up the candle that had long since gone out and placed it in Jason's hand as well. The shower door closed and the water began. Jason leaned to the right to place the candle on the sink, keeping his back to Sara.

Sara smiled when she caught Jason glimpsing toward the mirror for a look at her reflection. She purposely ran her hands all over her body before turning off the water.

When the water stopped, Sara turned, opened the door and took the towel, wrapping it around herself. "You have seen me before ya know," she yawned.

"I'm not taking anything for granted. If you want me to look, I'd be happy to…if not, I respect that," he smiled.

Jason swept Sara off her feet again.

Sara's eyes still drooped. "What happened with that Carlo guy? Did he tell you anything else?"

"Not much. He's being stubborn. But maybe a night in a warehouse tied to a chair might convince him otherwise. For now, let's get you to bed. He carried her into the bedroom and laid her down.

Sara held Jason's arm and sat up. "I need to put some lotion on," she said. "Especially after sitting in water for God knows how long."

"I can do that for you, if you'd like. You can keep the towel on and I'll do your legs, your arms and your back," said Jason.

Sara tossed the towel on the chair and lay on her stomach. "It's in my makeup bag, right there." Barely holding her arm up, she pointed her index finger toward a medium size blue canvas bag on the floor in the corner. "Vaseline Intensive Care."

Jason unzipped the bag and spread it wide. Right on top…the hand cream. He pumped a couple of squirts into the palms of his hands and began massaging at Sara's feet.

"That feels wonderful," said Sara, in between yawns.

Jason moved carefully up her calves to her thighs and stopped on her bottom. Sara had a huge bruise on her left hip, her arm and her face. He moved his hands gently over her bruises to her back, shoulders and arms. Sara's whole body sank into the mattress.

***

The sun separated the curtains and a stream of light fell across the left side of Sara's face. She heard birds chirping and everything felt right. But when she turned on to her back, she felt the ache in her arms and legs. Her pajamas were neatly folded on a chair to the right of the bed. She immediately stretched her hand behind her and felt the mattress. Jason? She turned. There on the recliner, Jason was fast asleep. His pajama clad leg stuck out from beneath the blanket, one slipper on and one slipper off. Sara picked up her pajama top and panty and put them on under the covers and sat up. *He must have been afraid he'd hurt me,* thought Sara. *He is so-o-o sweet.* She glanced at the clock radio…7am.

Sara slipped from between the sheets, retrieved her clothes from the drawer and her bag from the floor, and disappeared into the bathroom.

She glanced in the mirror. *Wow! No wonder I hurt. I look awful,* she thought, looking at the bruises that riddled her body. She set her makeup on the sink, washed up and began applying eyeliner, shadow and mascara.

Good thing I've modeled, she thought. *A little foundation, a little makeup - I know how to cover things up.* Within twenty minutes she was dressed and ready to go. Returning to the bedroom in a pair of jeans and a beige tank top, she placed her pajamas back in the top drawer, her bag on the floor and walked quietly to the kitchen, so as not to wake Jason.

In the refrigerator, Sara found eggs, microwave bacon, orange juice and milk. She heated the frying pan, put a little butter in for the eggs and placed the bacon in the microwave. She beat the eggs in a bowl with a little milk and poured it into the pan. Within thirty seconds, the smell of breakfast wafted through the kitchen.

It's so weird. It's like I'm living in some other world, she thought. I've been lied to, chloroformed, tied to a chair, dragged from a car and beat up...and now I'm making breakfast for a man I thought was trying to kill me. Whoa. I can honestly say, my life is anything but boring.

He really is a wonderful guy. It has to have been so hard for him...one minute feeling good about his accomplishments and the next...finding out someone is using them to hurt people.

Rounding the corner into the bedroom, Sara saw Jason on his side in the chair, still sound asleep, and tiptoed over to him.

"Good morning Jason," said Sara, in a whisper. *Well that's not gonna work*, she thought. Jason didn't move. Sara ran her fingers gently down his arm. She stared at how peaceful he looked and thought of last night. Leaning forward, she kissed him on the cheek. As she pulled away, he opened his eyes and the corner of his mouth curved up.

"Morning," he said. He lifted his nose slightly.

"Something smells good."

Sara smiled, realizing he meant the food.

"Morning, you," said Sara. "Eggs and bacon and it's about to be served."

Jason sat up and stretched for the ceiling, then popped out of the chair. Rubbing his eyes with his fists, he walked toward the kitchen.

"Hmmm! Nice," said Jason. "Can I shower after breakfast?"

"Absolutely!" said Sara. "Sit right here," she said, pointing to the dining room chair.

Jason took a seat and was done in minutes.

"Better than Mom's," said Jason with a smile. "Gonna take a shower," he said as he cleared his plate, rinsed it off and put it in the dishwasher. "Be out in about five minutes."

Sara glanced at Jason's plate, then hers. *Wow!* She thought. *I ate two eggs to his four and only half the amount of bacon and I'm still eating. Here, I thought I might've made too much.* She finished the last bite, gathered her plate, glass and silverware and walked it to the sink. Part way there, she stopped and walked toward the bathroom.

"Jason, what'd you find out last night?"

"Tell ya when I get out," said Jason as he turned on the shower.

Sara nodded and walked back into the kitchen. *Not much of a morning person.*

After wiping down the table, Sara walked down the hall and sat on the floor by the bedroom door. She listened to the water pulsating against the plexiglass walls of the shower stall. *Hmmmm, he's naked behind that door. I wonder if there's anything I need in there?* She thought. Her smile broadened. *After yesterday's shower, that's all I can think about.* She batted her eyes and leaned back into the doorframe. *I guess I'll wait.* She rubbed the palms of her hands on her jeans and licked her lips, then opened her eyes and shook her head.

"Focus Sara," she whispered to herself.

I wonder what happened with that guy last night? I hope he told Jason something worthwhile. But I don't know. This guy didn't seem to be the nervous type. Although, he might have been all macho with me because I'm a woman. Jason and Frank can be intimidating. But then again, Jason did say he didn't get much out of him. I think this guy would have to be afraid of something. Sara scrunched her mouth.

"Hmph, what would do it?" said Sara. *I mean everyone's afraid of something, so what would he be afraid of? What would he be afraid that Jason could do to him?*

"Rrrrring, rrrinnng, rrrrinng." Sara felt her phone in her pocket…not hers. She followed the ring further into the bedroom and found Jason's phone pushed between the creases of the recliner. She picked it up on the fifth ring.

"Hello, this is Jason Forest's phone," said Sara.

"Hello, Miss Sara. This is Frank. How are you feeling?"

"A little bruised, but other than that, I'm good."

"I am glad," said Frank. "Is Mr. Jason there?"

"Oh! He's in the shower. Hang on a sec." Sara walked to the bathroom door and waited. She put the phone back to her ear. "Can you hang on for one more second, Frank? I think he's about done."

"Yes, I can, Miss Sara."

Leaning toward the door, Sara tapped. "Jason, Frank is on your cell phone. I heard it ringing, so I answered it," said Sara.

"Hang on!" yelled Jason. Another five seconds and she heard the water shut off and the shower door open and close. Another ten seconds and Jason opened the door. He stood in a different pair of jeans and no shirt…his chest and arms still wet, brushing his teeth.

"Can you put him on speaker?" garbled Jason.

"I'm putting you on speaker, Frank," said Sara and she pushed the button.

"Hey, Frank. When can you pick us up? We've gotta get some more info outta that guy."

"I'm downstairs," said Frank.

Jason walked to the window, still brushing his teeth.

"So you are. We'll be down in three minutes."

"Okay!" said Frank. "I found something I think that you will be interested in, Mr. Jason."

Jason clicked off the phone and turned toward Sara.

"We're gonna give it another try. Problem is…we're not like him. We're not killers. We care about people and he knows it," said Jason. "Doesn't give him too much incentive to spill what he knows."

Sara reached for Jason's arm. "I was thinking about that this morning. I think I've got an idea."

Jason's eyes opened wide and he tilted his head. "What is it?"

"Well, do you have an empty syringe?" asked Sara.

"Yeah!" said Jason, cocking his head back slightly.

"Well, I figured, like you said, he doesn't think you'll kill him…but what if you don't, what if he kills himself, in a manner of speaking?"

"I don't get it? Why would he kill himself?" asked Jason.

Sara squeezed her eyes tight and tapped Jason's arm. "Hopefully, he won't--want to, that is. Because I'm proposing you fill up that syringe with something harmless like saline, and inject him, telling him it's the H1N1 shot, from phase II. Then, make him swallow an aspirin every hour until he tells us what we want to know."

Jason's mouth dropped open, his eyes fixed on Sara.

"Unbelievable. That could actually work. Because it'll be up to him whether he dies or not." said Jason. Jason took Sara's face in his hands and gently kissed her.

"You're brilliant."

Sara curtsied. "Thank you, sir."

Jason pulled a syringe from his suitcase, then rummaged until he found Anna's bottle of time released aspirin. He threw them both into a small bag.

"I'll have to stop at the lab for a quick second to grab some saline," said Jason as he headed for the door.

Sara tapped Jason's arm.

"Don't forget, I have Anna's funeral today at 11am."

Jason slowed down. "Of course, of course. Can you grab what you're gonna wear and bring it with?"

"Sure." Sara ran into the bedroom, retrieved her long skirt, brushed the dirt and stones from it and selected a black and gray shell with a pair of black flat shoes and threw them in a plastic bag she got from under the sink.

The two of them hurried downstairs to meet Frank. Another beautiful day…already seventy degrees with a clear blue sky that stretched for miles in every direction. A slight breeze tousled Sara's hair. Jason opened the cab door for her and stepped in after her.

"Frank, can we stop for a quick second at that lab I've been working out of. I need to get some saline," said Jason.

"No problem, Mr. Jason. It is on the way."

Frank pulled from the curb and Jason grabbed Sara's hand. "I'm so glad you're okay," whispered Jason.

"Me too," said Sara. She kissed her finger and touched the small bump above Jason's left eye. "Sorry about that."

Jason squeezed Sara's hand, then tapped Frank's shoulder. "What was it you wanted to show me, Frank?"

"I will show you when I pull over, Mr. Jason."

"Good enough," said Jason.

Sara ran her fingers up and down her legs, then touched Jason. "Did any of your calls pan out last night?" she asked.

"Yeah! The one guy in New York that I still trust," Jason hesitated. "His name is Alex. I got a hold of him last night and he gave me some information." Jason shook his head. "It's not good news, but it's good that we know."

"What is it?" asked Sara

"It's another list for a second trial. Apparently it reads, Good first run…second run, non-stopping…green light. He's gonna scan it and email it as soon as he can." Jason leaned toward Sara, resting his hands on her shoulders and looked her in the eye. "I can't be certain, but I think it means that because the first run went so well, meaning a lot of people were logged in as taking the Rilosac and then checked into a hospital following that, they feel it was successful. And the scary part is," began Jason.

"That's not the scary part?" asked Sara.

"No! Unfortunately, it's not. The scary part is that these assholes-sorry-jerks are running another test that I'm guessing doesn't contain a stopping agent in the Rilosac. Which means, anyone who takes the H1N1 vaccine, then gets the reflux and takes Rilosac, will have a heart attack and die," said Jason.

"Everyone that takes it?" asked Sara, her eyes squinting in disbelief.

Jason's eyes were lost in thought and Sara knew it.

"Is there more?" asked Sara.

"I don't know, but…"

"But what?"

I'm not sure if phase II requires taking Rilosac at all. It may just need a time released medication of any kind to follow," said Jason.

"So everyone who takes any time released medication will die?" asked Sara.

"Yes! Unless, I can come up with a stopping agent. And that is my plan."

"Won't it be pretty obvious to the police or FBI or somebody, if everybody starts dropping dead?" said Sara.

"The problem is, they're gonna ask what the last medication they took was. For some it'll be aspirin, for others it'll be a muscle relaxant and others a blood pressure medication. Any medication that has a time release factor in it will kick in with the time release factor from the H1N1 vaccine and will begin the symptoms of a non-stop heart attack."

"Massive heart attacks, all over the world?" said Sara.

"Yes, and the thing is, everybody will be looking at the wrong thing for the answer. It won't occur to them to look at what they took weeks ago. And by the time they figure it out, if they did…"

"It will be too late," said Frank.

Sara's eyes dropped toward the floor and her shoulders drooped.

Frank pulled up to the back door of the lab, Jason jumped out and in less than two minutes, he returned to the car.

"Got it," said Jason.

Frank took off for the warehouse where they had left Carlo.

"Frank, Sara came up with a great idea. I filled this syringe with saline, which is harmless, and I'm gonna inject Carlo with it. But, I'm gonna tell him it's the H1N1 vaccine from phase II. Then I'm gonna give him a time released aspirin every hour on the hour until he tells me who's behind this.

"It sounds like a very good idea, Miss Sara. Very good indeed," said Frank.

Frank pulled down a barren alley between two black brick buildings. Chains and padlocks, like prison guards, held each warehouse door tightly sealed. Frank stopped near the end of the alley, got out, and carefully navigated around the potholes and crumbling gravel to hold the door for Jason and Sara. They walked to Warehouse D and Frank put a key in the padlock. The chain fell to the ground and Jason pulled a steel door open, allowing a sweet moldy smell to escape. Inside, Sara heard Carlo cursing in Italian. She raised her hand to cover her nose as Jason reached in to his right and flipped on the lights. Three gigantic rats scurried for cover and Sara took a step back.

"It's okay, they only came out because the lights were out," said Jason.

Carlo stopped swearing and looked up with a smile.

It was a huge empty warehouse that smelled of oil and mold with an odd, sweet smell that lingered in the air. *It looked like they used to make some kind of food product here,* thought Sara. There were stacks of boxes at one end and parts of conveyor belts at the other with cords hanging from the ceiling. Rows of rusty metal chairs were stacked behind the door and a very old presentation screen hung crooked on the wall. In his black suit pants and white shirt,

Carlo lay on his side, his hands and feet bound to the chair with a chain that connected the chair to a pole in the middle of the room. Carlo had managed to rub a corner of the tape off his mouth.

Walking toward him, Jason reached down and pulled the chair to an upright position and walked slowly around to the front. He stared at Carlo and smiled.

"You think you're so smug, don't you," said Jason. "You may have kept the rats away, but they're not really what you need to worry about. I've been thinking about what you said."

Jason circled the chair.

"And you're right about what you said last night, that we wouldn't kill you, because we're not you…" Jason hesitated and paced back and forth in front of Carlo. "But, if you kill yourself, then I had nothing to do with it, right?" Jason ripped the rest of the tape off Carlo's mouth.

"What are you gonna put a gun in my hand and expect me to blow my brains out," said Carlo, laughing, leaning on the back two legs of the chair.

"Mr. Jason," interrupted Frank. "I need to talk to you."

Jason turned toward Frank, his eyebrows pinched toward the center. "Kind of in the middle of something, Frank."

"Yes, Mr. Jason, I know. But, I wanted to show you something, remember?"

"Yeah! Yeah! Sure," Jason pointed an index finger at Sara. "Don't go near him." Then he walked toward the door with Frank.

Sara glanced at Carlo and back at Jason and Frank. Frank had Carlo's black suit jacket and he pulled a stack of folded paper from the inside pocket. He turned the pages toward the end and Frank pointed at the bottom of the page. Jason's eyes expanded and fury filled him.

"Son of a bitch! You miserable son of bitch!" yelled Jason. He raced toward Carlo, fists ready. He grabbed Carlo with his left hand and his right fist pummeled Carlo's face.

Carlo's head hung to the right, blood oozed from his lip and cheek. Bringing his head upright, Carlo licked the blood away and laughed.

Sara wrapped her arms around Jason's chest and pulled him back. "Stop, Jason stop. We need to stick to the plan," she said.

Perspiration beaded up on Jason's forehead as he kicked Carlo in the shin.

"What's wrong with you? What was on that paper?"

Carlo's grin grew to take up his whole face. "Your boyfriend here just found out that your name is on the list for phase II.

"Shut Up!" said Jason.

Jason turned toward Sara, placed his hands on her arms and looked her in the eye.

"Sara, you're gonna be fine. You haven't taken any other medicine for the past few days, right?" said Jason.

Sara's face turned white. Her body went limp and Jason held her up.

"Sara, what's wrong?

Carlo laughed louder.

"Shut up," said Jason as he threw an elbow into Carlo's head.

Sara's eyes drifted as Frank placed a chair beneath her. She sat and Jason knelt down in front of her.

"The aspirin you took when you stayed at my house won't do anything. It has to interact within forty eight hours. You're gonna be okay, Sara." said Jason.

"He gave me an aspirin yesterday. I tried not to swallow it," said Sara, her eyes unfocused.

"But I heard you on the phone. You wouldn't do it. I thought you spit it out," said Jason.

"No, he pushed my face into the ground and held my mouth until I swallowed. It was already dissolving, so I did."

Jason's head fell hard in her lap. Tears ran down Sara's face and Jason kissed her.

"Listen! We still have thirty-six hours," said Jason rubbing his sleeves across his face. "It's gonna be okay. I promise." He lifted Sara's face. "Look at me, Sara. It's gonna be okay."

"Hey! What are you doing old man?" yelled Carlo.

Jason turned around and Sara saw Frank inserting a needle into Carlo's arm.

"I'm sorry, Mr. Jason, but I wanted to do it. I want him to know the fear of dying, what he's done to Miss Sara and all the others. I gave my mother insulin shots for many years, so I know how," said Frank.

"You sick bastard. Where did you get that?" yelled Carlo, squirming in his chair.

"He got it from me," said Jason.

Jason strode over to Frank and put out his hand. Frank deposited the empty syringe. "I gotta buddy in New York who sent it to me. It's from Phase II.

Carlo's face went still, his eyes squinting, his head tilted to the right.

"My name's not on that list. It has to be on the list," yelled Carlo.

"So, I guess it's up to you whether you die or not, because a Mr. Messinger isn't going to. You got his dose. His name was on the list. I was deciding whether or not to inject you with it, but I guess I don't have to make that decision," said Jason. He turned and nodded his head toward Frank. "Thanks!"

Turning back to Carlo, Jason snagged the bottle of aspirin from the bag he'd brought. He shook the bottle and read it aloud. "Time release…up to forty-eight hours of medication. Sounds like a good thing, don't you think?" said Jason.

"Are you crazy? What's wrong with you?" yelled Carlo. "You're supposed to be the good guy."

"I am the good guy. You look like you're in pain. Well, I wanna give you an aspirin to take away that pain. And, I think you'll need one every hour to be sure it doesn't come back. Unless, of course, you can give me a reason not to give you any," said Jason.

"You're bluffin'," said Carlo. "You haven't got the guts."

Jason pushed his face up close to Carlo. "You gave Sara a death sentence and you think I don't have the guts?" Jason turned and picked up a small pair of tongs and returned to Carlo. Leaning forward he forced them into Carlo's mouth. Carlo tried to hold his lips shut, but couldn't. Once in, Jason dropped the aspirin in the opening. He then pushed Carlo's head back and poured a bottle of water down his throat until he swallowed, choking and coughing.

Jason let go and walked a few feet away. "Now you can tell me who put you up to this, or you can die. And I'm guessing they could care less. Did they pay you enough to die?"

Carlo sat there, the front of his shirt soaked with water and drips of blood and the side of his face covered in dirt and oil.

"How about we start with something easy," said Jason. "Are you the one who broke into Mrs. McClusky's apartment and Sara's?"

Carlo brought his chin to his chest, raised his eyes to the left and down. "Why should I tell you anything now? You've killed me already," said Carlo.

"That's not true. Sara took an aspirin after she took the H1N1 and she was fine, because it was in the beginning, but the later it gets, the more likely it is to interact. And, here's the real reason you should talk. I work with enzymes, molecules, substances, all day long, every day.

I'm the one who discovered that time releases could work together. And I'm already working on something that will prevent the release factors from connecting and starting the arrhythmia. Give me some answers and I could help you too. But, if you don't help me in time to help Sara, I'm not gonna save your miserable ass."

Sara stood up. "Maybe we should leave him here until tomorrow. See how he feels then."

Jason looked at Sara, eyes pensive, mouth separated. "You could die," he whispered.

"Well, I'd rather you be working on a cure, then babysitting him." Sara's decibel level rose. "He's too stupid to give us what we want. He'd rather die for someone he doesn't even know," said Sara. "Come on, let's go."

Jason reluctantly followed and Frank did as well.

Carlo struggled in his chair, his eyes searching the room.

"Wait, wait, I'll tell you who hired me. I'll tell you what you need to know, but you have to promise me, if you find a way to stop this thing, you'll give it to me," he yelled. "Give me your word."

Sara, Frank and Jason stopped and slowly headed back toward Carlo. Jason brought over two more chairs and they all took a seat.

"I give you my word… so start from the beginning," said Jason. "But talk fast."

Carlo scrunched his mouth to the left and began. "I was contacted by phone and asked to do a job. At first it was a simple job. I had to retrieve a bottle of Rilosac and time release aspirin from your friend's apartment. Unfortunately, I didn't find either. I found out from the Apartment Manager that Sara…" he nodded his head toward her. "was her closest friend and took care of things for her. So, I decided to check out her place, but I didn't find it there either. I reported what I found, which was nothing, and that's when they decided you…" he nodded at Sara again. ". . . were asking too many questions. So, they wanted you to have an accident."

"Are you the one who untied the jig," asked Sara.

"No, I got a flunky to do it, at least he thought he did it. I had him purposely trip over it and I made sure it wouldn't hold," said Carlo.

"That was the guy who played my boyfriend for the shoot?"

"That's the guy. He hadn't gotten a gig in years, so I said I'd get him the job if he did this for me." Carlo turned his attention to Jason. "But your girlfriend here, has pretty good reflexes, or she'd of been gone."

Jason's fists opened and closed and Sara grabbed his hand in hers and squeezed.

"Did you try to kill anyone else because of it?" asked Jason.

"No, most people accept death, especially if it's someone older, that's why they targeted people over seventy. So, in case something happened, no one would put two and two together."

"How come I'm on the list then. I'm not even close to seventy," said Sara, crossing and uncrossing her legs.

"Because you're in phase II. They already know it worked with the old people in phase I and they made sure that those people were very healthy before it was released. So they've broadened the scope quite a bit," said Carlo. "Besides, you became a problem."

"So who are they?" asked Jason.

"Well, I always check out my assignments to a certain extent. Ya know, to cover my own ass. And, I found out it was a pharmaceutical company here in the states, New York to be precise. They're dealing with a terrorist from a third world country," said Carlo.

"What was the terrorist's name?" asked Jason.

Carlo hesitated. "If he found out I said anything, I'm as good as dead."

"Well, if you don't say anything, you are dead." countered Jason.

Carlo dropped his head and took a deep breath. "Mujahdeen Jihad," said Carlo.

Jason nodded his head toward Sara. "How did you know he was the one?" asked Jason.

"I kind of intercepted underground messages to a guy name Larz.," said Carlo.

"Do you have them?" asked Jason.

"Of course, I do. And when you find that back door or whatever, I'll let you know where to find em." He shot Jason a smug look. "Everybody's gotta have some collateral...right?"

Frank stood up. "I will go and check his car, Mr. Jason. He left it around the corner from the gas station where he stole my cab. That is where I found his jacket with the list. I will be right back, Mr. Jason…" he nodded, "Miss Sara." Frank limped toward the warehouse door.

"Oh! So now the limping cabbie is gonna be 007?" laughed Carlo.

"Go ahead, Frank. We'll be right here," said Jason.

Jason turned toward Carlo again. "How many people are gonna be affected by this phase II?"

"Well, you saw the list for Chicago…about fifty pages long, so I'm sure it'll cut down on the population," he said with a smirk.

Jason swallowed hard and stared at Carlo. "And what about phase III, the big one? How many people will be affected by that and how?"

"I don't know, probably most everyone. And they said something about not needing extra medicine," said Carlo. "Whatever that means."

Jason glanced at Sara. "That's what I was afraid of."

Jason got up and paced the length of the warehouse. After several laps he returned and sat down.

Sara's head swiveled as the door smacked open and knocked into a few rusty chairs.

"I've got them," said Frank, waving his hand in the air. "Underground documents, listing step by step instructions for the H1N1 drug and the Rilosac drug and how they would work together. They are written to Larz from Mujahdeen Jihad and the money changing hands is documented as well. There are a few other names mentioned too," said Frank.

"What the hell? How'd you find those?" said Carlo. He squirmed in his chair.

"This is great! Mr. Jason. Now you can call in the FBI and give them this information."

Jason put a hand on Frank's shoulder. "But I have to find a way to stop the time release in the H1N1 first. If I call the police or the FBI right now, they're not gonna let me figure it out. And by the time they've decided they can trust me, it'll be too late for Sara."

"He's right ya know," said Carlo, staring Frank down.

"I understand, Mr. Jason," said Frank.

"Did you find me a place to do some more testing?" asked Jason.

"Yes, Mr. Jason. I can take you there right now."

"That's great! You're amazing. I owe you big," said Jason.

"If you get these people caught and find something to save Miss Sara, I will owe you for life." said Frank.

"Sara, I need to go to this lab and test a number of different variables. It's gonna be a long process, but if you could come with, I could really use your help. It should shorten the time it takes, quite a bit. I need the results indexed with all the different samples, so I can get the right variable to stop the release factor that causes heart arrhythmia and ultimate heart attacks," said Jason.

"Of course. I'll do whatever it takes," said Sara.

Jason squeezed her arms. "Sara, we're not gonna let this kill you or all these other people. We're gonna stop them, but I need you to be strong, okay?"

Sara focused and swallowed hard. "Yes, I, I will be, I am, I mean, I'm good, really," said Sara.

"I know." He kissed her gently on the forehead and held her close. "We're gonna do this."

"Hey! What about me?" yelled Carlo.

"What about you?" said Jason.

"You're not gonna just leave me here, are you? I had to fight off those rats all night long. Besides, I gotta take a leak bad," said Carlo.

"Frank, can you take Sara to the car. I'm gonna help him with that," said Jason.

"Do not untie him, Mr. Jason. I do not trust him."

"Don't worry, I won't."

Frank walked out with Sara. When they got to the car, Frank turned toward Sara and put his arms out. Sara walked into them and Frank hugged her.

"Everything will be fine, Miss Sara. Mr. Jason is a very smart man…and I know he loves you."

"I know," said Sara. "I know." Tears ran down her face, but she did her best to hide them. After a couple minutes, they both got in the car and waited in silence for Jason.

Sara looked at her watch. It was 10:40am.

Jason opened the back door and jumped in.

"Jason, Anna's funeral, it starts in ten minutes," said Sara.

"I know, but I think she'll understand. I can call the Funeral Director and tell him you're in the hospital with an appendicitis attack. I'll ask if he can take care of things. Okay?"

"Okay!" replied Sara. "Okay!"

Frank pulled away from the curb and headed for the lab. It was only a few minutes from the warehouse.

Jason took his phone from his pocket and flipped it open.

"773-741-1922," said Sara. The Funeral Director's name is Mr. Morley.

Jason dialed and waited. "Hello, Mr. Morley, please. I'm a good friend of Sara Parkins. I'm calling to tell you that she was admitted to the hospital for an appendicitis attack. She's not going to make it to the funeral. Could you please make an announcement to those who attend?" Jason listened. "Thank you so much. Yes, I'll tell her. Thank you."

"What did he say," asked Sara.

"He said to wish you well and that you're not to worry. Everything will be taken care of."

"He is a wonderful man. I'll have to thank him later," said Sara. Her head dropped. "If I have the chance."

Jason lifted Sara's chin in his hand. "You're going to have tons of time. Don't worry."

Sara leaned back in the seat and rested her head on the side window.

CHAPTER 13

"Mr. Jason, the lab I'm taking you to is state of the art. Since it is Saturday, no one else will be there except for my friend, Mr. Steve. He also works with medicine and should be able to help. He said the lab has everything you'll need. Mr. Steve is a very dear friend of mine. He has worked at this facility for twelve years. He is taking a chance on getting fired by letting you in. But, I told him it was life or death. He is a very good man."

Jason placed his hand on Frank's shoulder. "Once I find the right drug to stop the time release factor in the H1N1, it'll all be worth it. And when it's done, we'll let the world know that Steve and this facility allowed us to save millions of people."

Frank drove down a wide alley behind a red brick building. The blacktop was smooth and plants lined both sides.

This is a lot different than that other alley, thought Sara.

Frank stopped ten feet from the only door with a keypad in it.

"We are here, Mr. Jason, Miss Sara."

A 6'5" man with sandy brown hair, blue eyes and thick glasses in dark frames wearing a white lab coat, white scrubs and gumshoes, stood in the doorway.

Jason stepped out of the cab and Frank took Jason's arm and pulled him close.

"God's speed, Mr. Jason," said Frank.

"I'm gonna need it," said Jason.

Sara heard Frank's well wishes and knew that Jason was right.

Jason offered his hand to help Sara out of the car. She pulled herself out, forced a smile and hugged Frank.

"You will be fine Miss Sara. You will be fine."

"I know," she replied. She looked into Frank's eyes and took his hands in hers. "Thank you so much for everything. You've been so wonderful through this whole thing." She swallowed and her eyes drifted. Leaning in to Frank, she whispered. "If he doesn't find something in time," Sara began, "promise me, you will not blame yourself for anything. We've only come this far because of you."

"Miss Sara, he will find something…" began Frank.

"Frank, promise me," said Sara.

"I promise, Miss Sara. I promise."

Sara turned and took Jason's arm. They walked around the car, past a dumpster to where Steve waited.

"I'm Jason. Steve, right?" said Jason, extending his right hand.

"Yes, it's good to meet you." He gave Jason a hardy handshake. "I understand we've got quite a task ahead of us."

"That's an understatement," said Jason, raising his eyebrows.

Steve typed his code in the keypad and pushed open the door.

"Thank you, Mr. Steve," shouted Frank.

"No problem, Frank. Any friend of yours is a friend of mine."

"Frank, you should go pick up fares," interjected Jason. You know, normal stuff, so no one gets suspicious. I promise I'll call as soon as we find something. Okay?"

Jason, Sara, and Steve walked in and closed the door behind them. Steve walked down a long hallway to a bay of elevators. He hit the button, the doors opened and they all entered. Steve hit LL.

"All the top notch equipment is in the lower level. It's sealed off for obvious reasons. But, I have the code and can get you in there. All I ask, is that you explain what you're doing as you go along," said Steve.

"Not a problem, Steve. I really appreciate this."

The elevator stopped and Steve held up his hand for Sara to go first and then Jason. "Hey man, I looked you up and you've done some really radical stuff," said Steve.

"Yeah! Well hopefully, I can find a way to reverse it," said Jason.

Steve exited the elevator and turned left. He inserted his left thumb print and used his right index finger to put the second code in the keypad. 304.5670.5189.

"Is that code regarding 'Teaching Quantitative Thinking?'" asked Jason.

"Wow! You are good?" said Steve.

"I have a photographic memory and recognized the sequence of numbers. And considering where we are, that made the most sense," said Jason.

"My boss comes up with these. It changes every two days for security purposes. But to be honest, half the time, I memorize the numbers, but don't think of what it relates to."

"If I worked here, I probably wouldn't either," said Jason.

Steve walked straight ahead and then turned left toward a large marble countertop. Empty test tubes and saline sat in a rack at the left, while a couple of high powered microscopes sat in the center.

"Frank gave me the low-down on what you're trying to accomplish, so I set up some of the obvious things you'd need. If something's missing, let me know and I'll snag it for ya," said Steve.

"Thanks. Do you have an extra log-sheet and a chair that Sara can sit on at the end of the counter? She's gonna log everything in as we go."

Steve walked across the aisle and pushed a chair on rollers over to where Sara stood and handed her an old log-in book. "These are old log sheets, so they don't use them anymore," said Steve. "As for the chair…if you sit on it and push the lever on the right, it'll go as high or low as you want."

"Thank you," said Sara. She sat down, pushed the lever and the chair raised up to the perfect height for the counter.

"Here, let me fill in the columns," said Jason. He took the log book and wrote above several columns and handed it back to Sara.

"Basically, I'll say the name of the drug and you write it in the left column. Then, I'll give you the information for the rest of the columns, okay?"

"Okay!" said Sara.

I'll be going back and forth between the drugs because I'll have to wait for the timing, so I need you to let me know as soon as there's a drug that has a P and a time stamp that is less than an hour.

"How many drugs are you gonna test?" asked Sara.

There are hundreds that are in pure form, but it might have to be a mixture, which gives it a much broader possibility and which will take a lot longer. I'm hoping a pure drug will do the trick, but I don't know," said Jason.

Steve handed gloves to Jason and put on a pair himself. "I might as well make myself useful. I can test them right alongside you for the Positive or Negative interaction. And when it gets a lot deeper than that, I can set it up for you. That should shorten the time substantially. Let me know the mixtures you want and I'll get them ready," said Steve.

"That'd be great, Steve. In case we need a drug mixture, Sara, start the sequence again and call it drug two. If you're ever unsure, ask me to repeat it, okay?"

Sara nodded and began writing down the first batch of drugs as Jason gave them to her. There were long periods of time where Sara watched Jason and Steve as they peered through the microscope and talked back and forth about a possible match. Steve would run and get another drug and they'd try that one too.

Sara looked at her phone. 3pm. Jason and Steve had been testing different drugs for over three hours. *I know how critical it is that they find the right drug,* she thought. *My life depends on it. But, I'm losing hope. I want to tell them to stop, so I can spend some time with Jason, but there are so many other lives at stake too. I guess if these are the last hours of my life, I can feel good that I'm doing everything I can to help.*

"CI 888 is a Positive," said Jason.

Sara picked up the red pen and marked it.

"AET is a positive," said Steve.

Sara marked it in.

"RA233 is a positive," said Jason.

Sara knew the timing was the important part. *Please God, let this work, she thought. I could have a heart attack at any moment. I know Jason will come up with something, but he needs time. Please give it to him.*

Jason looked up and stretched.

I hope Jason can't see how desperate I feel, thought Sara.

He glanced over. "Sara, are you okay?"

Sara pulled the corners of her mouth up. "I'm fine. You're the ones that are probably tired. Do you need a break?" asked Sara.

"Actually, I think that's a good idea. We're waiting on three possible drugs and I think it would be a good time to take a step back and see if we're missing something. What do you think Steve?" asked Jason.

"I've been learning so much, being able to see how you come up with the different variables. But, you're right. I think it's always good to regroup."

They removed their gloves and took a seat on the stools. Jason rolled his neck and stretched his arms above his head. "Feels good," he said.

Sara stepped behind Jason and massaged his shoulders and neck.

"That feels even better." He turned and kissed her on the lips.

Sara heard a phone ringing.

Jason found his phone and flipped it open. "Hello!"

"Frank, what is it? Slow down. What's going on? We'll be right down to let you in." He closed the phone.

"I'll get him," said Steve. Steve rushed to the elevator.

Sara turned Jason toward her. "What's wrong? Why is Frank upset?" said Sara.

"I'm not sure. Something about the FBI. They think I had a part in this."

"Oh! my God! What are we gonna do? If they take you in for questioning, it'll be too late," said Sara. She began to cry and Jason held her.

He let her cry for a minute and then he pulled her away and looked at her. "Sara, no one is gonna stop me from helping you, no one. Do you understand me. I'm not gonna give up, okay?"

"Okay!" She held on to him as Steve returned with Frank.

Jason moved Sara to the side and stepped toward Frank.

"Exactly what happened, Frank?" asked Jason.

"I had a fare at your building, Mr. Jason. And I saw the police passing around a picture of you. They started to question the cabbies as they pulled in. They came to my window and asked if I'd seen you lately. I said I had not seen you for a couple of days. Then they asked what places I had taken you to. I told them that I had taken you to Riggati's a couple of times and to Mulaney's pub another. I tried to get information from them by asking if I should be worried about you, Mr. Jason. They said that it was a matter of National Security, but that I should call if I see you. They had a man with them. He was tall and thin with blonde hair and a scar on his left cheek. I do not know who it was," said Frank.

Jason shook his head from side to side. "I do. That's Larz. He must know I've got information on him. He's trying to turn the tables on me. I can't let the FBI find me before I have the answer."

"I will do everything I can to help. How is it coming, Mr. Jason?"

"We've gone through close to fifty pure drugs and forty- eight mixtures. So, far, we've only found three that are positive. I'm gonna check now to see what the timeline is," said Jason. Jason went back to the table with Steve.

They both checked under the microscope.

"Mine's interacted," said Steve.

"Both of mine have too," said Jason. "Okay, so that means they're all under twenty minutes."

"That's good right?" said Sara. She immediately marked the time in the column.

"That's very good. The only thing is we don't know which one worked faster. And we need to isolate these to see if there is any negative response within the hour," said Jason.

Sara looked down at the floor. "We have to wait another hour?" Her voice was barely audible.

Frank walked to her side. "It is good news, Miss Sara. It means you are going to be okay,"

"Yes, I suppose it does. You're right. Thank you everyone. I really appreciate everything you've done," said Sara. "So, now what do we do?"

"We wait," said Jason.

"Mr. Jason, I can run and get some food for everyone. You haven't eaten in a very long while."

Jason and Steve slipped into their pockets for cash.

"I've got it," said Jason. He held his hand up, palm out. "You've gone above and beyond, Steve. It's the least I can do."

Jason turned toward Sara. "What would you like for dinner? How about some ribs, your favorite?"

"Actually, a Chicken Caesar salad would do for me," said Sara.

"Frank, you get whatever you want. It's on me," said Jason. "And none of us are gonna eat, if you don't get something for yourself."

"Thank you, Mr. Jason. I will be back as fast as I can."

Jason handed Frank a hundred dollar bill. "I'll have an Angus burger and fries," he said.

"Me too," said Steve.

"And I, as well," said Frank.

Frank pocketed the money and headed for the elevator. "I will be back before you know it."

"The kitchen is on this floor around the corner. We'll have to eat in there," said Steve.

Jason took Sara's hand and followed Steve through a massive array of countertops, test tubes and specimens. Sara glanced from side to side, taking in everything she could.

"I never really realized how much research goes into making one medication," said Sara.

"It does take quite a bit of time, but sometimes, it should take more," said Steve.

"I agree," said Jason.

Steve stopped short of the door to the kitchen, holding his hand out for Sara to go in first. There were five square and two oblong tables, a refrigerator, microwave and a sink. Two vending machines sat at the far corner of the room.

"Let's take a long table," said Steve. "That way, we can put all the stuff at the other end."

"Sounds good," said Jason, as they each took a seat.

"I have something to say," said Sara.

Jason and Steve turned toward her.

"I've been moping around here, when I realized I could be helping others."

Jason raised his eyebrows and looked at Steve.

Sara held her head high and continued. "I've had the H1N1 flu shot and I've had a time release aspirin less than 48 hours ago. Isn't there something you could learn from my blood? Since I'm still alive, for now, I think you should do some testing on me. Maybe put that drug you found in with my blood and see what happens."

Steve looked at Jason and Jason stared at Sara.

"Are you sure you'd be okay with that?" asked Jason.

"Of course. Even if it can't help me, if it can help other people, then that's what I want to do," said Sara softly.

Jason sat motionless.

Sara wrapped her hand around his arm and shook it. "Go, go get a needle or whatever you need to do these tests."

Steve and Jason jumped up and headed back to the lab. Within two minutes they were back with test tubes, a needle and a large rubber band.

Steve handed the needle to Jason, who sat down in front of Sara,

"Sara, I haven't taken blood from an actual person…at least not for a long time. The blood is usually given to me in a test tube. So, please bear with me."

"I'm okay. Take your time," she said.

Sara looked at Steve. "I'm going to talk to you while he takes the blood, so that I don't think about it, okay?"

"Talk away," said Steve.

Meanwhile, Jason tied the rubber band above Sara's elbow and found a vein. He cleaned the area and touched the needle to her skin.

"So, Steve, what do you like most about working here?" asked Sara.

"I think it's the excitement of finding something…"

"Uhhh!" said Sara.

"You okay?" asked Jason.

"I'm fine. Go on Steve," said Sara.

Jason inserted the needle a little further and began withdrawing the blood.

"Finding something," continued Steve. "Something that will make a difference in the world. The human body is so amazing and the more I learn about it, the less I know. Does that make sense?"

"Yes, actually, it does. And thank you for distracting me."

"Okay, Sara, I've got four test tubes," said Jason as he slid the needle back out. He put pressure on her arm as he placed the band-aid at the insertion point and kissed it.

"You were a great patient," said Jason. "We're gonna mix a little of your blood with the three drugs we found and maybe that'll help us even further. This was a great idea."

Jason and Steve disappeared again, returning ten minutes later.

"Now, not only will we know if the drug interacts well with the H1N1 flu shot and a Time Release pain medication, we'll also know if it works well once it's in someone's blood…yours in particular," said Jason.

"Rrringgg, rrrinng, rrringg."

Steve picked up his phone. "Hey Frank! No problem, I'll be right down."

Steve took off immediately to let Frank in, and Sara moved close to Jason.

"Jason, I want to tell you something, but you have to promise not to interrupt me"

Jason looked puzzled, but nodded his head.

"If for some reason, I don't get the medication in time…"

"You're not…" began Jason

Sara put her finger to his lips. "You promised."

Jason bit his lip.

"If I don't get the medication in time, I want you to know that I know you did everything you could. This was not your fault. You started out trying to find time release medications that would work together to help people. You had no way of knowing that some madman was using your information to plan some sort of devastation. Whatever happens, you need to keep going, to fix all of this for everyone else."

Jason's eyes welled up.

Sara ran her fingertips across his cheek. "Hey, you, I have never met a more caring and sensitive man in my life. Thank you for being who you are. I love you, Jason."

Sara kissed him gently on the lips as Frank and Steve rounded the corner with lunch.

"There's bottled water in the fridge," said Steve. "I'll grab some."

Once they all settled down, the only sound was that of chewing, swallowing or Sara's fork pushing the lettuce from one side of her dish to the other. It was 4:12 and they hadn't eaten since early morning, but Sara's appetite wasn't there.

"Steve, tell me how you met Frank," said Sara.

"Now that's a funny story," said Steve.

"Good, I could use some humor."

"Well, I had just moved to Chicago and I had dreams of being some big famous chemist. Frank picked me up for my interview here," Steve nodded at Frank. "I was so busy thinking of all the wonderful things I was going to accomplish, I stiffed him. I got outta the cab, said 'thanks' and went to my interview."

"You're kidding?" said Jason.

"No, it is true," said Frank. "He was very nervous about the interview and it slipped his mind. I did not want to make him feel bad, so I said nothing."

"So anyway," Steve continued, "as I sat down for the interview, I realized I never paid the cabbie. I jumped up and said, I've gotta go. I grabbed the first elevator and got down to the street level where there were at least fifteen cabs lined up. I walked up to every cab on the street, trying to find Frank."

"I was the seventh cab back," interjected Frank. "When he looked in, he apologized again and again. I knew right then, we would be friends."

"He wouldn't take the money," said Steve. "He said, 'anybody that would go to that much trouble to pay me was a good guy and deserved a free ride'."

"That's cool," said Jason. "What about the guy you interviewed with?"

"Well, after I told Frank what happened, he suggested I go back up and tell him." The left side of Steve's lip lifted and he shook his head. "Frank kept talking until I said I'd go. So I thought, what the hell? I've got nothing to lose. I'd already screwed up the interview."

"So what happened," asked Sara.

"Well, it turns out Mr. Meldon, the guy I interviewed with, knew Frank. Frank had called him while I was on my way up. I got the job immediately. Frank and I have been friends ever since."

"That's a great story," said Sara.

"Frank has always been a good judge of character, so I knew you guys were okay," said Steve. "This was a big favor, but I knew I had to do it."

"Thank you," said Frank.

"No, thank you. Maybe, what I wanted all along, just showed up. I could actually be saving lives."

"I sure hope so," said Jason. "Time to go see which ones worked and which ones didn't."

Sara collected the styro-foam containers and plastic silverware and put them back in their original bags.

"You can throw it in the trash can, Sara," said Steve.

"If there's trash in the garbage, won't they find out that someone was here on a Saturday?" asked Sara.

Steve nodded. "Thanks! Wasn't even thinkin'."

"No problem! I got it. There's a huge dumpster in the alley. I'll run it out there and be right back."

Steve reached above the vending machine. "Here, use these sticks to prop open the two doors. Just be sure to pull them out, when you come back."

Sara took the full bag and walked back to the elevator, went upstairs and outside to the alley. She opened the bin and tossed it over and turned to go back in. She removed the piece of wood in the outside door and pulled it tight. Before she went back downstairs, she took a tour of the first floor. She knew the guys wouldn't be done for a while and she wanted to keep herself busy.

Walking around to the front of the building, she found a beautiful atrium with a three story glass window looking out on the street. She sat on a stone bench and stared out the window, until in the distance she saw a group of people moving very quickly together. She stood up and moved toward the corner of the window and peered out. There were seven or eight men in black tactical gear. She looked at the name on the truck. S.W.A.T. They ran quickly toward the front of the building.

Sara backed up against the wall and put her hand over her mouth.

Oh my God, they've all got weapons. They must be here for Jason, she thought. She turned and ran to the back of the building and took the first elevator down.

The elevator door opened and Sara ran out and through the open door. She heard laughing and cheers.

"Jason," she screamed. "Jason."

The laughter stopped and Jason reached her in seconds. "What is it? Sara! Are you alright?"

Sara stopped, leaned over, one hand on her hip, the other on a formica countertop. She took a couple deep breaths and stood up. "They're here. And they have guns," said Sara.

Jason reached for her arm. "Who's here Sara?"

Breathing heavily, Sara continued. "The FBI or CIA or somebody. There are about seven or eight of them and they all have guns. They must be here for you, like Frank said."

"Sara, listen to me. We got the right mixture to stop it from happening to you. We've gotta get it in you now before you have a heart attack," said Jason.

"Oh, Mr. Jason, they probably saw my cab."

"It's too late to worry about that now. We need to delay them. Frank, can you stall them? Go out to the alley and tell them you were called here for a fare and the door was open, so you went in, but, no one was here. Can you do that?" asked Jason.

"Yes, Mr. Jason. I can do that."

"I'd ask Steve, but I need him to put together a capsule for Sara," explained Jason.

Jason ran his fingers from his forehead over the top of his head. "Okay! Sara, I want you to sit down at the counter where we were working and stay there please. Steve, I need a capsule filled immediately."

"You got it."

Frank took the first elevator up to the main floor.

Sara could hear something happening outside, then upstairs. Jason measured half of the mixture then stopped.

"Do you have a syringe?" asked Jason.

"Sure, I'll get one." Steve opened a drawer under the countertop and picked up two in his thumb and index finger.

"I think we're gonna need to get this straight into her blood stream," said Jason. Something could happen any minute and, if a heart attack is in progress, I don't know if it's strong enough to work. The capsule might take too long."

"Agreed," said Steve. "We have to get the liquid form of the drug measured and into a syringe immediately.

Jason glanced at Sara. "It might burn a little and feel a little strange, but it's best to get it in as quickly as possible."

Sara smiled and nodded.

Jason measured the amount of AET needed and filled the syringe. Footsteps of thunder crashed through the opening elevator door.

"Oh my God, I didn't take the door jam out," said Sara. She could hear them running, circling closer to them. She watched Jason trying to force the drug into the syringe. *C'mon c'mon c'mon, she thought. Please, please, please.* Jason finished and rushed to Sara's side. At that moment, a black clad arm wrapped around Jason's throat and forced him to the ground.

"Don't move. I'm Swat Team Commander Klaser and you're under arrest."

Five men pointed semi-automatic weapons at Jason. Sara quivered. Steve was dragged around the corner and walked back with his hands behind his head.

"Let me explain," said Jason. "I'm trying to help."

"You can tell it to the judge," said Klaser. "Miss, you okay? I don't know if you know Miss, but these men have done some really bad things. Did they give you anything?"

Klaser glanced at one of his men. "Brett, hold 'em" said Klaser.

Bravo Team Leader, Brett, took over holding Jason on the ground with his hands behind his back. He patted Jason down and searched for explosives.

"He's clean sir," said Brett. "Except for this. Looks like he was about to stick her with it." He held up the syringe and put it on the tabletop.

Brett pulled Jason to his feet and held him in a choke hold.

"So what were you trying to give the lady?" said Klaser.

"She needs it. Please let me give it to her. She could die without it." Jason struggled to get free.

"You're not going anywhere," said Klaser. "We've got two S.W.A.T. Teams here. Alpha and Bravo. Trust me son, you'd never make it out alive.

"I'm not trying to run. I'm trying to help Sara," said Jason.

"According to this guy. . ." said Klaser as he stepped aside. "It's just the opposite."

A head of blonde hair stepped through the line, stretched out an arm and pointed at Jason.

"That's him."

CHAPTER 14

Larz strutted between the two SWAT teams and pointed at Jason again. “He worked late every night. I should’ve known something was going on. He’s been making this stuff to kill people and it’s working. I’ve got proof that he’s the one that started this whole thing.” Larz spat on the ground. “He’s filth.”

Sara stood up, eyes filled with hate, her body shaking. “You’re filth. You’re the one who’s been soliciting a terrorist to kill people. Jason’s been trying to undo what you’ve done.” Sara looked at all the men in black, shaking her head. “Don’t believe him. We have faxes and paperwork to prove it,” cried Sara.

“Who do you think put you on the list?” said Larz.

“You’re lying. We have proof,” cried Sara.

“Is that what he told you?” said Larz laughing.

“Excuse me, sir,” said Frank holding up a stack of paper two inches thick. “It is true. This is the proof that Mr. Jason and Miss Sara are innocent. This man you have has been working with a terrorist named, Mujahdeen Jihad. This is his handwriting. And I am sure if you look for fingerprints, you will find his as well."

Larz's eyes shifted from left to right.

"You're bluffin', old man. You've got nothin'."

Klaser took the papers from Frank and thumbed through them.

"Looks pretty authentic to me," said Klaser.

"I don't know what you're talking about. They're trying to frame me," yelled Larz. He turned and dashed for the elevator.

Two members from Team Bravo stopped him in his tracks.

"Jack, Murray, bring him over here," said Klaser.

Bravo leaders, Jack and Murray cuffed Larz's arms behind his back and forced him toward Klaser.

Klaser stood inches from Larz's face. "So, you haven't been telling us the whole truth there, Larz?" said Klaser, jabbing him with an index finger. "You better start talkin'…and make it fast, because I really don't like being lied to."

Larz chewed on his lower lip and Klaser jabbed him again.

"Start talking. So this was really your baby, huh!"

"I had a part in it. But, it was his idea," said Larz, throwing his chin out toward Jason. "He's the brains behind it all. Who do you think devised a way to have time releases work together in the first place? It's all documented and it's his work."

Klaser glanced at Jason and back at Larz and then to Sara. "So, Miss, how do you fit into all this?"

Sara stepped forward, cleared her throat and swallowed hard. "I'm one of the people he…," Sara threw her finger out at Larz "he's trying to kill."

"Maybe we should all start at the beginning," said Klaser. "Why don't you take a seat Miss. You look a little shaky."

"She needs the shot," insisted Jason.

Klaser held a hand, palm up toward Jason. "Hold on a second. Let her talk. Maybe she can get you off the hook."

"I don't care. I just wanna give her the shot," repeated Jason, pushing forward.

"Brett, keep him quiet," said Klaser.

Brett held him tighter and jabbed him in the ribs. Jason buckled and gasped.

"Please don't hurt him. He's trying to save me," said Sara.

"Okay, so start at the beginning," said Klaser. "Why do you need a shot and what's he trying to save you from?"

"From dying," replied Sara. "It's a conspiracy that he…" she pointed at Larz. "is in on. He's working with a known terrorist to kill millions of people. And it'll work unless you let Jason stop it."

"And how do you know all this? How long have you known this guy, Jason?"

"Long enough to know I trust him. Jason developed the time release that went into the H1N1 vaccine and Larz put bacteria and other stuff in it to kill people."

"It's his time release that's killing people," shouted Larz.

"No it's not," yelled Sara.

Klaser turned nose to nose to Larz. "If I have to tell you to shut up again, it won't be your choice." Klaser returned his focus to Sara.

"Go ahead, Miss!"

"Anyone who received the vaccine from phase I. . ." said Sara.

"Phase I? Is there a phase II?" asked Klaser.

"Yes, and the shot I got is from phase II, which means if I don't get the antidote shot in time, I could have a heart attack and die."

"Whoa! That sounds like a pretty serious accusation," said Klaser.

"We have a hitman in a warehouse that knows all about it. You can ask him yourself."

"Why would a hitman want to kill you?" asked Klaser.

"Because I asked too many questions about my friend, Anna, who died after getting the vaccine. They said I was getting too nosey."

"Okay! Let me get this right," said Klaser. "Jason came up with the time release for the H1N1 vaccine and Larz contacted a known terrorist to use Jason's research to kill people?"

"Yes, Jason works in New York for the same company as Larz, but when he found out what Larz was doing, he knew he had to stop him."

Sara looked at Jason and smiled. "He didn't know that people like Larz were using his knowledge to do something evil. He knew if he came forward too early, they would think he did it and he wouldn't be able to find a drug to counteract it. When he found a list of people here in Chicago who had received the H1N1 and had reflux, he moved here to see if he could get more information to stop it and get the police to see it wasn't him."

"So, you're saying there is an organization dealing with a terrorist to kill millions of Americans through the H1N1 vaccine?" said Klaser.

"Yes, that's exactly what I'm saying," said Sara.

"They stole a release factor that Jason spent years perfecting. They used it to give reflux to anyone who received the H1N1 shot. Once the person has the symptoms, they usually go to the doctor and get a prescription for Rilosac. Of course, all of this is documented in a National Registry. So, now the bad guys know that it's working. The Rilosac triggers heart attack symptoms that last about an hour. Once again, most people check into the hospital and their name…,"

"Is on the Registry," interjected Klaser.

"Yes. After an hour, the heart attack symptoms diminish and the person is supposed to be fine. There's a problem though - if someone has taken another time-release medication, like an aspirin, it interacts with the previous time-release medication and a heart attack ensues."

Sara broke down in tears.

"So they'd die?" said Klaser.

"Yes," said Jason, lunging forward. "For God sake, let me give her the shot."

Brett tightened his hold.

"Release the choke hold, but hold him," said Klaser. "So Jason Forest is it? How does this work?"

Jason choked a bit and rubbed his throat. "It's like Sara said, the heart attack continues and the person dies. But, that was a test run," said Jason waving his hands frantically in front of him. "Phase II has already started and that purposely doesn't have a stopping agent in the Rilosac, the way phase I did. So they wouldn't need to take a third medication. They'd die after taking Rilosac. And there are rumors that there's a phase III. With that, if you take H1N1 and any other time release medication, it starts a heart attack that doesn't stop. Because people take all kinds of medications that have a time release, it will be difficult to pinpoint the cause before millions of people die."

Jason looked at Sara. "Sara is on the list for phase II. And Carlo, the guy in the warehouse, forced a time release aspirin down her throat over thirty six-hours ago." Jason looked at Commander Klaser, his eyes welling up, perspiration dripping from his forehead. "Please, I beg of you. I need to give her this shot. It'll stop the symptoms. If she begins to have a heart attack, it may not work."

"He's right," said Steve. "I've been working with him all day and night to find the right drug to counteract it. He found it."

"Alright, look if Sara wants…" began Klaser.

"Uhhh, ughghhhghgg. My chest, it's so tight. Oh God!"

Brett loosened his grip and Jason fell to the floor. My chest," said Jason.

"What's happening?" cried Sara.

"You think you're so smart, third in your class. Got all the answers," yelled Larz. "Your name was on the list buddy, not Sara's. I switched it." He threw his head back and laughed. "And it's too late to do anything about it."

It's impossible," said Jason. "I never had the H1N1 flu shot and I don't take medication."

"No, you didn't take it," said Larz. "But I followed you to Trattoria's the other day and I snuck in the kitchen and put it in the white sauce. Even you couldn't taste it. And it's Phase 3. You don't need anything else to make it work. Of course, you're the first, so good luck."

Jack stiff armed Larz in the ribs and he fell to his knees.

Jason lay on the floor clutching his chest.

"What about the shot?" yelled Sara. She grabbed the syringe and ran toward Jason. She inserted the needle into his arm and pushed the plunger in and removed the needle.

"Jason, Jason, please be okay! Please," cried Sara. She picked up his head and ran her fingers through his hair.

"That's karma buddy," said Larz.

"Shutup!" said Jack, as he tightened his choke hold.

Brett knelt at Jason's side.

"What can I do?" asked Brett.

"Pray," said Sara.

"His heart is still compressing," said Brett.

"Unless the shot kicks in," said Steve, "nothing's going to stop it."

Klaser stooped in front of Larz and pushed a sharp index finger into his chest. "If he dies, you're lookin' at murder one."

Klaser stood and looked at Jason. He turned back toward Larz. "That's if you make it outta this room."

"What about an aspirin?" asked Brett. "I've always heard they help."

Sara kept her focus on Jason, stroking his hair.

"If it weren't a drug-induced heart attack, they usually do. But, unfortunately, this is," said Steve.

Jason's chest continued spasming. Gasping for breath, his hand tightened on Sara's arm.

"Hang in there Jason. Hang in there. It's gonna work. Just give it time, it's gonna work," repeated Sara.

Jason's eyes met Sara's, the corners of his mouth lifted slightly, his grip loosened and his hand fell to the ground.

Kneeling on the floor, Sara held Jason's lifeless body in her arms.

Sara threw her head back. "No-o-o-o-o," she shouted. "No-o-o-o-o." She looked back down at Jason. His eyes still open, his mouth, a gash in his face. No movement, no breath, his arms hanging at his sides. Sara lowered Jason's head to the floor, tears rushing down her face, and gently closed his eyelids.

CHAPTER 15

Handcuffed and in Jack's custody, Larz stood ten feet behind Sara. Head down, Sara rose, turned and plowed into him, knocking him to the ground.

"You bastard," she yelled. "You son of a bitch."

Sara landed one punch. "You took him from me." She landed another punch.

The Commander watched, holding his hand out and to the side, keeping his men at bay.

"Why? Why?" yelled Sara, forcing her fists into Larz's face. "You're the one that deserves to die. You!" she yelled.

Commander Klaser flagged his men. Brett and Jack continued holding Larz, while Assistant Alpha Commander Cody stepped up and wrapped an arm around Sara's waist and slowly pulled her back.

"Miss, it's okay! You need to stop," said Cody. "That won't bring him back. You need to stop."

Sara continued swinging, screaming and crying.

"Miss Sara," said a voice behind her. "Miss Sara," yelled Frank. "It's Jason."

Sara's fist stopped flailing inches from Larz's face. She attempted to turn and Cody released her. She stared blankly at Frank, eyes blurred by tears, fist bloodied. Then, Frank stepped aside and Sara saw Jason's hand move. She ran to him and dropped to her knees.

"Jason," yelled Sara. She lifted his head and placed it on her lap. She felt for a pulse. "He's breathing!" she yelled. She turned toward the Commander. "He's alive!"

Turning back toward Jason, she ran her fingers down his cheek.

"Jason, Jason, are you okay?"

Jason opened his eyes and glanced up at Sara. "Well I'm looking at an angel, so I'm not sure," he responded. "But, my chest hurts."

The Commander and all his men began to clap, one after the other, until the whole room erupted in applause for Jason and Sara.

"Okay!" said the Commander. "Let's get movin'. We need to get Mr. Forest to the hospital to get checked out. I want him back here asap, so we can get that stuff out to the rest of the public."

"Yes sir, I took the liberty of calling the paramedics and they're on their way up," said Cody.

Sara pressed her lips to Jason's and breathed in his essence.

"I love you Jason. I am so-o-o glad you're okay," said Sara.

"So this is what it takes to get you to say you love me? If I'd of known, I'd of had a heart attack sooner."

"Stop that," said Sara.

Sara heard metal hitting metal and turned as the paramedics rushed through the doors and into the lab with the portable stretcher.

"Right this way," said Klaser, pointing toward Jason.

Placing the gurney along side Jason, they opened it and locked the legs in place.

The first paramedic placed the stethoscope under Jason's shirt and took his pulse at the same time. "Names's J.T. How ya feelin? Got any pain anywhere in particular?"

"I'll tell ya what, J.T. I'm feelin' better than ever. Got a beautiful girl takin'care a me and now I got the pros."

"Okay, well, Joe and I are gonna help you up on this gurney, nice and slow," said J.T., extending his arm.

J.T. got Jason situated and secured him to the gurney, then monitored his pulse. "Joe, start an IV drip and get him on a monitor,"

"Will do," said Joe.

Jason lay still. Sara's hand rested on his chest.

"Everything sounds pretty good right now," said J.T. "But we're not taking any chances. One of the SWAT guys said you had a massive heart attack. Hmmmpph! Hearts pumping pretty good right now."

J.T. and Joe wheeled Jason out to the ambulance in the back alley and Sara followed.

"Miss Parkins, Assistant Commander Cody'll be riding with you and Jason," said Klaser. As soon as he's up to it, we're gonna need Jason to manufacture that antidote.

"Hey! Commander. I think I'm good to go right now," said Jason. "Don't forget, it was medically induced, it wasn't a natural heart attack. I'm probably fine."

"Okay! It's the 'probably' that concerns me. Let the doctors check you out and if they're okay with you leaving, that'd be great," said Klaser.

"I know he'll want to get to it as soon as possible, but I've got all his notes," said Sara.

Steve stepped in front of Klaser. "Commander, I worked side by side with Jason on this. It's his find, but I can re-create it for you."

"Great! Brett, you stay here at the lab with the other guys. Let me know what Steve needs and we'll get it to him. I'm calling Washington to see how they want to proceed. But, I'd like to have something in place to begin with." said Klaser.

"Steve, I'll be back as soon as they give me the green light," said Jason.

"Mr. Klaser, sir," interrupted Frank. "That man that Mr. Jason and Miss Sara were talking about… he's in a warehouse about ten minutes from here."

"How d'ya know he's still there?"

Jason raised his arm and reached for Klaser. "Yeah! I forgot about him. He was hired by Larz to kill Sara and anybody else that got in the way."

"What's he doin' in a warehouse?" asked Klaser.

Jason grimaced. "Well, we sorta tied him to a chair and questioned him."

"Oh! ya did, did ya? And, if he was in on this, why would he tell you?"

Sara turned toward Commander Klaser. "Well, I kinda came up with an idea…"

"That I agreed with," said Jason.

"What was this idea?"

"To give him a shot of the H1N1, at least that's what he thought it was," said Jason.

"So you gave him a shot against his will?"

"Mr. Klaser, sir, I gave him the shot, not Sara or Jason. I did. He took part in killing my mother, sir," said Frank.

Klaser looked at the three of them. "So, let me get this straight. You kidnapped him, you…"

"No," said Jason. "I didn't really kidnap him. I stopped him from dumping Sara in Lake Michigan. He beat her up and shoved an aspirin down her throat and he said he was gonna push her off the pier. So, I got there and used chloroform, put him in the trunk, and…"

"You know what, I don't want to know any more," said Klaser. "He's in the warehouse, right? And he thinks he's gonna die?"

"Pretty much. I gave him a time release aspirin after Frank gave him the shot, the one we said was the H1N1. It was just saline."

"Got it! Okay! Well, let's go get him and see if we can get any more information out of him. Jack, Murray, let's go with… Frank, is it?"

"Yes, Mr. Klaser, Sir."

Frank layed his hand on Jason's arm and smiled.

"I will see you soon, Mr. Jason."

"See ya, Frank. Good luck."

J.T. and Joe lifted Jason into the ambulance and Cody helped Sara up after them. Cody and Sara sat on one side and J.T. sat on the other, while Joe drove.

Resting her hand on Jason's arm, Sara kissed him on the forehead. Jason reached over and took her hand in his. He felt something wet and ragged and looked down.

"Oh my God, Sara. What happened to your knuckles," said Jason.

"Oh! It's nothing," said Sara, pulling them away slowly.

Jason held on. "Nothing? It looks like you were in a fight."

Sara looked down sheepishly and Jason looked at Cody.

"Your girlfriend here went ballistic on that Larz guy when she thought you were dead. She pounded him pretty good," said Cody with a smile.

Jason smiled. "Really?" He pulled her hands up toward his lips and kissed them. "Sara, your poor hands. Do they hurt?"

"They're okay!" she said softly.

J.T. reached for Sara's hands. I'll clean them up and put some ointment on them. They'll be good as new."

The sirens blared and the lights swept off the buildings and through the ambulance. Within minutes they pulled into the ambulance bay at the hospital and Joe rolled Jason through the Emergency Room, straight to a doctor.

A tall, lanky man with a receding hairline, wearing glasses and a white lab coat stood in their path.

"I'm Doctor Hager, the Chief Resident, I've been expecting you."

"I'm Assistant SWAT Team Commander Cody. Mr. Forest here had a heart attack brought on by a medication."

"Did someone here give it to him?" asked Dr. Hager.

"No, sir. Just making you aware of the situation. We need him released as soon as possible…healthy of course," said Cody, nodding to Sara. "It's a matter of National Security."

“Should we be worried about him or the safety of my staff?”

“No sir. He’s one of the good guys,” said Cody.

“I’ll take care of him personally,” said Dr. Hager. He turned toward the nurses’ station and raised his right hand. “Page Dr. Coburn and Dr. Stern. Have them meet me in 3H, at the end of the wing stat.

“Thank you, sir,” said Cody. “I’ll need to be in the room with you to make sure he’s okay and I’ll need to know exactly what test is being run and why?”

J.T. buzzed by on his way out. “You two, take care.”

Cody and Sara followed Dr. Hager as he rushed past crash carts, wheelchairs and orderlies into a room at the end of a long hall.

“Okay! These are the tests I’m gonna run. First, an EKG. It’ll give us a graphic record of the electrical activity of his heart as it contracts and relaxes. It’ll also detect abnormal heartbeats, areas of damage, inadequate blood flow or heart enlargement. Then, we’re gonna do some blood tests to check for enzymes or other substances that are released when cells begin to die. These are called "markers" measuring the amount of damage to his heart.”

Dr. Hager glanced at Jason. “By the way, there’s no pain involved in these tests.”

“I’m good with that,” said Jason.

“Finally, I’ll do a Nuclear Scan. This’ll show areas of his heart that lack blood flow or may be damaged. It’ll also reveal any problems with the heart’s pumping action. To do this, we inject a small amount of radioactive material into his arm. Then, we position a scanning camera over his heart and it records whether the nuclear material is absorbed by his heart muscle. If it is, he’s healthy; if not, his heart’s been damaged. The camera helps us evaluate how well the heart muscle pumps blood. Now, there's another test called a Coronary angiography. But I don't know we'll need to do that. Let's see the results of these tests first."

Within ten minutes, a doctor hooked up a heart monitor to Jason, started an EKG and drew blood. Within an hour, all the tests had been completed.

"Just give me a couple of minutes to look over the tests and if all looks good, I'll release him myself," said Dr. Hager.

Sara leaned toward Cody. "Wow! It's amazing how fast things can get done, when you know somebody."

"Yes, ma'am."

One doctor removed all the probes from Jason while another doctor checked his heart and another his blood pressure.

Ten minutes later, Dr. Hager came back to Jason's room.

"Sorry, it took a little longer than I thought…"

Sara's eyes opened wide. "Is there something wrong?"

"No, actually I was just double checking, because his heart is in amazing shape, even for someone who hadn't had a heart attack. Commander, you said it was induced by a medication?" asked Dr. Hager.

"Yes sir. I'll have one of my men contact you and give you all the particulars. Right now, you need to release him, if he's okay."

"It's just that we've had a couple of other similar cases," began Dr. Hager. "They each received good test results after suffering a heart attack and arriving here. But not long after, the arrhythmia started up again and went into a full-blown cardiac arrest that we couldn't stop."

"How long did it take, before the heart attacks started again, sir?" asked Cody.

"Three to four hours was the longest time period in between," said Dr. Hager

"Sir, I'm going to give you a number to call, if you get any new cases in," said Cody.

"Is there something going on that we should be on the lookout for?" asked Dr. Hager.

"It's not something I can discuss right now sir, but if you'll keep us informed, we'll let you know when we have something concrete. I'll wait while he dresses, sir – and we'll keep an eye on him."

"That's good," said Dr. Hager, "because the others didn't make it, no matter what we did."

Sara's mouth dropped and she stared at Jason as he walked toward Cody and her.

"What are you looking so glum about?" asked Jason. "They said I'm in great shape."

"Dr. Hager said that this has happened to other patients recently. They had the same symptoms and the tests said they were fine. But then the symptoms came back and wouldn't stop," said Sara. "They died."

"Sara, we know why they died. You gave me the shot. And it worked. Don't worry, I'm fine." Jason turned toward Assistant Commander Cody.

"Can we go now?"

"Yes sir. Follow me." Cody started and then stopped abruptly.

"Hold on a second." He pushed a button on his belt and adjusted his mic. He stood for a few moments without saying a word.

“Roger that.” Cody clicked the button off on his belt.

“Is there a problem?” asked Jason.

“Apparently the guy in the warehouse was dead when they got there.”

CHAPTER 16

"Dead?" Jason's face went ashen. "I swear we didn't do it. We just talked to him and…"

"Sir, it was a hit. Apparently someone found out he didn't get the job done. And some of our intel picked up a possible ID on another hitman. So we're gonna have to move. We've got a truck outside with one of our guys driving and the rest of the team are on their way as back-up."

"Oh my God! Jason, what are we gonna do?" asked Sara.

"Ma'am, you're not going to do anything, except what I tell you to do…if you wanna live. Understood?"

"Yes, of course."

"Stay directly behind me," said Cody.

Sara followed them as they walked out of the hospital to a waiting S.W.A.T. truck. The sun was out and people milled about.

I don't know what it is about having the sun out, that makes things a little less scary, but I'm glad it is, thought Sara. *You're not afraid Sara. Look at the beautiful burgundy ripple inset in a perfect blue sky. Everything is fine,* she told herself.

Cody made his way to the front of the truck and glanced inside.

"Hey Brett. Thought you were back at the lab," said Cody.

"Yeah! Well when they heard about a second hit man, they sent me right over."

Brett craned his neck around the outside of the truck. "Jason, you can sit up front with me. It's not as bumpy a ride and all the glass is bullet proof."

"Ma'am, do you mind sitting in the back?" asked Cody.

"I can sit in the back," said Jason.

"Sir, sit in the front please," said Cody.

That sure seemed to be more of a command than a suggestion, thought Sara.

"You've been through a lot and we wanna make sure you stay healthy," said Cody.

Jason glanced at Sara. "You okay?"

"I'm fine. Go, sit up front," said Sara.

Jason nodded and took a seat next to Brett.

"Brett," yelled Cody. "Let me know if you notice anything funny."

"Roger that," said Brett.

Cody walked Sara to the back, then opened the rear door exposing a metal cavity with twelve metal seats that folded down from the wall by leather straps. Sara stepped up and Cody brought a seat down for Sara. "Take a seat ma'am."

"Could you please call me Sara. You're making me feel old. Even though next to you, I probably am."

"Yes ma'am, I mean no ma'am, er Sara, you're not old."

Sara smiled. "Thank you for that."

Cody closed the huge metal door and locked it.

The truck pulled away and there was silence. *If there was ever a sound for no sound, this was it,* thought Sara. Cody sat directly across from her, his back against the wall, legs shoulder-width apart, hands on his thighs, firearm in its holster.

I can't even hear him breathe, Sara thought. *I don't wanna stare, but it's hard not to. I mean he's like someone from a movie.* Sara clicked off items in her mind. *Black matted gymshoes...probably for speed; a knife in a sheath attached to his ankle; a serrated circular piece of metal sticking out of a leather pouch on his thigh; a canister in a belt around his hips; two guns, one larger than the other and a pair of goggles. Wow! He's got dozens of different size pockets sewn into his fatigues...looks like there's something in each of 'em. I wouldn't wanna mess with this guy. Thank God, he's on our side.*

Sara locked eyes with Cody, then immediately looked away. She eyed a steel box locked tightly by a heavy padlock sitting at the back of the truck behind the front seats. It was the only other thing in the truck.

Sara leaned forward and removed a tube of pearl lipstick from her purse, unscrewed the top and began applying it to her lips. Holding her purse on her lap, she leaned forward again to replace the cap, when the truck shifted unexpectedly to the right, and her head snapped back. Her lipstick shot through the air and put a two-inch mark on Cody's right shoe.

Cody pushed the button on his belt.

"Got trouble?"

Before Brett could answer, the truck swerved again and gained speed. Sara slipped from the seat onto the metal floor and glanced up at Cody.

"Stay down Sara. In the corner, by the metal box. Everything's fine."

Sara's heart began racing. *Everything sure doesn't seem fine,* she thought.

Small sounds, dinging sounds. "What is that?" she asked.

"Gunfire, Sara. But they can't get through the walls of this truck. Sounds like it's coming from in front of us."

The truck pulled to the right.

"Must've gotten one of the tires," said Cody, his voice level. He stooped down in front of Sara. "Sara, when we stop, I'm gonna get out and you need to lock the door after me and keep it locked." He handed her a walkie talkie from his belt. "I'll radio you when you should open the door. If I tell you to open the door, but I use the word 'old' in anything I say, it means they're out there with me. Don't open it."

"Well, what about you and Jason?" asked Sara.

"I'll take care of 'em. Back-up's on the way."

Cody pushed the button again and listened.

"Roger that, a ten count, North side. Got it."

The truck's tires squealed and at one point the truck almost tipped over. The back end swerved completely sideways, then stopped. Cody unlocked the door, jumped down and closed it behind him.

Sara immediately stood and locked the door. She looked down and noticed a key. *It must've fallen from one of his pockets,* she thought. She picked it up and turned it over and over in her hand as she sat back down in the corner by the steel box, shaking.

Oh God! Please let Jason and Cody be okay," she thought. She heard another shot and then the bullets stopped, but she could hear cursing. Someone slammed something up against the outside of the truck. Sara put her ear to the wall, but she couldn't make out anything being said. She glanced down at the walkie talkie and rubbed her thumb over the Listen button to see if that might work. Nothing! A few more times, something smashed up against the side of the truck. Perspiration ran down Sara's neck and every muscle in her body tightened.

She heard a crackle on the radio and hit the listen button. It was Cody.

"Sara, it's safe to come out. We've got 'em. I'm not too old for this job afterall."

Sara jumped up and went to the door. She stopped in her tracks. *He said, 'old'. I'm not supposed to open the door if he says 'old'. What should I do*," she thought. She looked down at her hand, where she turned the key that fell from Cody's pocket over and over again,

"Oh God, please let it be," she said. She bent down in front of the steel box and put the key in the lock. It fit. She turned it and lifted the lid. Every kind of gun imaginable. She picked up a smaller one and looked in the chamber to see if it had any bullets in it. It was as though she were twelve again.

"It's loaded. Okay, now what? Is there a safety?" She cocked the gun back and placed it by her cheek to get line of sight.

"Oh God! I haven't fired a gun in eighteen years," whispered Sara to herself.

The walkie talkie crackled again and Sara pressed the button and listened.

"Sara, you can come out now. The lock's a little old, just give it a push."

There was the word again, 'old'. "But, I can't just sit here." She moved toward the door and it crackled again. Sara pushed the button and heard a different voice, it was Brett.

"Sara, it's good. Everything is under control. Come on out."

There was a muffled 'no' in the background.

Why did Brett call me? And where's Cody? Something weird is going on, thought Sara.

Sara clicked the answer button. "Brett, how's Jason? And where's Cody? Are they okay?"

"Yeah, They're both okay. In fact, Cody is walking around the back of the truck to meet you right now. Go ahead and open the door."

Sara glanced in the box one more time. There was one of those round serrated black Karate things. It looked really sharp. She grabbed it.

"Okay, I'm gonna unlock the door and come out."

Sara's hand shook as she slowly opened the door. They were in an alley with the back door facing a dead-end. As she pushed the door to the left, she saw a black matted gymshoe with the declining rays of the sun pooling across it. She started to say, "Cody," when she noticed the shoe…no lipstick…this wasn't Cody.

In a split second, Sara took the serrated circular weapon, aimed and spun it to hit an inch above the shoe.

Someone screamed in pain.

Sara swung the door open and saw Brett fall backwards, losing his hold on Jason, who had a bloodied lip.

"You bitch," Brett yelled.

As Brett attempted to pull the star from his ankle, Jason scampered to safety behind the truck.

"You're dead," said Brett, brandishing a gun.

On the ground against a wall to the right of Brett, Sara saw Cody, bound and gagged, blood oozing from his leg.

"Please don't hurt him," said Sara. "Please."

"The two of you, are nothing but trouble. Couldn't mind your own damn business. Now you pay and so does he."

Four feet in front of him, Brett turned toward Cody and pointed the gun at his head. Jason crept around the truck and lunged toward Brett.

A single shot rang out.

Sara screamed. She dropped to the ground shaking. The gun slipped from her fingers. Total silence. Jason lay on the ground, hands stretched above his head in a pool of blood. Cody's focus went to Sara. He worked the gag off his mouth.

"Sara, Sara, it's okay. It's okay," said Cody.

Jason lifted his head and saw Brett laying a few feet above him, blood pouring from his chest.

"What happened?

"Sara stopped him cold," said Cody.

"What? How?" What do you mean?" asked Jason.

"I think she's kind of in shock. Go be with her. I hear my guys comin' now," said Cody.

Jason jumped up and ran to Sara.

"Sara, Sara, it's okay." Jason saw the gun in her lap. "Where did you learn to shoot like that? You saved Cody's, life, - and mine."

Sara buried her head in his chest and Jason held her.

The second S.W.A.T. truck pulled down the alley and before it stopped, Klaser, Jack and Murray jumped out and ran toward Cody and Brett.

Cody worked his way up the wall and began to hop on one foot toward Klaser.

"What the hell happened here?" said Klaser, pointing to Brett.

"He's a double agent, Sir. Working for the other side. He knocked Jason out, faked a hi-jacking, and layed on the steering wheel pretending to be hurt. When I went to check on him, he shot me in the leg."

How'd you land the star?

"I didn't," said Cody. "Sara did."

"No shit!"

"No, sir."

"What about the gunshot?"

"That was Sara too, sir."

"Wow! Alright then," said Klaser. "We've got a medic truck with J.T. and Joe right behind us. They'll be here any minute."

Ambulance lights cascaded off the crumbled brick and sirens bounced off the walls.

"Here it is now. Murray, take care a Brett. Get any weapons he might have on him, got it?"

"Got it, sir," said Murray.

The paramedics lifted Brett onto a stretcher.

"Is he gonna make it?" asked Klaser.

"Yeah! Looks like it missed his heart by an inch. Did a lot of damage though," said J.T.

"Get him in the ambulance and then come back and take a look at Assistant Commander Cody," said Klaser.

"Will do," said Joe.

Klaser cut Cody free as Joe and J.T. returned with a second stretcher.

"Hey buddy, let's get you up on this thing and take a look at that leg," said J.T.

Cody looked back at Commander Klaser. "I'll fill in the details later, sir."

J.T. wrapped Cody's leg. "You both got pretty lucky today. Looks like that star in your pocket deflected the bullet and it went straight through the fleshy part of your leg. Missed the bone entirely. We'll have to let the docs take a look, but it looks like some antibiotics and staying off it for a week or so might just do the trick," said J.T.

Sara wrapped an arm around Jason's and walked toward Cody.

"I knew you wouldn't leave like that," said Sara.

"You might want to sign up for the S.W.A.T. team," said Cody.

“That’s okay. I think that was the total sum of my tomboy days, right there.”

Klaser stepped toward Sara. “By the way, the CIA caught Mujahdeen Jihad. They found him in Jamal with twelve of his operatives. We’ll get the rest of the intel from Brett.”

Klaser turned and put his hand on Jason’s shoulder.

“Ya know, if you weren’t so damned determined, we wouldn’t of known what hit us. We owe you a lot.”

“You can say that after we get this drug out there for everybody,” said Jason.

“Well, Steve has been following your notes and we’ve got it started. Do you think you’re up to going back there now?” asked Klaser.

“That’s exactly where I wanna go,” said Jason.

“Me too,” said Sara.

“I was hoping you’d say that. I asked Frank to order ribs…said they’re your favorite.”

CHAPTER 17

Jason, Steve, Sara and Frank along with Klaser, Jack and Murray, filed into the kitchen at Steve's lab.

"Whew!" said Sara, holding her hand under her nose. *This must be what a men's locker room smells like. No one's taken a shower all day and the tension makes for an interesting blend - blood and sweat mixed with the chemicals in the air along with that bleach they used to sanitize the kitchen.*

Klaser stood at the foot of the table and a tall gray haired man stood in the doorway looking in.

"First of all…good job," began Klaser. "Sara, you were amazing."

Sara blushed and squeezed Jason's hand.

"Believe me, I didn't even know what I was doing most of the time."

"Well, if that's the case, keep it up," said Klaser. "You saved Cody and Jason. And believe me, we'll be talking about that later. I've talked to the President, the Director of the CIA, the Director of the FBI and the Mayor of Chicago. Everybody's got a hand in this to make sure we can stop what these assholes…"

Klaser motioned toward the kitchen door. "To explain the rest to you, here's FBI Director, Richard J. Branowski.

The tall, gray-haired man walked over, cleared his throat, and placed his hands on the table.

"Good evening, everyone. Thank you, Commander Klaser. This is what's going on at our end. While Jason was on his way to the hospital to get checked out, I hand picked the top six research doctors from all over the country and we're flying them in by Lear jet. They've been in the air for over an hour and should be here at about 9:30 this evening. All they know is…it's a matter of National Security and they're being asked to come and support their country. When they get here…Jason, I'd like you to explain exactly what's happened."

Sara glanced at Jason and squeezed his hand once more.

"I think you can explain it to the doctors better than anybody," said Branowski.

Jason nodded.

Branowski continued. "There are ten FBI agents here with another ten guys from the Alpha and Bravo S.W.A.T. teams - most of whom you've already met," he said, waving his hand, palm up, about the room. "There's another twenty Chicago police officers outside the perimeter. So, I'd say we're pretty protected. As you know, Jihad and his operatives were apprehended in Jordan by the CIA, but we've been informed there may be one or two more undercover operatives, here in the States. So, we still need to be careful, because he or she could be anybody."

"Sir, does my boss know what's going on here?" asked Steve.

"Don't worry…we rarely take over a medical facility without getting an okay first. We've talked to your boss and we let him know you've been a crucial part in saving hundreds of thousands of people. He's sent out notice this evening that the plant will be closed Monday for upgrades," said Branowski.

"Upgrades?" Steve tilted his head slightly.

"Yeah! Well your boss let us know how many capsules we could crank out at a time, so we're having three new fillers permanently installed."

"That's awesome," said Steve. "He's been trying to get those requisitioned for the last two years."

"Well, it's nice to know the FBI is good for something," said Branowski. "And for those of you who don't know, those are machines that'll be used to fill the capsules. I believe that'll make a total of five, I'm told." He glanced at Steve for confirmation.

"That's correct, sir."

"Each machine needs to turn out 100,000 pills…" began Branowski.

"Wow! How long will that take?" asked Sara. "There might be somebody out there having a heart attack right now!"

"That's a good point and that's why we've been able to get all this done so quickly. And to answer your concern, Sara, we'll be sending capsules to the hospitals within the first hour to help anybody in immediate need. In fact, that's something we thought of asking you to do, if you're willing? Some people might need a little persuading."

"Absolutely, anything you need," said Sara.

"Of course, you'll have an FBI agent with you and someone from the S.W.A.T. team at all times."

Jason glanced sideways at Sara.

"And Jason, we'll need you to test a couple of capsules in each batch, okay?"

"Sure, no problem, Steve and I can test two for every 500. But I would suggest we send syringes to the hospitals, not pills. If they're in the hospital with chest pains already, the pills will take too long to make a difference."

"Okay, said Branowski. "In about an hour and a half, this place'll be buzzing and there won't be any time to relax. No breaks or down time. We've ordered dinner and they should be delivering within the next few minutes. Thanks to all of you for your help. You'll all be receiving commendations for your work on this."

"I don't need to eat and I definitely don't need a medal. I just wanna get started," said Jason.

"Me too," said Sara. Frank and Steve nodded.

"Well, I prefer everyone eats, so no one passes out half way in. And given everything you two have been through…a good meal's not a bad idea," said Branowski. "When the rest of the medical researchers get here, I'll go over everything with them while you eat and then I'll introduce you. Jason, you'll be leading one team and Steve, you'll be leading the other." He turned and looked at Frank. "Frank, is it? Jason requested you stay on to help him out…if you're up to it," said Branowski.

"Yes, sir, thank you, sir."

"Okay! That's all for now. I'll be back," said Branowski. As he left the room, the muscles in Sara's back relaxed.

"Commander Klaser," said Sara.

"Yes."

"How's Cody? Is he gonna be okay?"

"He's doing really well. It was a flesh wound, through and through. In fact, if I know Cody, he's not gonna be at that hospital for long. He's not the kinda guy to just sit around. Klaser lifted his nose and turned. "Whoa! Something smells really good."

"Well, don't look at me," said Jack.

"He said good, not good and ripe," said Cody, as he made his way into the kitchen, hobbling on one crutch.

A wonderful smell sifted into the kitchen right behind him and a silver haired man poked his head around the corner. "Who wants ribs?" he yelled.

"Henry, what are you doing here?" asked Sara.

"I heard you guys were hungry, so I brought my ribs. I know you like 'em." He pushed in a silver cart with fifteen bags, plastic silverware and napkins. "Each bag has enough for four hearty appetites. And, it's on me by the way," said Henry. "The least I could do."

Cody snagged a bag and tucked it under his arm with the crutch and hobbled over to the table. Murray and Jack picked off another bag, which Klaser immediately snatched from them and divvied up.

"Hey! Code, hear the bullet missed everything. No muscle either, huh!" laughed Murray.

"Can it," said Cody as he tipped Murray's chair back with his crutch.

"Alright, alright, just kiddin'."

Henry walked toward Jason and Sara and extended his hand. They both took his hand in theirs.

"I wanted to say a proper thank you to you for finding the men who killed my Gladys."

"There's really no need. She was a wonderful person," said Sara. "And Frank here had a huge role in all of this coming together."

"That's not surprising. We go way back," said Henry. He took a seat by Frank and filled their plates.

It sounds like a mess hall of frat boys, thought Sara. *But it's nice.* She turned toward Jason and leaned in close, so he could hear her.

"You know, if you hadn't cared enough to check into something you knew wasn't right, hundreds of thousands of people, maybe millions would be dying all over the country. I'm really proud of you," said Sara.

Jason took her face in his hands and looked into her eyes. "Sara, I'm concerned about you visiting the hospitals. I know you'll be with an FBI guy and someone from S.W.A.T., but that didn't go so well last time. Why not let them take care of it," said Jason.

"Well, like Director Branowski said, I think he wants me to go because I'd have a softer approach then these guys." She glanced around the room at the guys gobbling down their ribs, stealing each others fries and knocking into each other. "And to be honest, I think he's right. There are gonna be a lot of scared people out there. I could let them know it's okay. And, if I can do that, I really want to."

"Okay! But why don't you request Cody to be the guy from S.W.A.T.. I know he's hurt, but I trust him and I think he'd feel good if you did. You know the only reason he got tied up is because Brett threatened to kill me unless he gave up his weapon."

"I knew," said Sara. "I'll ask him when he's finished eating."

Sara glanced to her left and noticed Frank and Henry talking. She turned and pressed her lips to Jason's ear.

"I think Frank and Henry need some cheering up."

Jason stood. "Attention! Attention everybody! Tonight is for Sara's Anna, Frank's Mom, Elizabeth, and Henry's sweetheart, Gladys. May they rest in peace."

Everyone stood.

"To Anna…here, here, to Gladys…here, here, to Elizabeth…here, here"

Sara noticed an emptiness in Frank's expression as they cheered on his Mom.

They all sat back down and continued their meal.

Jason had finished off a full rack of ribs when Branowski popped back into the lunchroom.

"Jason, a word?"

Jason grabbed an alcohol wipe and cleaned off his hands, then followed Branowski into the lab.

The S.W.A.T. guys finished up as well. After Jack, Murray and Klaser left the room, Sara approached Cody at the other end of the table and took a seat.

Cody scrunched his lips and looked down.

"Been meaning to talk to you, Sara. Really sorry to of put you in that situation. And…"

Sara placed her hand on his arm and shook it. "Hey! You were great. You saved Jason and I really appreciate that. And, I was wondering, if you're up to it, if you could be my guard. The CIA director said I'd have one S.W.A.T. member and an FBI agent with me, and there's nobody else I'd rather have protecting me, than you."

"Really?"

"Absolutely."

Cody nodded his head and stared at his food.

"Here comes, Commander Klaser. I'll let him know," said Sara.

"Cody, you up to working today?" asked Klaser.

Cody rubbed his sleeve over his eyes and attempted to stand.

"Actually, Commander," interrupted Sara. " I've asked Assistant Commander Cody if he would mind being my bodyguard when I bring the syringes to the hospital. I hope that's alright."

"Sara, if that works for you and the Assistant Commander, it works for me."

"I'm good!" said Cody.

"Okay, why don't you go sign-in for your detail and find out which of the FBI guy's is coming with you."

"On it!" said Cody. He wiped his hands on his pants and grabbed one crutch and hopped out of the room.

Klaser took Cody's chair and sat down.

"Sara, I haven't had the opportunity to apologize to you and Jason for what happened today. I'm really sorry. It's hard, when it's one of your own men. Not much else I can say. He's been with us for about six months now. I know it's a little scary, but I want you to know, he's the odd man out. It's never happened in my unit before. I feel bad that I trusted him."

"Commander, you don't have to apologize. It wasn't you and you had no way of knowing…" began Sara.

Jason rounded the corner and waited for Sara and Klaser to finish.

"Believe me," continued Sara. "Trust is a difficult thing. You want to and if there's no reason not to, you do."

She rolled her eyes and looked down. "I've had issues with trust myself."

Jason touched her hand. "We've all had our issues…with trust," added Jason. "You can only do the best you can and when you realize you put your trust in the wrong person, you fix it. Hell, that's why I'm here."

Klaser stood and extended a hand to Jason and left to join his men.

"Jason, Cody's gonna be with me, along with an FBI agent," said Sara.

"Good, I feel more at ease now."

"Mr. Jason, Commander Klaser said you requested me to be here. What is it you would like for me to do for you?" asked Frank.

"Are you kidding me, Frank, you're my strength. You've been amazing through this whole thing. I want you around me. You keep me motivated."

"But, I have done nothing, Mr. Jason."

"Nothing?" said Sara and Jason looking at each other in astonishment.

"You kept me sane," said Sara.

"You got me a small lab to work in, the same day I asked," said Jason. "And you let us stay at your condo, when you knew we were in danger."

"Not to mention," added Sara. "You and your wife stocked it with everything we'd need. You're an angel, Frank." She leaned over and hugged him hard.

"Thank you, Miss Sara."

"And," continued Jason, you contacted Steve, who's been an enormous help."

"Well, I'll be honest," said Steve. "When Frank called me, I really wasn't sure I wanted anything to do with this. But I gotta tell ya, for the first time in years, I feel like I'm doing something really important. And it never would have happened, if it weren't for you, Frank."

Frank took Jason and Steve's hands in his.

"You've all allowed me a way to keep my promise to my Mother," said Frank.

Director Branowski popped his head around the corner. "Jason, the FDA has approved your drug. Good work! You can start setting up anytime."

Sara looked at the food and then at Henry.

"Director Branowski," said Henry. "There's plenty of ribs with my special sauce, not to mention potatoes and fries here. Maybe you and your men would like some. They're really, really good."

"We've been smelling that great sauce down the hall for a while. I'm sure they'd love it. Thanks."

Jason and Director Branowski disappeared into the lab. Within five minutes, ten FBI agents entered the kitchen.

"Director Branowski said…" began the first Lieutenant.

"Help yourself," said Sara smiling.

The agents took over the picnic style table with the one square table at the end. Sara and Jason shook Henry's hand, and Frank walked Henry out.

***

The three new fillers were installed and working. Steve ran over the specs and Jason checked the drugs and set the machines for the right amount of milligrams and a buffer to be put in each capsule.

Steve flipped on the switch for the first filler, the second and the third, while Jason flipped the switch for the fourth and the fifth.

"Sara, we're gonna fill about one hundred syringes. Every time we get twenty five, you can take them to a hospital. Branowski said they're keeping tabs on any emergencies coming in. We'll go to the hospital with the most calls. Okay?" said Jason.

"Sure, I'm ready."

Sara watched Jason measuring and filling syringe after syringe. *I love his intensity and his desire to make a difference. I think that's what I love about him most,* she thought. Her mind started to drift and she remembered the first day she met Jason. *He was cute and I was scared. I hadn't had a lot of good relationships in the past and I figured why would this be any different. I guess looking at all that's happened, one might still wonder,* thought Sara. *But, the good has definitely outweighed the bad.*

"Sara, are you okay?" asked Jason.

"Yeah! Just day dreaming. Sorry! Are you ready with the first twenty-five?"

"Got 'em right here," said Jason. He dropped them in a canvas bag and handed them to her.

"Wow! I didn't know syringes came in a light lavender?" said Sara.

"It's their old stock. Steve asked that we use those first," said Jason.

"Let's go, Sara. Agent Carmichael'll be riding with us," said Cody.

Agent Carmichael walked up behind Sara.

"You can call me Carmichael."

"Oh! Well that's much less formal," smiled Sara, glancing at Cody.

"Sara, wait a second," said Jason. "See how many people are in Frank's family that have taken the H1N1 vaccine. We need to give him a capsule for each, Okay? And, Steve and Henry's family too. But, we have to keep track of each capsule, so if you can list the names of the individuals getting one and mark them off, that'd be great. Oh! and also, could you get a count on how many people here tonight have family members that need the capsules too? "

"No problem!" Sara turned toward Cody and Carmichael. "Cody, Carmichael, can you handle this with your teams?"

"Be right back," said Cody.

Agent Carmichael got out a pad and paper to make a list, starting with CIA Director Branowski. Meanwhile, Sara found Frank and Steve and got the information needed. Carmichael was back within ten minutes. Cody was back in eight.

"Cody?" asked Sara. "How many?"

Cody handed her a list. "For both squads, we'd need eighteen, if we're including immediate family."

"We've got twenty six," said Agent Carmichael, handing her the list.

"Jason, Frank is gonna need three. No one in Steve's family got the flu shot. Oh! and I checked with Henry and he didn't either. Here's the list for Klaser's team and Branowski's."

"Great!" said Jason, as he scooped out forty seven capsules.

Sara put them in separate baggies and handed them out.

"Here you go, Sara," said Jason. She turned, but Jason turned her back toward him. "Here." He took a capsule and gently parted her lips. "You need one too, just to be on the safe side. Add your name to the list, okay!"

Sara smiled and kissed him gently, took a gulp of water and swallowed the capsule as she wrote her name on the list.

Director Branowski walked his men over to Jason, and Klaser did the same.

"Jason, can you give a quick explanation on why they need to take these capsules. These guys only know they're here to protect," said Branowski.

Jason stepped forward. "I've got a lot to keep up with over here, but Sara knows exactly what's going on and she can fill you in…Sara."

Sara turned to face everyone. "I'll make it simple. If you've taken the H1N1 vaccine, it will ultimately kill you. Jason developed the time release that was supposed to be in the vaccine, but a terrorist by the name of Jihad used Jason's research to manufacture a different time release with a bacteria in it. The vaccine that's out there now, is phase III, the worst."

Commander Klaser stepped in.

"That's why you need to take the pill you've just been given. It'll kill the bacteria and stop the heart arrhythmia. Apparently, Phase I was all about covering their tracks, Phase III is just lethal."

Jason finished another twenty-five syringes and walked over to Klaser.

"If Jason hadn't thought fast on his feet, we'd be running in circles, not knowing why people are dying," said Klaser. "That's why these guys added different time releases to the mix. Kinda like a phone line or internet connection…the more twists and turns it takes, the harder it is to figure out where the call is actually coming from."

Klaser glanced at Jason and Sara. "Because of Jason and Sara's questions and research, Jihad was captured, but not before he sent a huge shipment of the lethal H1N1 to hospitals all around the U.S. That shipment was Phase III. We've estimated about ten thousand people received that. These guys know what they're doing, but so do we. We have the list of people who've gotten it. And we've sent emails to every institution that gave out the vaccine and they'll be setting up clinics tomorrow to hand out the capsules."

Klaser placed a hand on Jason's shoulder. "Some of you know Jason went into cardiac arrest himself and got a shot and made a full recovery. A shot isn't necessary unless a heart attack has started. So, men, I suggest you take your capsule." Branowski grabbed a bottled water, flipped off the cap, popped the capsule in his mouth and took a swig. His men followed.

Sara underlined two names on the list and pointed them out to Branowski. "They both need a shot," said Sara.

"Agent Camden, Agent Serenson" called out Branowski. "Where's Agents Camden and Serenson?"

Camden went to the bathroom…said he was feeling nauseated," said Agent Carmichael.

"Jason, that's one of the symptoms," yelled Sara. Sara took off for the men's room with Jason and Branowski right behind her. Sara stopped short of the door and Jason pushed through it. Agent Camden was on the floor in the corner clutching his chest.

"My arm. I've got pain in my arm," said Camden. Jason dipped into the bag of syringes and stuck one into Camden's arm.

"Agent Camden, let me know if the pain subsides," said Jason.

Branowski stooped behind Jason and Sara knelt down and put his head on her lap.

All of Branowski's agents stood inside the door watching.

Branowski looked up at them. "This is what we're trying to stop. Has anybody seen Serenson?"

Cody made his way to the other end of the bathroom. "Serenson's over here sir. He's dead."

CHAPTER 18

Branowski looked at his men. “We have to stop this now,” he said. Has anyone in any of your families had the H1N1 shot Friday or after?”

Staring at his men, Branowski’s eyes dropped and he grabbed his cell phone. “Oh my God! My wife. I think she said she was going Friday.” His hands were shaking as he attempted to dial her number.

Sara reached for his phone. “What’s the number, sir?” asked Sara.

“312-231-4871,” said Branowski.

Sara dialed and waited. “Is this Mrs.Branowski. Please hold for your husband.” She promptly handed the phone to him.

“When did you get your flu shot?” asked Branowski. “I know you were busy all week…I need to know now.” His voice raised. “When did you get it? You got it Thursday? No! God, I’m thrilled. I love you. Gotta go. I’ll talk to you later.”

"Camden, how are you feeling?" asked Jason.

"The nausea is going away." He lifted his arm and clenched and unclenched his fist. "My arm isn't hurting any more. Wow! It just came outta nowhere."

"When did you get your flu shot?" asked Branowski.

"I got it Friday morning sir, why?"

"At least it took a few days. We gotta get out there and give these people their shots and their capsules."

"We're ready to go," said Sara.

"What about our families?" asked Agent Carmichael. "I'd like them to get the capsule as soon as possible. I thought maybe Frank could deliver them to our homes."

"Mr. Branowski, sir. I would be honored to deliver them personally to each of your homes." said Frank.

"Jason, you okay with that?" asked Branowski.

"Absolutely!"

"Okay! Steve, ya know where there's a copier around here? We need to give a copy of this list to Frank," said Branowski.

"Down the hall and to the left," said Steve.

Carmichael grabbed the list and headed down the hall.

Back in less than thirty seconds, Carmichael handed it to Frank and flipped open his cell phone.

"Honey, a guy named Frank will be coming over. He's gonna give you, your Mom and the kids a capsule to take. Take it right away." He paused listening. "No, it's fine. I'll explain everything later. Take the capsule. You'll hear a news bulletin on the TV within an hour. Okay! honey. I'll talk to you later. Love ya!"

Branowski approached Frank.

"Frank, stop at your house first, then continue with the list," said Branowski.

"Are you sure, sir..."

"Stop at your house first," re-iterated Branowski.

Frank smiled, nodded his head and left.

Branowski and Klaser cut Sara, Cody and Carmichael off at the door.

"Listen, be careful out there. Don't forget, there's still one operative lurking around somewhere. He or she may be unaware of Jihad's capture," said Klaser.

"Carmichael, I want you on at every second, got it?" said Branowski. "Assistant Commander Cody's already been hurt. It's your responsibility to get those syringes there and keep everybody safe."

"Yes, sir."

"We'll be fine," said Sara.

Cody leaned his crutch up against the wall.

"What are you doing?" asked Klaser.

"J.T. gave me a shot. I have no pain in my leg at all right now. And I don't want anyone getting the idea that I can't handle things," said Cody.

Commander Klaser was going to question that decision, thought Sara. *But, you could see it in Cody's eyes that he meant business.*

Klaser took a call and held up his index finger. Moments later he clicked off the phone.

"Okay! It's started. An elderly woman was brought in to St. Cecelia hospital three minutes ago with chest pains. She got a flu shot on Friday. You need to get there fast."

"Ma'am, you follow Assistant Commander Cody and I'll be behind you," said Carmichael.

"That's fine, but..." began Sara.

"Call her Sara," said Cody, turning his head toward her.

"Ye-e-e-s please!" said Sara.

"No problem, Sara it is," said Carmichael.

"And the guys call me Code," said Cody.

Cody held his weapon at ready. *I can barely tell he's favoring his good leg,* thought Sara. They walked Sara out to a bullet proof car, supplied by the CIA.

"I'll drive," said Carmichael. He took the two bags of syringes from Sara and put them on the seat in the front. "Sara, you and Code will sit in the back.

"Okay," said Sara and she climbed in after Cody.

"I heard you were supposed to keep that leg up for a while," said Carmichael, as he pulled away from the curb.

"I'm good," said Cody.

Sara immediately wrapped both hands around his foot and carefully lifted it up and rested it on her lap. "Lean against the door, so it can be completely stretched out," she said.

His eyes opened wide, Cody grabbed the headrest in front of him and settled himself in the corner.

"I know you're not used to being helped, but that's what I do," said Sara.

Cody smiled and relaxed his leg.

Sara's smile grew as she leaned back in the seat.

Up front, Carmichael flipped on the red flashing light and siren. Taxis honked and then pulled to the side - the sounds of the siren drowned out their cursing. At a sharp left turn, the bags slid off on to the floor and under the seat.

"Geez, almost knocked Sara off the seat," said Cody.

"Sorry! Light was changing and sometimes people don't stop." said Carmichael. "Okay kids, we're here." He reached under the seat and retrieved one of the canvas bags.

Cody was up and out before Carmichael put the car in park. He held the door for Sara and then directed her behind him. Carmichael followed close behind, watching rooftops and windows. They entered the hospital and were greeted by the Chief Resident. Agent Carmichael stepped up and extended his hand.

"I'm Agent Carmichael and we've brought some good news."

"Glad to hear it. I'm Dr. Socol. Got a call from Commander Klaser. Said you'd be stopping by. Twenty-five syringes, right?"

"Yes sir," said Agent Carmichael.

Sara stepped between them. "And, to put her mind at ease, I'd be happy to talk to the woman that came in," said Sara.

"Appreciate it, but it's not necessary. We've got it from here. He took the bag and walked down the hall.

Sara pushed a small dimple out of her right cheek. *I guess they really didn't need me to make a difference afterall,* she thought.

"Sara, he's bein' a jerk. If someone comes in at the next hospital, you can talk to em,' said Cody. "I'll make sure of it."

They returned to the car, and headed for the next hospital. It took about seven minutes to get to Rush, where they dropped off the other twenty-five syringes, then they headed back to the lab.

Sara sat quietly as Carmichael pulled away from the curb, when Cody got a call from Klaser.

"No way! You're kiddin'. That sucks! Okay, will do," said Cody.

"What happened? What's goin' on?" said Sara.

"Carmichael, go around the block," said Cody.

"Huh!"

"Director Branowski got a call from Doctor Socol at St. Cecelia … that first woman died. Sorry, Sara. She got the shot and she died anyway. Looks like this stuff doesn't work on everybody," said Cody.

"No, no, something's wrong. I have a bad feeling about this. We need to go back. I need to see that woman," said Sara.

"Sara, she's dead," said Carmichael. He got an incoming call and clicked his earpiece, He nodded his head again and again. "Yes, sir. Will do."

Sara turned toward Cody. "I know it sounds crazy, but I need to see her. Please?" asked Sara.

Carmichael clicked off the earpiece. "Looks like the doc gave her the shot himself. Said she didn't respond at all. Nothing we can do. I guess the whole deal's getting put on hold, but we do have to pick up the batch of syringes we dropped off. "

"Hey! We gotta go back anyway," said Cody. "I'll get ya in to see her." He glanced at Sara. "It saved Camden. Maybe Jason needs a little more time to work on it," said Cody.

"They don't have more time," said Sara softly.

"I'll wait out here and watch for any unusual activity, plus I'll keep an ear to the radio, in case any other hospital calls," said Carmichael.

Cody held the door open for Sara and walked by her side.

I can't even tell he's been hurt anymore, thought Sara.

They made their way to the reception.

"Excuse me! Can you tell me where the woman is that came in with chest pains?" asked Sara.

Cody flashed his S.W.A.T. badge and the receptionist walked them to the curtained off room.

"I'm sorry, but she passed away," said the nurse.

"Did she get the shot?" asked Sara.

"Yes, I saw the doctor give it to her myself. I'm sorry!"

Sara turned toward Cody. "I left the list in the car. I'm gonna check to make sure this woman was on the list. Maybe she actually had a natural heart attack." She turned to go when Cody grasped her arm.

"Sara, you stay here. I'll go get the list."

"Okay! she said. Sara glanced at the woman lying there and immediately thought of Anna. *About the same age…another life taken for no reason. Why didn't the drug work?* she thought. She began to smell the antiseptic again, the death that lingered in the air. She noticed the cold stainless steel and white walls that surrounded her.

"Do you need anything else," asked the nurse.

Sara glanced back at her.

"I'm sorry, kinda got lost for a minute. Reminded me of a friend. What's your name?" asked Sara.

"People call me Jen," she answered.

"I'm Sara." She paused. "Jen, can I ask you a favor?"

"Sure, what is it?"

"Can I see the syringe? I'm sure the doctor gave it all to her, but I have to make sure it's empty. So many people have worked so hard on this and I have to know if the whole syringe was used."

"Sure, I put it in the box myself." She opened a metal box on the wall and there was only one syringe in it. She held it up for Sara.

Jen's face contorted, her eyes pulling to the right. "Sorry! It's totally empty."

"Thanks Jen. I appreciate it. Can I take it with me?"

"Sure, I'll put it in a plastic sleeve, so you don't get stuck."

Sara watched as Jen slid the syringe into a heavy plastic sleeve, holding it out in front of her. Sara noticed the light burgundy in Jen's scrubs, show through the bottom half of the syringe as it dropped in. Sara's eyes opened wide.

"Oh my God! Jen. Can you hold that away from you please?" asked Sara.

Jen's eyes opened wide. "O-o-okay! How's that?" asked Jen, holding it out to her right.

"That's perfect, absolutely perfect." Sara could see Jen was even more puzzled.

"Jen, this is really important. You said that the doctor gave her the shot. Was it Dr. Socol?"

"Yes, why?"

"Did you see where he got the syringe?"

"A white canvas bag. That big FBI guy handed it to him," said Jen.

"Did the FBI guy hand him the bag or the specific syringe?"

"He reached in the bag and found one. I don't understand any of this. Making me a little nervous," said Jen.

Sara put her hands on Jen's arms. "I'm sorry. I promise I'll explain everything, but right now I've gotta make a call. Thanks so much. You really helped. Oh! Can you get me the canvas bag with the rest of the syringes?"

"Sure!" said Jen.

"Oh! and Jen. Please don't say anything to anyone else for now. Okay!"

"Okay?"

Sara flipped open her phone as Cody returned. She put her index finger up in front of her.

"Jason. No, no, wait…It does work. I'm still at the hospital…Listen to me. The doctor didn't give her your shot…no, I'm not protecting you…I asked the nurse to show me the syringe, just to make sure it was all used. But it wasn't our syringe. This syringe is white. Remember, you gave me the old stock, a light lavender…Yes, I'm positive. I don't know…yes, Cody's right here."

Sara handed the phone to Cody.

"Yeah! I just heard myself. Don't worry. Nothin's gonna happen to her on my watch." He clicked off the phone and handed it back to Sara.

"So, let me get this straight. They didn't use one of the syringes we brought for this woman?"

"That's right."

"Sara, can I see the syringe?" asked Cody.

Sara removed the syringe from the sleeve and handed it to Cody. "And you're sure this wasn't like the others?"

"Positive," said Sara.

Light footsteps quickened around the corner. It was Jen. "Here's the canvas bag. Good luck with whatever you're trying to figure out," said Jen, exiting quickly.

Cody opened the bag and took out a handful of syringes, laying them on the counter. He put the white one in with them.

"You're right. Definitely not from this batch. But who knew that Jason was gonna use these purple ones?"

"Nobody but Steve and I," said Sara.

"Alright, so for now, let's say it's not Steve. If that's the case, there would have to be something on this syringe that would tell the doctor to use it. Cuz, if it was in with a bunch of white ones, he'd have to have a way to recognize it."

Cody ran his fingers and thumb all around the syringe and stopped his thumb on the plunger.

"Here, Sara, this is it. There's a very tiny piece of medical tape on the bottom. Feel it?"

Sara ran her thumb underneath and looked up at Cody. Then she picked up a lavender syringe and rubbed her thumb underneath that plunger.

Her face lit up. "That's it. That's how he knew which one to use without being obvious. Jen said Dr. Socol put his hand in the bag and found one, like he was looking for a specific one." said Sara.

Sara poured the rest of them out on the counter. "One, two, three, four…twenty-two, twenty-three. There's one missing," said Sara.

"Don't you mean two. There were twenty-five to begin with," said Cody.

"No, remember Jason took one for Agent Camden, so there were only twenty four to start. "

"So," began Cody. "The good doc must've lifted one, giving the impression he used it."

"If we search him and find the syringe, we can prove it was him," said Sara.

"Okay! Settle down. You're not searching anyone. You come up with the ideas, but I'll do the follow through."

"Alright, alright," said Sara. "So, it's Doctor Socol right?"

"It would appear to be," said Cody.

"We should get Carmichael," said Sara.

"Actually, when I went out to the car, he wasn't there. I figured he was taking a…" he glanced at Sara. "Using the bathroom. Sara, I need you to stay somewhere safe, while I figure out what's going on."

"Me, too. That's why I'm staying with you."

"No, it's too dangerous…" began Cody.

"Oh! And being here with a crazy doctor and who knows who else, isn't?" She shook her head. "I'm staying with you."

Cody rolled his eyes and bit his lower lip. "Alright, but if I yell for you to get down, I want you on that floor in a second flat, got it?"

"Got it," said Sara.

Cody clicked on his headset. "Gotta call Klaser. This is Assistant Commander Cody. We've got a situation here. The doc's definitely in on this...yeah! He marked the syringe, so he knew which one to give the woman.

Somebody didn't want this stuff getting out to the public. We might still have a couple players. Yes sir!...Stubborn sir…no sir…yes sir!" Cody turned away from Sara, but she could still hear him. "What do we know about Carmichael? Yeah! that'd be good. Roger that." Cody clicked off his headset.

"What did he say? What are we supposed to do?"

"You're gonna do exactly what I tell you to do." Cody dipped his head, eyes, razor sharp. "I'm serious."

Sara looked him in the eye. "Were you referring to me, when you said stubborn?"

"Yes, Sara, I was," smiled Cody.

Sara smiled too. "I know I can be."

"Alright, Klaser has men on his way and we need to wait," said Cody.

Cody stood behind the curtain, watching the hallway, when Jen returned.

"Excuse me! Are you Assistant Commander Cody?" she asked.

"Yes ma'am. Can I help you?"

"An Agent Car-something asked if I could give you a message."

"Okay!"

"He said that Doc's a player and he's in the side alley. I don't know what that means," said Jen.

"Do you know the best way to get there?" asked Cody.

"Yeah! I'd go all the way down this corridor to the cafeteria. Cut through there and take a left to the first set of doors. It's where they take the trash out," said Jen. "Some people smoke out there."

"Thanks."

Cody turned toward Sara. "Listen!..." he took one look at Sara's face and hesitated. "Just stay behind me," he said.

Cody took off down the hall with Sara on his heels. Pushing past carts and interns, they made it to the cafeteria where the dinner crowd was long gone. Cody pulled out his gun and cocked it. Sara slowed to an arm's-length behind him as they crept toward the door to the alleyway.

Knees bent, eyes focused, Cody slowly pushed the door out toward the alley. Sara remained behind him at the door. She watched as Cody surveyed the alley. To his left sat one dumpster about fifty feet away. A lone light shined above it. Holding his hand out behind him, he motioned for Sara to stay put, then he slipped around the right side of the door. Sara waited impatiently for Cody to return. She heard something and saw a paper fluttering beneath the dumpster. Cody had heard it too, and walked slowly toward it, passing the crack in the door that Sara peered through.

WHAM!!! Sara pushed forward, a black clad arm around her throat and a gun to her head. Cody turned, gun aimed and rock steady. Sara gulped, nerves on overdrive. *Not again*, she thought.

"Carmichael," said Cody. "Shoulda known."

Carmichael backed Sara over to the fence opposite the building.

"Just couldn't leave it alone," Carmichael growled in her ear. Heat poured down her ear canal. "Now your buddy here's gotta die…and he didn't really have to."

Sara scrambled to get free, but Carmichael tightened his grip. *Oh! God! Oh! God! This can't be happening,* she thought.

She watched Cody as he moved in a half circle, keeping in front of Carmichael with his gun aimed and ready. She watched his eyes as he assessed the situation.

"So how's this gonna play out. You shoot me, you shoot Sara, then what?" asked Cody.

"First off, you're gonna drop the gun and kick it over here. Cuz if you don't she dies first. And don't try anything funny."

"If she dies, you're next big boy," said Cody.

"So, is that the way you're gonna play it. Lose the hostage, then kill the perp," said Carmichael. "See, at the FBI, we actually try to save the hostage. But then again, you guys always were a little backwards."

Cody held his position, eyeing Sara and Carmichael.

"You're not gonna win this time. Your buddy, Brett, wasn't up to killing you. But I am. Even if you do hit me, my fingers already squeezed on this trigger and she'll be gone too." He pushed the gun further into Sara's neck, her head tilted to the right.

Sara saw a white lab coat emerge from the open door.

"Say a word and I'll blow your head off," whispered Carmichael.

Sara looked at Cody and then moved her eyes past him, hoping he'd notice.

"Haven't you taken care of these two yet?" asked Dr. Socol. His gun was at the back of Cody's head. "Or do I have to do it myself?"

"He is S.W.A.T. sir," said Carmichael "Another weapon trained on him is always helpful."

"Drop the gun now, son, or she's as good as dead," said Socol.

Cody breathed out and dropped the gun.

"Kick it over here," said Carmichael. "And get down on your knees."

Cody kicked it toward him and knelt down.

"So, now that it's two against one. How's this gonna work?" asked Cody.

Dr. Socol threw a knee into Cody's back. Cody's head went back and Socol kicked him in the side.

"Don't. Please don't hurt him. If he weren't protecting me, you'd be dead," yelled Sara.

"You were afraid of this pansy," said Socol, looking up at Carmichael.

"Not exactly, Doc."

In split second timing, Carmichael extended his arm and pulled the trigger. The shot rang in Sara's ears and a dot of blood appeared on Dr. Socol's forehead. His eyes turned in and his body flew backwards, while his gun slid by Sara's feet. Sara screamed and looked away. Once she realized where the gun was, she took a swipe at kicking it back toward Cody, but missed.

"Feisty one aren't ya?" said Carmichael.

"Why did you kill him? Wasn't he working with you?" said Cody.

"Not the way I'm gonna tell it. See, I came in and the Doc there was holdin' Sara, kinda like this." He tightened his hold around her neck. "And you, well you were right where you are, on your knees. When I came in, he got scared and killed Sara. Then he turned and shot you, and I got him right between the eyes. Of course, I feel awful that Sara and one of our finest S.W.A.T. members had to die. But, it's the price you pay to save others," he laughed.

"So, what are you waiting for?" said Sara.

"A buddy of mine. Actually, he's a buddy of yours too. Can't wait to see your face. I love surprises, don't you?"

"Sara," said a low husky voice from behind the dumpster.

"Wait for it, wait for it," said Carmichael.

I don't know that voice" said Sara. "Who is it?"

Sara looked to the right and out from the shadows came a man, a man Sara didn't think she knew. Shoulders back, head held high. His walk held a confidence and a sophisticated demeanor. As he moved beneath the light, Sara saw his face. There was a depth to his eyes that scared her. A swagger that defied fear.

"Frank?"

CHAPTER 19

Sara called his name, but still she wasn't sure it was him. He was different.

Cody turned his head to the left to see for himself.

"Thanks for showing up, buddy," said Carmichael. He squeezed Sara's face and turned it toward him. I couldn't pass up that look."

Sara's mouth hung open. *Not Frank, not our Frank. How could it be?* she thought.

"You helped us through all of it. How can this be?"

"I helped you with what I wanted to help you with," smiled Frank. "No more, no less. You were such an easy mark."

Frank walked past Cody, toward Sara. He was rugged and suave. Not at all like the Frank she knew, the Frank, Jason and she knew.

He placed his hand on her cheek. "You're a typical blond," he said, giving her a gentle slap. "I'd kinda like to get a little first. Maybe just a kiss," he said pushing up against her.

"Well make it fast Frank, cuz they're on the way," said Carmichael.

Frank grabbed her face in both hands and dipped her down and out to the right. Before Sara knew what happened, Frank had kicked the gun back to Cody. Cody snatched the gun, rolled to the right, aimed and pulled the trigger. Carmichael's gun fell to the ground and his body was not far behind. A large red dot appeared in the middle of his white shirt. Oozing from the center out, one fiber at a time, it spread like a weed, branching across his chest. The blood was quickly absorbed by the cotton fibers and the excess blood pooled on the ground around him. His grin faded and his eyes rolled back in his head.

"Sorry, Sara," said Frank, as he brought her back up.

Sara shook in his arms as she stared at Carmichael's lifeless body.

"I don't understand, you don't even look like you…and, and you don't sound like you either."

Cody was on his feet with an arm wrapped around her waist to keep her from falling.

"Frank works for the government as a secret operative. Even the CIA and the FBI didn't know about it. He's way under cover. I only found out about him today, Sara. He couldn't chance telling anyone else for fear someone would be listening." said Cody. "They've been following intel about this drug for a while."

"Boy, was I glad to see you." He patted Frank on the back.

Sara's jaw still hung loose as she stared at Frank.

"It's true," said Frank. Problem is, we didn't know who was running it. For a while, we thought it was Jason. Still weren't sure, when he showed up here. We had to keep an eye on him."

Sara turned her head toward Cody. "So, Cody, are you really a S.W.A.T. guy, or is that a cover?"

"No, I really am, Sara."

She turned toward Frank. "Is there anyone else who isn't who they say they are?"

"That, I couldn't tell you," said Frank. "Partially, because I don't know and partially because it's confidential. But as for Carmichael, the first time I met him was about twenty minutes ago. I'd set myself up as a contractor, but I didn't know who my contact was. He knew who I was, so I couldn't take the chance of saying anything to anyone. It could've been anybody. I mean, we'd been talking on the phone, but he disguised his voice and I never saw him in person. But I knew Cody was one of the good guys."

Frank hugged Sara. "I'm really sorry about all this, Sara. You and Jason are good people and if it weren't for the two of you, we couldn't have gotten done, what we did."

"What about Carlo? Did you kill him?"

"No, Sara. I'm guessing Carmichael was tracking him all along. It was a clean hit by a professional. And he obviously didn't let Carlo talk at all, cuz Carlo was onto me the last time we were at the warehouse," said Frank.

"What do ya mean?"

"When I found the documents in the car."

"Yeah! He did seem surprised. But why? They were in the car, right?" asked Sara. "What's the big deal?"

"Yeah! They were in the car, but they were in a secret panel underneath the chassis, adjacent to the gas tank. He didn't expect me to find 'em. When I came back with 'em, I was taking a chance he'd figure me out."

"Then why did you?"

"To prove that Jason and you were innocent."

He leaned forward and whispered in her ear. "I was never here, Sara. Just you and Cody, to protect my cover…okay?" He kissed her on the cheek.

Cody pressed the button on his belt. "Assistant Commander Cody here. We're in the alley outside the cafeteria at the west end of the hospital. It's all clear. Doc and Carmichael are down."

Within minutes, heavy feet came thundering down the hall and burst through the alley door, guns and rifles prepared. S.W.A.T. and FBI with the Chicago Police Department not far behind.

"Cody, got your message. So everything's good?" asked Klaser.

"Yes sir." Cody looked around and Frank was already gone.

"Assistant Commander Cody took care of everything," said Sara. She stared directly into Cody's eyes and nodded her head.

"Good work, Cody," said Klaser.

"Uh! Yeah, yes sir. Just doin' my job."

"Sara, Sara, Sara, where are you?" cried Jason, as he came running down the hall toward the open door.

Sara raised up on her toes, kissed Cody on the cheek and ran through the door into Jason's arms.

"My God!" said Jason. "I'm so glad you're okay! He pulled her in tight to him, holding her head to his chest.

"When I heard something was going on, I was afraid…afraid that…"

Sara pulled away and pressed her index finger to his lips. "Jason, I'm fine. You were right to want Cody to protect me. He did. He saved my life."

Paramedics, S.W.A.T members and FBI agents swarmed the room as Jason held Sara in his arms.

Klaser and Branowski walked toward the two of them.

"Just got intel that Larz dropped a note to the Chicago Lake News through a friend after we took him in. It gives detailed information about all of this," said Klaser. "Of course, it's not the true version…and I'm sure they'll find info that it was your research that started this. And if it gets out tomorrow morning, we're gonna have riots all over the place," said Branowski.

"We also found out that the editor-in-chief over there, received the H1N1 vaccine yesterday morning, the third phase. We need to get a shot over to him and stop that paper from going out."

"Can we go with?" asked Jason.

"He's a hard-nosed newspaper man. And we definitely want him to know we have the truth on our side. Having the two of you there to explain it in detail…well, that might make the difference," said Branowski.

"Are all the bad guys caught now?" asked Sara

"Yes!" said Branowski.

"Then I say 'yes', let's go."

"Commander Klaser will be with you. Since you have a good history, Cody, I'd like you to go too." said Branowski.

Sara backed into Jason as the paramedics wheeled the two dead bodies past them.

She leaned into Jason's ear. "I'll be glad when my excitement consists of watching my national commercial aired. I used to think my life was boring, but now I'm thinkin' I've been pretty darn lucky."

***

It was 11:02pm when a black sedan pulled alongside the thirty-six story, 462 foot majestic Chicago Lake News Building. Sara remembered the first time she'd walked around this building. The neo-Gothic architecture was astounding, boasting stones from all over the world, with plaques indicating where they were from: The World Trade Center, The Parthenon, Pearl Harbor, The Alamo, and The Cathedral of Notre Dame. The list went on and on.

It seemed only fitting that this is where we'd stop the chaos, thought Sara. *And make a difference*. The night was still and the air was calm as Jason and Sara stepped out of the car. Sara glanced in front of her and saw a long light cascading onto the street. Her eyes followed the light up to a line of 4th floor windows. *That's where it's going to end,* thought Sara. *Finally, we'll stop the madness that killed Anna and the others.*

Sara and Jason followed Branowski and Cody as they made their way through the shadows into the building foyer and entered the elevator. Jason held Sara's hand as the doors opened on the 4th floor.

A man with brown hair, oval-rimmed glasses, worn jeans and a button down shirt stopped as Cody entered the room. He quickly exited and returned with a shorter, bald disheveled-looking man.

"I'm Clyde, the Editor-in-Chief," said the bald man in a low raspy voice. "How can I help you?"

"We're here to talk to you about a story you received about widespread heart attacks," said Klaser.

"It's too late," said Clyde. "We just released this headline." He handed the front page to Klaser. *Massive heart attacks plague the Nation...Who's Next?*

The lead-in read: *In Chicago alone, dozens of healthy people have already died of massive heart attacks. Several others are hospitalized. The culprit is still living with us...what is the government not telling us?*

Sara glanced around the room. The women stopped working at their desks and a few of the men stood and leaned on their cubicles watching, expectant.

"Look, I know you think you've got a great story here, but we've got a better one for you and it's an exclusive and it's the truth," said Klaser.

"This is Tom, my assistant," said Clyde. He then took the clipboard and pen from Tom and pressed the pen firmly on the paper. "Send the copy to print, Tom," he said. He initialed it. As he turned to walk away, Clyde clutched his chest and fell to the ground.

Cody rested his hand on Tom's shoulder and held him there. Klaser kneeled next to Clyde and wrapped a rubber band around the Editor's upper arm. Pulling a syringe from his pocket, Jason inserted it into the largest vein he could find.

A woman at the back of the room stood and picked up the phone.

"I'm-I'm calling 9-1-1," she shrieked.

Two men emerged from their cubicles and rushed toward Clyde. Cody raised his rifle and stepped in front of them.

"What have you done to him?" cried another woman.

Sara stepped up onto a chair. "Everybody just stop, it's okay. They're saving him. The story you were given is only a half-truth. We're here to tell you the whole truth, if you'll listen."

"I've already called '911'" said the woman at the back.

"That's good, that's good," said Sara.

"What happened to him?" demanded Tom.

"He's having a heart attack. But.." Sara raised her index finger. "The shot he was just given is gonna save his life. And we already called the paramedics too. They're on their way up."

Sara then walked to the center of the room and sat on the corner of a desk while Jason and Klaser stayed with Clyde.

"He'll be fine," said Sara. "Take a seat, please…let me explain."

"How come he's not moving?" yelled one of the men who ran forward.

"He will," said Sara. "He will."

"I'm not moving until he does," said Tom. Everyone in the office froze. One woman finally fell to her knees and began to pray.

"Come on Clyde. You can do it. Come on back," said Jason, waiting for some sign.

The pinky on Clyde's left hand moved, then his index finger.

"His fingers moved," yelled Tom.

Jason raised Clyde's head and Klaser took his pulse.

"He's okay!" shouted Jason. "He's okay!"

Clyde opened his eyes slowly, creasing his forehead. Jason and Klaser lifted him to a chair.

"What the hell just happened?" said Clyde.

"You had a heart attack," said Tom. "Before they ever touched you."

"Ding." The elevator door opened and the police and paramedics entered.

J.T. and Joe wheeled the gurney over and helped Clyde onto it.

"I'm not going anywhere 'til I get an explanation. Did I have a heart attack…like the people in the story?"

"Yeah, ya' did," said Jason.

"So what happened? Why did the pain stop?"

"They gave you a shot," said Tom.

"Jason and Sara will explain everything," said Klaser. "Then you can send out your paper."

"Better be good- and the truth," said Clyde. "Because heart attack or no heart attack we're not gonna stop it, unless it is."

Cody wheeled the gurney over to where Sara sat. Jason followed. Tom, the Assistant Editor took notes while Jason and Sara explained the entire story from start to finish.

"So that's the whole thing," said Jason. "It started as something to help people and went horribly wrong. And I'm sorry for that. But, as you saw with your boss, we did find a way to counteract it. So, please don't put out a story that'll scare everybody into thinking they're dying and that the medical facilities and the government are doing it to them."

"If you do," interrupted Sara. "There'll be people who need medical attention that'll be afraid to come in and others that'll be coming in for indigestion. Let the government officials dealing with the hospitals, help these people." She looked at Clyde. "Just like we helped you."

"So what do you propose?" asked Clyde.

Commander Klaser stepped in. "The story needs to go out, but now it has a positive ending and that needs to be the most important point of the story."

"Hey, listen," said Clyde. "You told us the story, but we decide what goes to print and what doesn't."

"Okay, the main thing is, we don't wanna cause a panic. If that happens, a lot more people'll get hurt. Do they need to know about the terrorist who was trying to kill them? Yes! But they need to know he was caught and it was through a great deal of bravery that it happened. They also need to know about the H1N1 vaccine and the days it was received that are in question. It's important they come in, but they need to do so in an orderly way. If there's anything that you don't agree with, let me know and I can do my best to work with you on the facts. My men will contact the news stations tomorrow morning, after your paper comes out. That gives us time to contact and inoculate the individuals who are in the most danger. It also gives you a scoop."

Klaser looked Clyde straight in the eyes. "So, can you help us out?"

"Give me that clipboard," said Clyde. "And the sample front page."

Cody took the clipboard and page from Tom and handed it to Clyde.

Clyde crossed out the headline on the clipboard and wrote:

True bravery against a known terrorist saved our city from a medically induced death. Are you at risk? Here's what you need to know...

Clyde signed off on it and handed the clipboard back to Cody, who handed it to Tom. Clyde then turned toward Jason.

"Here, you might want to keep this. It'll remind you of what could have happened. You know Jason, knowledge is a wonderful thing, but it's a scary thing too. Look what I was about to print. But because of you, I didn't. I think we've all learned a lot from this."

"You're absolutely right sir," said Jason as he accepted the sample first page.

"Tom, did you get all that info down from Jason and Sara's explanation?"

"Sure did."

"Good. Put it into a coherent story and run it by Commander Klaser and get it out yesterday. Got it?" said Clyde.

"I'll have it ready in ten minutes," said Tom.

"Alright then, I'll be back as soon as I've been checked out at the hospital."

CHAPTER 20

In black silk pajamas, Jason walked over to the DVD/VCR player, inserted the DVD and walked back to bed, where Sara, wearing one of his lumberjack shirts, waited for him.

"I can't believe it's only been a month since I first met you," said Jason, sliding between the sheets and pulling Sara toward him. "So, where is that lingerie you said you were gonna wear?" said Jason. "You look amazing in it."

"Underneath," she said coyly.

She turned and took his face in her hands and kissed him passionately and Jason reciprocated, placing his hands on her hips and pulling her closer.

"Wait, wait, wait. I thought we were gonna watch the medal ceremony?" said Sara. "I was so nervous when it happened, I don't even remember what they said."

"You? What about me. I kept wiping my hands on my pants, I was perspiring so much." Jason rolled his eyes playfully. "Okay! I'll turn it on. But, if it gets boring, I'm getting' busy and that shirt's comin' off," he smiled.

"Agreed!" said Sara.

Jason clicked on the television, then the DVD and hit play. The National Anthem began and Sara removed Jason's hands from her hips and placed them over his heart with hers and smiled.

As soon as the song was finished, Jason's hands resumed their original positions and Sara snuggled close.

Sara snatched the remote and hit pause.

"Jason, why wasn't Frank given some kind of an award? He did so much. And, he wasn't even at the Award Ceremony."

"Well, Klaser said that he didn't want a medal. He was happy that things turned out like they did. But Klaser got word out to the government and they decided to send him and his family back to Africa to help build a small medical facility in his home town. From what he said, Frank was elated."

"Really!!! So, do think we'll ever see him again?" asked Sara.

"You know what! He gave me a card at the end of that crazy day. I'd forgotten about it." Jason walked to the dresser and retrieved a small folded card from the top drawer. He handed it to Sara. She opened it and read it aloud.

Mr. Jason and Miss Sara,

You are like family to me and I do not know how to thank you enough for what you have done. Thank you for the small part you allowed me to play. Mr. Klaser has offered to help me set up a small medical facility in the town where I grew up, in Africa. I could not refuse. I will miss you. And yes, Miss Sara, you will be seeing me again. Be at peace and love each other.

With much love, Frank.

Sara had tears in her eyes. "I'm going to miss him so much. He's been like a Dad to me. Always watching out for us. I hope we do see him sometime."

"I'm sure we will, Sweetie. Now let's watch the rest of this thing," said Jason. He hit play and wrapped his arms around Sara.

"Wow! That place was beautiful," said Sara.

"What place?"

Sara pulled away and sat up next to him. "The Palmer House, you know, the place where we got the Medal of Valor from the head of the CIA." Sara's eyes expanded.

"Oh! That place," said Jason. "I'm kinda busy in this place," he smiled.

"You promised we'd watch it," said Sara, squinting her eyes at him.

Jason propped himself up and pressed an index finger on the volume. "There, now we can hear it, even if we don't see everything. Jason wrapped his arms around her and she lay her head on his chest.

The camera zoomed in on Commander Klaser escorting Jason and Sara up a formal staircase to a two story gilded lobby with marble-topped tables, velvet seating, and a ceiling mural depicting Greek mythology.

"Wow! Look at the ceiling. But it looks like a lot fewer people than I remembered. I felt like the whole city of Chicago was there," said Sara.

"That's called nerves, Sweetie."

"Ooooh! This is when you get your medal," screeched Sara, and she pulled herself to a sitting position.

Jason reached for the remote, but Sara got it first.

"Fast forward through this part," said Jason in an exacerbated sigh.

"No! This is the important part. I want to watch you get your award," said Sara. Her eyes were fixed on the TV, while Jason attempted to cover his face with a pillow.

"We, as a country…" began CIA Director Holden. "…we're fortunate enough to have side-stepped a catastrophe. Due in a huge part to the four individuals on this stage. Millions of people would have died if not for the fast thinking, dedication and patriotism they displayed. So without further delay…" He turned, sweeping his arm out to the right.

"Mr. Jason Forest, please step up."

"Yayyyyyyyyyy!" cheered Sara. She clapped and removed the pillow from Jason's face.

"I just…"

"Shhhhhh!" said Sara. "You look so handsome in that black suit. You look adorable."

Jason rolled his eyes.

"I saw that," smiled Sara, as she turned back to the screen.

"As CIA Director and on behalf of the President of the United States of America, I would like to present you with the Medal of Valor. Your hard work and tireless effort saved the lives of millions of people. If not for your relentless research and intellect as a scientist, this country would have had a true catastrophe on its hands. We thank you for your patriotism."

Sara jumped from the bed and ran into the other room and returned with the medal. She walked toward the bed in a procession of steps and held it out in front of her, nodding her head at Jason, to receive it.

Jason shook his head, but obliged.

Sara placed the red/white/blue ribbon around his neck. Hanging from it was a blue-enameled, five-pointed, upside-down star surrounded by a wreath of laurel. The medal, suspended on a gilt disc bearing the letter "V" surrounded by a wreath of laurel in blue with white and red edge stripes.

Sara placed her lips on Jason's ear. "You know what this gold center stripe stands for?"

"What?" said Jason, playing along.

"Honor," she smiled. "I'm so-o-o proud of you. Ooooh! Listen! He's gonna read the other side of the medal." She turned it over as the Director read the inscription.

"FOR EXTRAORDINARY VALOR ABOVE AND BEYOND THE CALL OF DUTY."

The camera panned the crowd as they all stood for a three minute ovation. Sara clapped frantically and planted her lips on Jason's and kissed him hard.

"Okay! That's it." He picked Sara up and brought her down on top of him. He scooped the medal off his neck and tossed it on the chair beside the bed.

"Don't you want your medal?" said Sara.

"No! I want you," he said, turning her over, so he was on top.

Sara could hear Holden talking in the background, something about Cody becoming a full-fledged Commander and getting a medal too. Jason unbuttoned each of the buttons on Sara's lumberjack shirt and kissed beneath them, when Sara heard Steve receiving another sort of medal and just as things were getting good, Jason jumped up…

"What's wrong?" said Sara, breathing heavily. Then she heard.

"And last, but certainly not least...Miss Sara Ann Parkins, please step up," said Director Holden.

Jason quickly rolled over next to her. "Okay! Now it's your turn."

"Oh! No, let's keep doing what we were doing. We don't have to watch this. It's the same thing we just heard." Sara threw her leg over Jason and ran her hands across his chest.

"Oh no you don't! You made me watch." He lifted Sara up and turned her around toward the television. Wrapping his arms around her, he kissed her neck.

"Oh! Look at that dress," Sara began. "Do you think it was too short? I didn't even get a chance to comb my hair before I walked up there."

Jason placed his lips next to her ear. "You looked beautiful…still do. Shhhhhh!!!"

"As CIA Director, Michael Holden, on behalf of the United States of America, I would also like to present you with the Medal of Valor. This is an unusual award to present to a civilian, but again, you are indeed, an unusual woman."

"That's for sure," said Jason.

"Even after being kidnapped," continued Holden. "Almost killed twice by people you were told you could trust, you continued to offer your services to help in a crisis without any thought for your own safety."

"You're my hero," whispered Jason.

"Stop it, you." said Sara, trying to turn around.

"You saved our very own Commander Cody in one of your moments of bravery and I must say remarkable marksmanship. Your selfless acts will not be forgotten."

The cameras panned the crowd and once again, the auditorium erupted in applause with another three minute standing ovation. Sara struggled to get free, still watching the video.

"Okay! You can turn around now," laughed Jason.

Sara leaned on her right arm to turn, when she suddenly stopped.

"Oh my gosh! Rewind, rewind," said Sara.

"You wanna get your award again?" said Jason.

"No! no, no. Go back and make it go in slow motion," said Sara.

Jason pressed his index finger on the Rewind button and then Play in slow motion.

"What are you looking for?"

Sara saw him in the shadows. She leaned back and thought of the first day Frank had given her a ride. *He must have known all about me and that I lived on the same floor as Jason,* she thought. *Wow! There's probably so much more going on in life that I have no idea about.*

"Sara, what are you looking at?" said Jason.

"I'm sorry! Go back a little again and then go forward slowly," said Sara.

"Are we talkin' about the tape?" said Jason smiling.

Sara scrunched her mouth to the left and raised her eyes.

"Yes, we are. Ooooh! Look!" she yelled "Right there…up on the second level by that post. See him walking to the door. It's Frank. He's got that swagger, that confidence."

"Are we talking about the same Frank?" said Jason. "I mean I love the guy, but confidence and swagger, I don't think so. And look, that guy doesn't even have a limp." Jason looked at Sara and smiled. "I think you're delirious from a lack of physical contact."

Sara's eyes grew big and two rows of pearly whites appeared. "I don't know what I was thinking, but, you're right."

With that, she slipped between the sheets and slid on top of him.

Jason stopped the video and as he was about to hit the off button, he saw Sara on screen.

"Your commercial," said Jason.

"What?" Sara turned around. "Oh my gosh! It is."

Sara watched as Adam moved in close to her, wrapped his hand with the glass of wine underneath the chiffon cover-up around her waist. With the other hand, he topped off her glass.

"You're beautiful," said Adam. "To us."

Jason growled.

The two took a long sip and Adam pulled her in and gently kissed her. She smiled, pressed her lips to his and rolled her head back.

Bringing her focus back to Adam, Sara raised her eyebrows and pouted her lips. "More please," said Sara.

Adam glanced at the bottle of wine and then at her and smiled. He pulled her closer and filled her glass.

Sara smiled again.

"Mmm-mmm," Sara ran her tongue over the lip of the glass. "A hint of chocolate."

The tagline read: *You're good people and you deserve good things in life. Boudenae can keep your passion surging.*

"Excellent job, Sara. But, he better not keep anything of yours surging," said Jason.

"Not even close," giggled Sara.

With that, Jason depressed the Off button, then tossed the remote on the chair.

"Now, where was I?" he said.

She gently took his hands and placed them on her hips, while she kissed his chest and ran her leg up his.

Removing the pearl bra, Jason cupped her breasts in his hands and gently kissed them, while sliding off her pearl panty. Laying her on her back, he pressed his lips against hers, then tenderly ran his tongue down to her shoulders.

Sara arched her back and sighed as she grasped the sheets below and bent her knees.

Rolling on his side, Jason pulled Sara on top of him once more and squeezed her tight. Sara kissed him, pulled back and inched her way down Jason's thighs to his calves, running her hands down his sides and removing his silk pajama as she went.

Jason's mouth dropped open and his eyes rolled back as goosebumps rose on his skin. Reaching his feet, Sara dropped the pants to the floor and ran her tongue slowly up the inside of his calf to his inner thigh.

"Mmmmmm, you taste good," she smiled. "And you feel great!"

"Yes, I do," smiled Jason. "I feel wonderful right now."

Sliding her hands beneath him, she pulled him closer. She tossed her hair playfully to graze his lower abdomen and hips, kissing him softly. She lay her cheek against his skin, to feel his skin against hers. She then inhaled his scent again and again.

Rolling his head from side to side, he moaned, then reached down and slowly lifted Sara up to eye level.

"I love you Sara Ann Parkins. My turn to make Sara feel good."

Jason smiled, knelt beside her and leaned toward her lower stomach. Holding his arms on either side of her, gently, he allowed his tongue to explore her belly button. Sara swooned and let out a small gasp. He lifted his right hand and traced the outline of an invisible panty. His fingers slid around the top of her thighs and crossed over two inches below her belly button, until his hand slid straight down, and parted the way. His head lowered and the heat grew in every inch of Sara's body.

Sara ran her fingers through the back of Jason's hair and clenched her hand, while trying to catch her breath.

Drawing her in with every breath, Jason lifted her bottom and Sara released her passion.

"I want you," she screamed.

Jason turned toward Sara and brought his eyes level with hers.

"I wanna look in your eyes when I make love to you."

Her eyes opened wide. “Me too.” Sara wrapped her hands around his muscular arms and pulled him toward her. She slid her hands to his bottom and guided him in.

“I love you Jason Forest. Now, more please. . .”

Love penetrated their thoughts, their bodies intertwined until their passion found each other and released. Droplets of sensuality ran from skin to skin as they fell asleep in each other’s arms.

CHAPTER 21

"There's always tomorrow for dreams to come true" played and vibrated on the nightstand. "The time is 1:37am," announced Sara's cell phone. Sara's leg lay wrapped around Jason and her face nuzzled under his chin.

"Sara! Your phone," said Jason.

"Oh! I thought I was dreaming." She reached over, pulled it from the side table, clicked it and put it to her ear to listen.

"Who is it?" asked Jason.

"It's not a call…it's a reminder message," smiled Sara.

"Oh! What's it reminding you of at this hour?"

Sara put the phone on the side table, smiled and nuzzled back under Jason's chin.

"It's Anna's birthday today. She was born at 1:37a.m., January 1937. She loved to be called exactly when she was born." Sara looked up at the ceiling. "Happy Birthday, Anna!"

"Happy Birthday, Anna!" said Jason.

Sara turned over and Jason wrapped his arms around her.

"It all started with you, Anna," whispered Sara. "You helped us save millions of people. Love ya!"

Sara giggled. "Oh! and you were right. He's definitely a catch."

Jason smiled and pressed his lips to Sara's head.

She turned and looked Jason in the eye. "I'm so proud of all your discoveries in medicine. You were so determined to find a way to comfort people over long periods of time without them having to take something every few hours…and you did."

Jason smiled.

"And ya know what?" said Sara.

"What?" said Jason.

Sara turned to spoon with him. "You're my Jason time-release. One in the evening and I'm good until morning. Although one more time…hmm."

With that, Jason turned her toward him.

"Well, it just so happens, this particular kind of medicine, can be administered as needed."

The Catwalk

Jeannie Brown

Available **May, 2012**
in Paperback or Download

The Catwalk is the 2nd novel, in the Sara Parkins/Jason Forest Series. This time we're reunited with Sara, a glamorous actress with a national commercial under her belt, as she's chosen to be the lead model in the Catwalk, an endangered species, charity extravaganza to be held at Windsor Castle in London.

While out on a romantic evening celebrating with her sweetheart, Jason Forest, a prominent research physician, Jason's shot by an unknown assailant. When Jason's body disappears, Sara investigates and is caught up in a deadly conspiracy of global proportions. As she searches for Jason, Sara discovers that an international drug cartel placed a hit on him and a reclusive scientist, who's made a major stem-cell research breakthrough. The Cartel will stop at nothing to get this research and kill anyone in their way – including Sara.

From Chicago to London, a deadly game of cat and mouse ensues. While the lives of those Sara holds dearest are at stake, she struggles to discover who she can trust, how to prevent the stem-cell research from falling into the Cartel's hands - and most importantly, whether Jason is dead or alive.